It was raining on Wednesday when Avion made her way home. Her long brown hair plastered to her back giving her the resemblance of a drowning rat. Her clothes likewise glued to her torso, making her shiver violently. She'd had a coat up until her boyfriend Damion, had sold it for beer money two weeks ago, and Avion couldn't afford to replace it, so she ran through the rain as though running alone would cheat the raindrops from soaking her, it didn't but in her mind, had she walked, she'd have been much worse. Her fingers were blue by the time she fumbled for the door key and let herself into the dingy flat that was home. The familiar stench of damp assaulted her nostrils, making her shiver again. She silently cursed Damion for spending the heating money on cannabis, and now they had to freeze. The floor was cold, they could never afford a carpet and the rugs Avion brought were soon ruined with cigarette burns, so she had stopped trying to make the hellhole into a home. She was glad that they still had some gas in the camping stove canister, enough to make a cup of tea with at any rate, and that'd warm her for a short while, so with trembling fingers she lit the stove and filled the camping kettle, then organized her tea into a mug with sugar. There was no point checking the fridge for milk, for starters it didn't work anymore, no electric, and for seconds Damion would've helped himself to it and not bothered to replace it. His money was his alone, and her money was his also, after all he was the man who had the wages, higher than hers, and as he was the main provider it was his right to take her money to help with things, he didn't ask her for rent so it was only fair she cough up to help him out. The kettle began to sing, and Avion poured the hot water over the tea bag, it seemed such a waste, when she could've used the water to wash herself, or wash the dishes, but hell she was cold, and in need of a hot drink. The wind chose that moment to hammer the rain against the window pane, so Avion stuck her tongue out at it in a childish moment of triumph, *you can't get me now na na*. She hugged the cup closely to her, absorbing as much warmth as she could, then she wandered through to the bedroom. Damion hadn't bothered to make the bed, but then he never did. His clothes were lying all over the floor, and the stale waft of old sweat lingered in the air. He had once spray painted obscene words on the walls in a fit of anger, they were a constant reminder of a very bad day. "Here lies the slut." With a large arrow pointing down to the side of the bed that Avion slept on. On better days she had asked him if he'd remove it, and he always promised he would, but then Damion's promises tended to be a bit like miracles, nonexistent. Avion had long since stopped seeing the filth and mess that constituted their home, rather she felt grateful they even *had* a home. They didn't have a bed frame, just a mattress on the floor, apparently it was her fault because she had landed on it too hard when he threw her across the room. Avion tutted to herself, a small part of her knew it wasn't her fault, but it was just easier if she agreed it was. She put the tea down and peeled her soaking clothes off, putting them on the radiator to air as opposed to dry, because that didn't work either. She reached into her bag and recovered a soggy sandwich, which tried to disintegrate when she held it. It was heaven. Her old lady wouldn't miss the bread and cheese, and whilst Avion felt guilty about stealing it, she consoled herself that she didn't steal very often. Who'd have thought a cheese sandwich soaked in rainwater could taste so good? She closed her eyes, imagining it was steak instead. *No amount of imagination is going to make soggy cheese taste like steak.* Avion laughed to herself, she couldn't really remember what steak tasted like, but soggy cheese was close enough today, heaven only knew when she would taste food again. She grabbed a damp towel and began rubbing her hair dry, vigorously putting warmth into her veins as she did so. As she rubbed her head she found herself drifting back to the days when Damion was a blond haired, skinny lad with a sweet way of talking that had folks believing butter wouldn't melt in his mouth. His true colours came out when he was drunk or high on cannabis, and at first that hadn't been often, but as the years rolled on, it became almost a constant. Avion never knew what kind of mood he would come home in, nor what it was about her that made him so angry. She had tried to leave him, she had even run to a refuge to escape him, but he always found her, would swear to God he loved her and would change, but he never did. Avion had begged people to listen to her, but Damion had that charm about him, his adoring smile, and his beautiful eyes with long black lashes, it seemed no one would think ill of him, but Avion of course was a gold digger. A gold digger! She snorted into her tea. Damion didn't have high wages, he worked as a free-lance skivvy on a building site, getting paid under the table. True he could get good money at times, but good money didn't go towards bills and food, just cannabis and baccy and booze. Avion wasn't allowed to work anywhere public, her job was as a cleaner for an old lady who was blind, someone who couldn't ask questions about bruises. Yet Damion loved her, and told her so, especially after he'd been a bit mean and broken her arm or covered her torso in bruises, she had to tolerate rape on a constant basis because that was her duty as a woman, to provide the pleasures for the hardworking man. She almost believed it, except that she worked hard too. According to Damion, cleaning a house wasn't hard work, but carrying planks around, or bricks or buckets of cement was bloody hard work, and his sweat was proof of that, made worse because they didn't have the money to use a launderette. If she dare wince from the pain he caused her, because she was still purple all over, he would chastise her by telling her she was a wimp and stop making a fuss, just a few bruises, was nothing at all. Avion rubbed her legs and arms with the now very damp towel, she covered her legs in talcum powder just so the denim wouldn't stick to her sore skin, then fought to wriggle into her jeans. Job done but she didn't have another bra to wear, so she put on a jumper and hoped Damion wouldn't notice. It was Wednesday night, Damion would be playing snooker, drinking what money was left, away, so perhaps he would come home drunk again, and fall asleep, giving her a night off from the awkward fondling, and often over-too-soon sex, thank God. Avion smiled as she finished her now cold tea, and fished in her bag for her own personal secret, something that only she knew about herself, and it made her feel superior that people like Damion only thought they knew everything about her, there was still one thing they would never know, and this was it. Carefully she positioned herself by the window, squinting in the diminished amount of light the dark skies gave her, she opened up a small piece of linen with a tiny needle attached. Avion smiled at the picture she was creating, not with silks, she could never afford cottons or silks, but hair was free. Avion took hair from hairdressing shops and she would dye it in the colours she could use in an embroidery. Delicate tiny stitches that made up complex pictures, using one or more strands of hair to create shading and depth. It took a long time to make her work, but that was partly because of its nature, but mostly because she had to be careful no one found her out. Avion couldn't imagine how her life would be if people actually did know all that there was to know about her. This small secret was hers and hers alone, it made her survive all the smart arses who claimed they could read her like a book. This was her book, a book that held her hopes and fears in neatly sewn stitches of hair, sometimes she used words, though words could be read, so often she stitched pictures, something that made her smile, or something, other than bruises, that made her sad. The birthday cake her employer had for her 90th birthday, was carefully reconstructed on a cloth, with a happy smiley face. The first and only flower Damion had given her, a stolen daisy from a graveyard bouquet, it was the thought that counted; he'd told her with that adorable smile that melted her heart, so she had stitched a heart beside the flower. The feel of the warm sun on her face in summer, she dare not show more than her face in summer, too many scars for people to ask her about. Her coat when it was new, before Damion ruined it by letting a cut on her arm bleed into it, happy memories, but also sad ones. The old fashioned pram with a baby sleeping within it, a face so pale it could only be dead. The writing on the wall over her side of the bed, a constant reminder of her worthlessness. A woman huddled in a dark corner hugging her knees close to her chest, a representation of what she'd become, skeletal arms a warning of what lay ahead. Then there were those silly moments, like the soggy sandwich she was about to stitch, or the only time Damion tried to put up a cupboard in the kitchen, and it had fallen off the wall nearly knocking him out. The pages told her story of three years of existence, not living, Avion would never bring herself to call it that, living meant more than fear, she was certain of it, even if she couldn't remember what life before Damion had been like. And so she stitched, a little bit of her emotions soaked into the thread, giving her work a hidden feeling that only she could detect. After about an hour, the light finally gave out on her, and sadly she had to admit defeat and put her work away, not daring to light a candle they couldn't afford to replace. Avion was unbearably cold and shivered violently, so she wrapped her jumper about her and crawled into bed, perhaps Damion would be too drunk to care that she hadn't got undressed, even so the sheets were damp and cold, and Avion shivered just as much, as she wondered how much longer she could sustain this kind of existence. Her stomach ached from hunger, her arms were bone thin. Damion had found the perfect excuse for her starved appearance, he told folks she was anorexic and he was doing his best to keep her alive, what a hero he was for caring for her so much. Not for the first time did Avion wonder what the hell had attracted her to him, but she knew the answer, the same thing that had people believing his every word. His charm, his looks, his devotion to her. Avion had to admit, his devotion to her had made her feel so important in the beginning; it was only as time moved on that she came to understand that devotion was a misinterpretation for possessiveness. Damion had gotten into so many fights over her, and she had got so many beatings because a stranger had looked at her, talked to her, and God forbid that she smiled or laughed at another's jokes. He hated her to wear low cut tops, that's what whores wore, but that didn't stop him admiring other women who wore them. Perfume made her smell like a sewer, but her own stench was worse, being unable to shower or take a bath. If she wore make up she looked like a clown in his eyes, but he flirted outrageously with women who caked themselves in the stuff. Yet she loved him, or at least she couldn't imagine a world without him, that was love right? To need someone so bad, you couldn't bear to be without them, and he did keep the roof over their heads, just, so it wasn't all bad. When he wanted to be kind, he was so adorable, the way he looked at her, like she was the only one in his life who mattered. The way he could hold her so gently when he had hurt her so bad, he hadn't meant to lose it, and he was so, so sorry. He had even taken the day off work once to look after her, and she swore he had cried when he thought she was asleep. It was his sea blue eyes and dark lashes that lingered in her mind as she eventually slipped into sleep.

Chapter 2

Avion woke to loud snoring. Thank the Gods he had obviously come home too drunk to give a shit for her, so she carefully slid off the mattress and crept into the bathroom, where she ran her finger under the tap and used it to rub her teeth. The toothpaste was for Damion, he had to look his best when he went out. Avion had to ask to use it and sometimes he made her pay for it. Avion understood that, she didn't pay rent, so she ought to pay for anything she used in the flat, like toothpaste. She also kept a spare toothbrush at work, and brushed her teeth every day in the old lady's bathroom, it always amused her that Damion never asked how come she always had white teeth! Exiting the bathroom, she walked straight into his skinny bare chest.
"Fucking look where you're going bitch." He squawked, rubbing his eyes which were bloodshot. Avion cringed, that was Damion talk for, hey babe, look where you're going.
"Sorry she mumbled" and walked around him.
"Where you going anyway?" He asked frowning at her.
"Work. It's Thursday." She reminded him. His face dropped and he paled. "Fuck." He moaned miserably.
"What?" Avion asked, fear running through her veins. When Damion swore in that way, it usually meant he had done something really stupid, and today wasn't a letdown.
"Gimme some money, I got to pay Danny for a loan he gave me."
"I ain't got any money Damion, you took my wages last pay day." Avion tensed, knowing what was coming and it did, right on cue, a hard slap around her face.
"You fucking useless piece of shit, you know I always need extra mid-month, you ought to know better by now." Another hard slap had her head snapping to one side, her

neck cracked loudly. Tears welled in her eyes as she tasted blood in her mouth. "I'm sorry." She whispered.

"What you got I can sell?" He demanded. Avion panicked.

"I got nothing, you know I got nothing." She pleaded, as she followed him into the bedroom. He tipped the contents of her bag over the bed and not for the first time, Avion held her breath, trembling with fear. Her secret was hidden away in the lining of the bag, but he could find it if he looked. He threw the bag to one side and poked through her meagre belongings. A comb. An old nail file. A picture of her and Damion in happier days. Tissues. In frustration he swiped the lot onto the floor, then went to the chest of broken drawers, and chucked the contents of every drawer onto the floor. His clothes not hers, she didn't have a change of clothes anymore. "You must have something. Your hiding stuff from me again ain't ya?" He turned on her and slapped her again, this time Avion saw stars in front of her eyes, she cried out at the unexpected assault.

"Damion please. I ain't got anything, I swear." She pleaded but he just hit her again, and then he kicked her, and then he punched her over and over. Avion curled up into a ball and waited for it to stop. Each punch raining down on her side, her ribs, her head. Each kick hitting her arm, and her legs. She saw the darkness at the edge of her vision and she all but beckoned it over, as she welcomed the solace of unconsciousness that seeped towards her, the promise of sleep, of not feeling any more.

When Avion woke up it was dark. Not the absolute darkness of silence and solace, of being pain free. Not floating like some people might explain it, for Avion it was sitting with her knees bunched up waiting, she hoped for the spot of light that would grow into a tunnel, filled with hope and freedom, but as usual she would not be rewarded this time, and sure enough she found herself in complete darkness. This came with sound, cars on the street, voices in the distance, and pain, oh God it came with pain. Complete darkness came with swollen eyes and lip, with an endless ache like a thousand dwarves were all hitting her with replicas of Thor's hammer. It came with red hot pokers burning into her nerves and all she wanted to do was scream and scream, but she couldn't even wail or moan, her throat was too dry, so she screamed in her head and drifted back into absolute darkness where she could sit and wait in silence, without pain. She had no idea how many times she drifted from one darkness to the other, but eventually she could make out the voices, they were closer, as was the traffic outside, all those cars and lorries rushing to get to some place or other, whose engines broke into her solace, whose fumes lingered like death on the windowsill. She heard the soft patter of bare feet on the linoleum floor, the rustle of a body sitting nearby.

"Come on Avi, no need to keep milking it. I know I hit you too much ok? I get it."

It was the usual fake caring, and Avion didn't want to hear it any more.

"I know yer alive, I felt yer pulse. You're just fucking milking it now and it's boring." He nudged her leg with his bare foot, sending spears of agony racing to her brain. Avion moaned softly.

"See! I fucking knew it." The relief in his voice far exceeded his concern, and that made Avion smile inwardly. *Shitting yourself were you?* She wondered silently. They both knew that one of these days Damion *would* be shitting himself, because one of these days, she wouldn't wake up again, no matter how long he sat beside her. As she became more aware of her surroundings, she wondered what had happened when Danny had come for his pay back, she was certain Damion wouldn't have been home. If Damion couldn't sweet talk his way out of a situation, then he took the other road and legged it, which made Avion wonder how he'd gotten out of it, and she wasn't likely to be told.

Healing was a slow process, made all the more tedious because Damion was nagging her to get better more quickly. He hated buying burgers and chips every day, twice a day, and Avion was heartily sick of eating them, but he seemed to think this was the best diet for recovery. Avion hated him hovering around her, moaning that he was losing money not being able to work. It didn't seem to occur to him that if he hadn't beaten her in the first place, he wouldn't have to be looking after her now, but she had long since learned that Damion had his own peculiar logic to situations, namely, he wasn't to blame for anything. She hated it most when he didn't wake her up if she'd fallen asleep, when the dreaded food arrived, then she had to chew her way through cold burger and cold chips, otherwise she had to suffer his constant whining about her ingratitude. After a week, he insisted she try and stand up, and he pulled her to her feet uncaringly, causing her to suck in her breath through the pain of stiff and healing bruises, and tender scar tissue.

"See, knew you were ok." He enthused. Avion was glad to be able to stand, and she did her best to walk and get moving, so she could go back to work, if she still had a job to go back to.

***

Monday morning was a dry but cloudy day. Avion was glad to be sitting on a bus, a real luxury that Damion had begrudgingly allowed her. She arrived at her employers' house, a large house with iron gates, and a few short steps from pavement to front door. The front door was unlocked but that was normal. Mrs Parker was blind and relied upon visitors for assistance, so she never locked her front door. Avion walked down the long hallway to the back of the house, where Mrs Parker would be sitting in her parlor room, brail reading, or snoozing.

"Hello?" She called cautiously.

"Arh, my cleaning girl has arrived." Mrs Parker chimed cheerfully. "Where have you been?"

Avion swallowed down the lump in her throat. "I um, I was sick Mrs Parker. I'm so sorry, I really am."

Mrs Parker held out her hand for Avion to take. "Now, now my dear. Your boyfriend was kind enough to call in and explain everything to me."

Avion went cold as ice, if Mrs Parker could have seen her, she'd have watched the blood drain from Avion's face. "H, he did?" she asked, unable to hide the slight tremble in her voice.

"Yes dear. He said you got bad cramps sometimes, you know, girlie things, but you'd be right back as soon as you were over it." Her smile was strong and sincere, causing a tear to slip down Avion's cheek.

"Such a nice young man, full of worry he was." Mrs Parker continued. "You know if you'd just use a mobile, he could've saved himself the trouble of coming to see me."

Avion listened in terror, which was one part anger. How dare Damion invade her work space and charm Mrs Parker into his vile confidence, now she would be another person who would always take his side. Avion felt her heart sink into her stomach, now she would have to look for another job again. Damion always ruined her hopes of employment, he would worm his way in with people, and then he would manage to persuade them that Avion was the meanest person alive, and that he was the victim of her demands. She really liked Mrs Parker as well. She removed her hand from the older one, whose grip was surprisingly strong given Mrs Parker's age.

"I'll um, get started then." She almost mumbled, her eyes darting around the room to see if anything was obviously missing. It wouldn't surprise Avion if whilst Damion was sweet talking her blind employer, he wasn't also filling his pocket with an ornament or two that he could hock later.

"I could really go a bit of toast truth be told." Mrs Parker said without any indication of what Avion was panicking about.

"What? Oh, yes, of course, toast." Avion said distantly. She paused to finish sweeping the room with her glance, before turning towards the door.

"He didn't steal anything, probably because I gave him the money for his taxi fare."

Avion tripped over the rug in shock, and Mrs Parker giggled softly.

"Taxi fare? You gave him money?" Avion was having a heart attack, she was certain of it. Her heart jumped all over the place and her chest had constricted painfully.

"Well of course I did! I'm not some money grabbing old biddy you know. He took the time and trouble to come across town to see me, of course I was going to pay his fare. What's fifty pounds to someone like me?" she laughed kindly.

"H how much?" Avion was whispering now, unable to find her voice at all. So Damion had talked her employer into handing over fifty quid for a taxi trip she was certain didn't cost that much.

"I also told him to feed you properly, you're so skinny. He promised he would. I hope he did?" She tilted her head to one side and Avion realised she was supposed to answer.

"Yes. Yes he fed me." She said in a flat deflated voice. *He fed me burgers until I almost begged him to stop.* Well that explained why he had bothered to buy food in. Avion walked into the kitchen, and leaned on the butler sink wondering if she could avoid throwing up. If Damion had gotten away with this once, and he had it seemed, he would do it again and again, which meant Avion would get beaten more often just so he could go running to Mrs Parker for financial aid. She wretched. The mere thought of Mrs Parker being used this way was enough to turn her stomach, but what could she do? She couldn't tell Mrs Parker what Damion was, she was well and truly in his clutches now. She could only protect her by handing her notice in, but then Damion would be furious, his new life line taken away, wouldn't be good for Avion. *Damned if I do and damned if I don't.* She put the toast in the toaster and

stood outside the back door gulping copious amounts of fresh air, to calm her giddiness and nausea. *How long before he is expecting me to ask on his behalf for money?* Could she do it? She already knew the answer. The toaster pinged with enthusiasm it had no right to, and Avion buttered the bread without knowing she'd done so. She took the plate into the parlor, and handed it to Mrs Parker.
"My dear, why don't you make yourself some as well, seems rude of me to sit here stuffing my face while you watch."
"Thanks but I am good. I'll go start in the bedroom." Avion got up and left the room, tears streaming down her face. She knew she couldn't leave, Damion would be straight round here whining to poor Mrs Parker, and Avion would be right back here when Damion dragged her in, having gotten her job back, selfish as she was for handing in her notice in the first place. She sobbed too loudly and paused in her work to see if Mrs Parker had heard her, but when no comment came floating up the stairs, Avion carried on cleaning, chastising herself for not being more careful with her crying. The only thing she could do was to try and warn Mrs Parker about Damion, if she chose to ignore her, then at least she could say she had tried, so at lunch time when they both sat eating cheese sandwiches, Avion tried to broach the subject.
"Mrs Parker, I think I need to tell you something about Damion, and I'm really sorry he came here." Her voice wobbled a bit.
"Oh don't be sorry dear, he was so kind. Even made me a cupper tea."
Oh Gods, the kitchen! Avion hadn't thought he would wander around the house, of course he would, he was light on his feet that one, why wouldn't he snout about and steal from another room. She leapt from her chair and dashed into the kitchen, only for Mrs Parker's voice to follow her. "I don't keep the crown jewels in the kitchen, who does that?" she chuckled again. Avion returned to the parlor.

"You don't understand Mrs Parker." She began, her voice choked with emotion. Mrs Parker levelled her gaze straight at Avion, as though suddenly she could see. "Think I don't know that boy's type? His gentle sincere voice etched with distraction. I may be blind Avion, but I can see through most people. I can tell a liar by their voice and your young man is full of them. I can tell insincerity a mile off, and your young man reeks of it. I played along as I have with you. Think I can't feel how dreadfully thin you are? You deserve better my girl, but who am I to tell you how to live your life? I'm just an old woman you work for. Sure I gave him money, can't take it with me can I? Though I'd rather give it to you than him." She paused to listen to Avion's sobbing. "Tsch. Why do you young uns always think we old folk are soft in the head? Think I never lived my girl? I may be blind but I used to kick up me heels in my day." She grinned and her eyes sparkled. "I can tell you, there are advantages to being blind, especially when it comes to young men!" she burst out laughing at Avion's sharp intake of breath. Mrs Parker nodded like a demented nodding donkey on steroids. "Oh yes." She said hissing the s into a long sound. Avion bit her lip. "You're not saying what I *think* you're saying are you?" She asked incredulously.

"And what do you *think* I'm saying Avion?"

Avion paused, she was quite unwilling to think nice old Mrs Parker was a pervert. "Um, well don't blind people have to um, feel or something?" Avion couldn't hide her smirk and was grateful Mrs Parker couldn't see it, then she remembered she could *hear* it, and Avion blushed.

"Like I said, advantages my girl." And Mrs Parker grinned again, then they both laughed, and Avion realised she couldn't remember when she had laughed, or laughed so much.

Chapter 3

Each day Avion ate with Mrs Parker, it was amazing to have food inside her again, and food that had real taste. They had both laughed at the burgers and chips Damion had insisted she eat, and Mrs Parker allowed Avion to make her omelettes and other simple foods, she knew it wasn't really for Mrs Parker's benefit, but for her own, so she didn't say anything.
"How come you never tell me to leave Damion?" Avion asked one lunchtime.
"None of my business dear, besides you think you love him, so why would I suggest you leave him? You chose him in the first place right?" She tipped her head to one side and paused in her eating.
"True. I did choose him, and I suppose I did love him once."
"You don't anymore?"
Avion considered this question. "I don't think I do, no."
"You don't sound so sure."
"I fell for his charm, his total obsession with me made me feel special, and he always seemed to listen. He was kind back then."
Mrs Parker was nodding. "Just like any other regular man then." She added, which made Avion smile, how wonderful this old lady was to understand her. "So what changed?"
Avion had to think about that, as she often had. "I'm not sure. He used to smoke cannabis from time to time, and he'd get a bit jealous when under the influence, but I never really bothered about it. We'd argue, but that was it. Then one day he asked me for money for some smokes, and I asked him why he couldn't use his own money. We ended up having a row about it. He said it was none of my business, but if he wanted me to give him money for smokes, surely it became

my business? Anyway, it all got out of hand and then he slapped me, called me a selfish bitch. He paid the rent, never asked me for any rent money, so I ought to give him money when he did ask for it, he said it was the least I could do."
"Yet you stayed?"
Avion nodded, then realised Mrs Parker couldn't see her. "Yes I stayed. I often wonder why, but truth is I loved him. I hoped it was a one off thing, he was so sorry afterwards, and he promised it wouldn't happen again, and stupid me believed him." Avion hung her head, it all sounded so pathetic, when it was far more complicated than simply one thing or one incident.
"Of course you did. Love makes us blind my dear, and women always want to see the good in men regardless of their failings."
Avion could've hugged her. "How come you are the only person who has ever understood me?" She choked out. Mrs Parker smiled sadly.
"I have raised a monster of my own and my grandsons are also monsters." Her face was sad. Avion couldn't imagine any son or grandson of Mrs Parker's being bad, she was kindness, how could she raise bad men?
"I don't believe you." Avion replied softly.
"Why not? Because I have money? Because I am kind? Or is it because I am blind? Why couldn't I raise a bully?"
Avion couldn't think of an answer, so Mrs Parker gave her own. "I married a wealthy man, but he didn't get wealthy by being a kind or generous man, and he didn't raise his son to be soft either, although Ethan started out like Damion, his father had to teach him how to be a bully of worth." She smiled with the memory.
"That's an odd thing to say." Avion pointed out and Mrs Parker chuckled. "Well yes, I suppose it is, thing is there are bullies like Damion who are worthless, and there are bullies like Ethan who have purpose, and by that I mean they are bullies in business. Ethan used to take drugs, and drink a lot,

and he had no problem knocking girlfriends around, so his father took him in hand, and my son had to learn the difference between being a worthless bully and a meaningful one. He has never hit a woman since." A smile spread over her wrinkled lips.

"Does his wife know what he is then?" Avion couldn't hide her curiosity, to think kind Mrs Parker could be so open about powerful men, or in Damion's case a man who thought he was powerful.

"Ooh yes, she knows. See her own father is a powerful man and hard as nails, so Ethan dare not put a foot wrong, though he worships the ground Catherine walks on, she's his wife."

"Sounds wonderful, to have a man that will protect you and care about you for all the right reasons." Avion couldn't help but envy Catherine, if only Damion could've been like that.

"You said you had grandsons?" Avion remembered. "How many?"

"Mrs Parker smiled. "I have five grandsons and one granddaughter. All grown men now, one boy is married and the granddaughter is also married, though no great grand babies yet." She chuckled proudly.

"Do you think you will have children one day?"

Avion stayed silent for a long time. "No. I can't. Damion put an end to that dream."

"Oh my dear, I'm so sorry. I should have thought before opening my big mouth." Mrs Parker seemed genuinely upset.

"It's not your fault Mrs Parker, you couldn't know." Avion leaned over the table and gave Mrs Parker's hand a reassuring squeeze.

"Do your family ever visit you?" She'd never seen anyone visiting her employer.

"Oh yes." Mrs Parker smiled. "They are always popping in, usually of an evening, though the boys are always very busy, they dote on me, I am quite the luckiest granny really. If they can't come in person they normally phone."

Avion just couldn't imagine being cared about that much, and she was glad Mrs Parker had family who cared, too many old folk had no one at all.

"Forgive me for asking." Avion ventured. "You don't have any family pictures displayed."

"Arh!" Mrs Parker slapped the table and rocked backwards. "There's a good reason for that my dear. My son and grandsons are somewhat well known and recognised, and I should not like to make myself a target for anyone who thinks they might use me to get one over them, besides what does a blind person need of pictures?" She smirked.

"What sort of business do your family do?" Avion asked, then realised that was rude of her, when Mrs Parker had never asked her about her private life. "I'm so sorry, I should mind my own business." She quickly added.

"Yes you should, but I like you Avion, and I find I like telling you about my boys. Ethan didn't do anything until he married Catherine, and I often wonder what she saw in him, given she is so very religious, but they work very well all things considered. It must work well, who in their right mind names their children after angels and saints?"

Avion's eyebrows hit her hairline, as her eyes widened and she let a huge grin split her lips. "You're kidding me?" she gasped. Mrs Parker found great joy, in once more making Avion smile and laugh.

"Well four angels and one saint, to be fair."

"Name them, please?" Avion drew out the please to make it sound longer. Mrs Parker rolled her blind eyes. "In no particular order then, we have Michael, not so unusual, but then it goes Raphael, Uriel and Gabriel, the Saint being Cuthbert."

Avion burst out laughing. "Oh my! Why on earth would she call her son Cuthbert?"

"Something to do with his birthday, they both share the same day March 20th, and Catherine is Catholic, which is why she has so many off spring."

"Poor boy, man." Avion laughed. "His life must be hell."

"Yes." Mrs Parker nodded sympathetically. "Yes it was, but Cuthbert is also a monster, and he soon made people realise a name is just that, and as he shares absolutely nothing else in common with his namesake, other people soon learned to respect him. If I told you he is called "Cut", that should tell you exactly what kind of man he is."

Avion stopped laughing at the serious face Mrs Parker wore. "I'm sorry, I didn't mean to make fun of him, it's just not the sort of name I imagine a monster having. Actually it's not the sort of name I imagine anyone having."

Mrs Parker tipped her head to one side and back again. "Well that's Catherine for you." She said matter-of-factly.

"What about her daughter?" Avion asked to get off the awkward moment.

"Kristine. Perfectly ordinary." There was a pause before Mrs Parker continued. "Names are beside the point, it always makes people laugh when I tell them I raised monsters but they all, bar one, have angelic names! Catherine's father and mother made their fortune after the war, they began a housing business, which made them a fortune, when Catherine married Ethan; he was trained into the business. The boys have all been trained as estates professionals but they have also expanded into other businesses, gambling casinos, science laboratories, health care, hospitality, media, television, you name it, one of them will be owner, silent partner, have a share in, dah de dah." She waved her frail bony hands airily in a circle. "Kristine is at university studying business law."

"Wow, what a family." Avion breathed.

"Do you have any family?" Mrs Parker asked her.

"My mom and dad disowned me when I left Damion after he'd hit me for the fifth time, but he went to see them when I was at work and when I got home my dad threw me out, called me a lying, attention seeking cow. I have never gone back to them."

Mrs Parker had pressed her lips together so hard, they made a thin, grim line across her face. "Some people are not best suited to be parents Avion, but I firmly believe that families are made stronger by their bonds to each other. I am sad yours have cut those bonds, not surprising you cling to Damion, I expect he is all the family you have?"

"Yes." Avion whispered, lowering her head. The big antique clock on the sideboard began to chime four o'clock.

"Gracious Mrs Parker, I am so sorry, we gossiped the afternoon away. I will make it up tomorrow I promise." Avion stood quickly collecting the plates, her mug and the tea cup and saucer Mrs Parker used, taking them into the kitchen, and filling the sink. "There's no rush on my part." Mrs Parker said as she tapped her cane towards the kitchen doorway.

"Sadly there is on mine. Damion will never believe in a million years we were chatting, he will accuse me of all sorts."

"Then leave those things and get yourself off home my girl. I wouldn't want to be the reason that boy beats you again."

***

It was a blessing Avion made it home before Damion, though going back to a cold damp flat wasn't something she had ever looked forward to, nowadays, it was far far more depressing. She often found herself imagining what it might be like to have a filthy rich man in her life, who loved her so much he would do anything to keep her safe, to want for nothing, to be free to come and go wherever she pleased, but most of all she imagined what Mrs P's grandsons might look like, tall dark and handsome no doubt, and of course very intelligent, far out of the reaches of someone like Avion. No rich man with a good education and wealth would look once let alone twice at a nothing like Avion, but hell she could dream. Dreams were the only things that kept her alive. When Damion wanted sex, she lost herself in her dreams though rough and unromantic as his kind of sex was, the men in

Avion's dreams were experienced and knew how to make a woman feel special. Truth was, she'd never met a man who romanced a woman, they only existed in love stories, and she was so damaged internally from the beatings that sex with any man would be agony, not just Damion. She often cried silent tears at night, wishing she had been able to be a bit smarter, have a nice body and be desirable to a man with a career, but each morning she woke to Damion snoring, a cold damp bed, vile writing on the walls, a filthy toilet because she couldn't afford cleaners, the stale stink of tobacco or cannabis, beer and sweat. The living room was permanently in darkness because the council hadn't got around to replacing the window pane Damion smashed in temper, and they had instead, a board up to keep the weather out. Each morning she watched her boyfriend dress, his ribs straining unhealthily against his skin, tattoos stamped in an ad hoc way, a spider web spread across his neck, a Nazi swastika on his bicep, a naked woman languished invitingly down his other arm, his skin bleached from lack of sunlight, though he tanned well in the summer, his eyes once beautiful and alluring, were more often than not blood shot these days, his once vibrant lips were pale and he often scowled, never laughing unless he was with his mates.

"Don't forget we're going out tonight." He said looking down at her. It was pay day for them both, so he would drink and smoke most their money away, she would have a cold shower, wear her only dress, one with long sleeves and high collar, because she was too afraid to let anyone see her scars, she would sit invisibly at the table, while Damion laughed and joked with his friends, their girlfriends, flaunting all they had, flirting with Damion. He would keep an arm around Avion's shoulders, pulling her to him when he expected affection, and he would suck her tonsils out in front of them all, just to show the other women what they couldn't have. Avion wished she didn't have to suffer such humiliation, but she did her best to ignore the saliva he dribbled into her mouth, the vile taste of his breath, alcohol soaked and baccy suffocating, she suffered his quick groping of her breasts, and the teasing he gave her for not being as big as Jock's girl up top. She even pretended not to have caught him tonsil tasting and groping Jock's girl outside in the car park. Yes it was pay day and her man was going out to have some fun, and Avion was going out to be embarrassed.

***

Mrs Parker noticed. "Everything alright?" She asked poking at her salad sandwich. Avion frowned. "Yes I think so why?"
"You're very quiet today and I can feel the atmosphere like a depressive cloud." She looked up from her plate into Avion's lowered face.
"It's pay day."
"I seem to recall pay day is meant to be a good day, not a depressing day?" Mrs P pondered.
Avion shrugged, then sighed heavily. "Perhaps it would be a happy day if I didn't have to hand over my wages and watch Damion drink the lot away."
Mrs P studied her plate again. "I suppose that might depress me too. It's your money Avion, he has no right to take it off you."
"He does though. I don't pay rent, so I agreed my wages pay for a night out, except it's your money he is pouring down his throat, and that seems unfair to you." Avion explained. Mrs Parker snorted, making Avion look up surprised.
"What you use your money for is no concern of mine. It's wages girl. If I'd given you a loan, then I might add the condition, it be used for the purposes you requested it for, then if Damion poured it down his throat you'd have a reason to feel bad, but it's wages. I can see how it might feel disrespectful, after all, you earned it and he is drinking it, but don't feel sad for me Avion. It's money and I am blessed to

have more of it than things to spend it on." She gave Avion a tight smile, but Avion just sighed again, and let a tear roll down her cheek. She could've spent her money on some soap so she could scrub her skin, or shampoo to wash her hair, food so she didn't have to suffer hunger pains, God forbid she might even buy a change of clothes, another bra, some more pants, anything, anything but bloody alcohol. The tears rolled freely. *It's your own fault Avion, you chose him and now you're stuck with him, made yer bed, now lie in it girl. Feeling sorry for yourself won't make the situation go away.* Yet she had dreamed of a better life, she could taste it. She had lost herself so badly into the dream of being desired and wanted, that reality was becoming too much of a heartache to handle. She would always have Damion, he owned her, her life was all about his tempers, his needs, beatings, rape and being put down, living like a tramp, and never ever escaping, *oh silly me, why did I dream of being liked? Mrs P feels sorry for me, that's the closest I get to being liked.* It was one of those million moments that she had lived over the last three years, how do you escape a monster like Damion? Whatever those grandsons were, none of them were as bad as Damion, nothing and no one was as bad as Damion and hundreds of men like him, men who'd been beaten as kids, had alcohol issues, drug addiction, always a good not-their-fault reason for being the lowest kind of humans imaginable, and Avion stupid young Avion, blinded by those beautiful eyes, long lashes and quirky smile, his easy charm his devotion, that turned out to be jealousy, she'd been so gullible, so easy to seduce, desperate to have a guy as cool as Damion, the envy of her friends at the time, now she had no friends, they'd all moved on, got married had kids, and found lives for themselves, but Avion. Hadn't she saved them from Damion? Sacrificed herself so that no other woman had to go through what she did? It was a nice twist of fantasy, when the truth was, it was Avion who could not walk away, Avion who longed to die so that the beatings would stop, she hadn't saved anyone anything; her whole life was a bitter, bitter lie.

"You going to eat that or keep dissecting it? You made it, you ought to know what went into it." Mrs P was watching her cleaner with milky eyes that held a steady gaze. Avion swiped her tears away, How was it that Mrs P always caught her out like this?, then she realised it was the soft sound of her sandwich being picked at and shoved around the plate, The bloody woman had the hearing of a vampire. Mrs Parker was right though, she had no right to put her sorrows onto other people, so taking a deep breath, Avion took a mouthful of salad sandwich and chewed it. She should be grateful for the food, but tonight was pay day and everything tasted like cardboard.

"There is a good chance I won't be in to work on Monday." She advised her employer, "So don't be surprised if Damion turns up and tells you I have girlie issues again." She almost added not to give him money either, but she knew that'd be a waste of time, if Mrs P wanted to give her money to Damion, she would, and there was nothing Avion could say to prevent her.

***

Damion arrived home by slamming the front door so violently the whole flat shuddered. Avion cringed, this could only mean he was in a temper already.

"Fucking whore where are you?" He shouted. Avion stood in the doorway to the bedroom, her arms crossed defensively across her stomach. As soon as he saw her he punched her in the eye. "Fuck you bitch, cos of you I am short in my wages. I gotta pay for this shit hole, and now I will be short an it's all your fucking fault."

Avion felt the sting of the blow, felt her eye closing up immediately, tears welled but she said nothing, too afraid that whatever she did say would earn her another punch, but turned out, saying nothing earned her the punch anyway. "Damion stop it." She begged.

"Why should I? I work fucking hard for my wages, and cos of you, I am short this month. Which means I can't go out and get off my face can I?" He punched her again, but she put her arm up to protect herself, the force behind the blow sent her arm numb. Avion sobbed.

"You had to have a fucking week off didn't you? Cos of that I am a week down, and you're going to fucking make it up. You hear me?" He was screaming with rage, right into her face, well arm, seeing as she dare not remove it. He stormed into the bedroom, heaving her frail frame out of his way. Avion fell hard against the hallway wall, bruising her opposite shoulder badly. He grabbed her bag and turned the contents out onto the bed, snatching up her envelope of cash, he ripped it open and counted the money, then smiled evilly.

"Good ol Mrs P, she knows how to keep in my good books." Avion sobbed. Mrs Parker had covered her week off by paying her double for that week, just so that Damion wouldn't hurt her, but he had. He turned to Avion.

"Why ain't you ready?" He sneered at her, and then walked into the bathroom. Avion looked at the money spread all over the bed. She could grab it and run, the temptation was powerful, but where would she go? Not to Mrs Parker that was for sure, Avion would never bring the likes of Damion into her life if she could avoid it, and she hadn't done such a good job so far. If she ran, Mrs P would be the first person Damion went to, and she had no doubt he would beat the old woman to death trying to find out where Avion had run to. So Avion sobbed, used some loo roll to wipe her eyes, and blow her nose, just as Damion emerged from the bathroom. He wore a white t-shirt, black jeans and an old leather jacket with a skull and cross bones on the back.

"Shit Avi, comb yer fucking hair, gees but you have to show me up don't you?"

"I don't want to go out." Avion tried to stand her ground. Damion ignored her scooping her wages up and shoving the notes into his jeans pocket.

"Are you listening to me?" Avion said more firmly. Damion paused and then stopped.
"No. I ain't listening cos you're being a spoilt brat again, life ain't all about you stupid tart."
"No, cos it's all about you int it?" she barked, surprised by her own bravado. Damion raised his head to look over at her. In an eerily calm voice he said "I am going out Avion, and if you've an ounce of sense in your pathetic body, you'll come along as well, otherwise, you can expect me to beat the holy fuck out of you when I get back."
She knew she was beaten, she knew what he'd do, and she was still terrified enough to fear that beating more than she yearned for the death that'd stop it. Avion turned to the door, and opened it, then waited dutifully on the door step until Damion had finished locking the place up. *We ain't got anything to steal.* She observed, through one eye now the other was suitably swollen.

***

Of course people stared at them as they walked down the street, Damion whistling happily, and Avion with her good eye glued to the ground. She could feel her arm stiffening from the bruises, aching and aching, hardly mended from the last round of punches he'd rained down on her. She followed him into the local bar, the same bar they always frequented. Stone floor and dark walls. The tables and bar sticky from cleaning fluid, and the place heaving with desperate people, trying to escape the monotony of their tired lives. Damion pushed his way to the bar, clutching Avion's wrist creating another bruise.
"Hey Day, how yer doin man?" The bar tender shouted over the boom boom of a base thumping from the loud speaker. Damion replied and ordered drinks. He then pushed his way to the corner table his mates were already occupying. A loud shout of joy and cheering went up at the sight of him, and

Damion enjoyed the recognition, toasting them all. Avion slipped into a corner seat, sipping her wine, at least it helped wash down the taste of blood from her split lip.

Every now and then, Avion would glance up and see the throng of people happily knocking back beer, laughing and joking. There were empty glasses all around her but her first and only glass of wine was still half full in her hands. She was so tired, and just wanted to sleep, but she was often bumped or jostled by someone wanting to pass her to go to the toilets, or they were messing about across the table, giving the bar maid the glasses that were empty. It was around midnight when the group decided they were going to a night club. Avion heaved herself to her feet, her head swimming as she did so. A strong hand grabbed her arm, another bruise, and steadied her, then he laughed shouting at someone
"She can't handle a glass of wine!" Lots of laughter then. Avion was dragged along with the crowd and deposited onto another sofa, but this time there were bright flashing lights, headache inducing, more booze, more loud music and she flopped over to one side unable to stay awake any longer. She instantly felt grateful for absolute darkness and the silence that came with it. *This time? Surely this time*, she hoped.

Chapter 4

She was dancing in the arms of Damion, although he didn't look like Damion, dressed in a tuxedo, light on his feet, his arms strong but respectfully holding her as they gently smooched their way around a dance floor, that was empty save for them. She loved him and she felt so lucky and happy. There was something not right about the perfection of it all, but she didn't want to question it in case it all disappeared, she was happy, they were dancing, it was perfection, then he bent down and kissed her lips, the softest of brushes, flesh against flesh, she felt heady, exhilarated. He parted his lips to speak "I - have a heartbeat." He said and Avion came crashing back into reality. No exotic man would say that in the middle of a dance, she tried to open her eyes but only one seemed to be working. A brilliant bright light flashed into her vision and the voice said she had concussion. There was music thumping in the background, traffic mumbling somewhere nearby, voices, some loud others just chatting. "Avion can you hear me?" A man said, she nodded slowly.
"Do you know where you are?" he asked. Sadly Avion did, so she nodded, then told the voice.
"Do you know what day it is?"
This was a bit harder as it had to be past midnight, so it wasn't Friday any more. Avion took a chance on saying it was Saturday.
"Ok, can you tell me how you got a black eye?"
This was the moment, this was her opportunity to spend the weekend away from Damion, to sleep in a real bed, to eat food, to be cared for. Yet it wouldn't just be the weekend, it would be longer, and what of Mrs Parker? She expected Avion to be at work on Monday morning, if she was absent,

she'd be waiting for Damion to descend upon her, and he would. Knowing Damion, he'd be straight round there giving her some sob story about how Avion had fainted, got concussion and was in hospital, and could kind Mrs P give him some money for the cab so he could go visit his girl who he was crazy about and worried sick for. Then there would be the questions from the doctors, the social services, the mental health people, and the police, who might arrest Damion, who might charge him with assault, and she would have to testify, and he would look at her with an expression that promised murder once he got out, let off, whatever.
"I walked into a door frame at home and didn't realise how bad I had injured myself."
She felt so depressed, but she couldn't deal with the questions, with the looks she'd get, half sympathetic half accusing. She didn't want to be judged, or patronized, or talked down to, she just wanted to be left alone; she wanted Mrs Parker.

At A&E they were kept in a corridor, the paramedics wishing they could leave to attend other Friday night catastrophes, more deserving than the thick twit who walked into a door and gave herself delayed concussion. Two hours later, Avion was examined again, given the all clear and sent home, this time by bus. Damion had hovered in the background all the time, asking constantly what was going on, was his girlfriend being admitted or what?

They had barely got home before he started at her.
"I ain't fucking taking another week off for you." He made that quite clear. "If you want fucking food, get yer own." What with Avion had no idea.
"You fucking ruined my night, you was determined, I shoulda known."
Avion let herself drift away as he banged on and on about how bad done to he was, and how he didn't know why he put up with her. In the end his words were just background noise to the arms that held her again, the soft voice that crooned in

her ear and those lips, *now where were we?* She woke with a start, ewk!, those lips belonged to the paramedic when he leaned over to check her breathing. Avion tried to forget the less than attractive man with a tickly beard, and concentrated on what might have come next.

Saturday was spent in a dreamy blurr, no food, and only water because she had caught Damion beside her. He would've refused but had she died, that might look bad on him, so he had begrudgingly given her a glass of tap water. She made it last, but when her bladder threatened to wait no longer, she was forced to try and get up. It was a good thing, she needed to start moving again, her arm ached, and her eye throbbed. She put cold, wet tissues on her bruises and swollen eye, so that by Sunday evening it had gone down sufficiently for her to be able see a tiny bit out of it. Damion had disappeared soon after he'd given her the water, leaving Avion on her own after all, though hospital would no doubt have been cleaner and warmer, she was still able to rest without his moaning and snapping at her.

***

Not for the first time did Avion thank her lucky stars Mrs Parker was blind. Her eye was black and purple and her cheek still swollen, her arm was the same, but when Avion walked into the back parlor, Mrs Parker was not alone. Sitting at the table was a young woman in her thirties, with long blond hair which was scraped back into a tight bun. Her face was heart shaped, with almond eyes black lined with long dark lashes and painted dark eyebrows. Her nose was slender and long meeting sweet heart shaped lips, and softly highlighted cheek bones. The woman wore a suite comprising a grey waistcoat, and pencil skirt, with a jacket hanging from the back of a chair, she wore a cream blouse. Avion stared at her.

"Oh my!" The woman gasped at the sight of Avion. "Oh you poor girl, come sit down here." She jumped out of her chair, and Avion wished she'd bolted upon first sight, but it was too late now.

"What happened Avion?" Mrs Parker asked in a stern voice. Avion burst into tears, not of self-pity, but from embarrassment. The young woman slipped into the kitchen and brought a cloth with ice wrapped inside.

"Here put this on your face while you get it out your system." She said kindly, rubbing Avion's shoulders in a mothering way.

"Talk to me Kristy." Mrs Parker said softly.

"Black eye, swollen cheek." The woman reported. Mrs Parker's lips thinned. Avion found a voice in amongst the sobs.

"He was short in his wages cos I took a week off, you know." She said. "Said it was my fault he couldn't have a night out, and he hit me."

"Didn't he see your wages?" Mrs P asked quietly.

"Yea, but he hit me first, then emptied my bag and took my wages, when he saw what you'd done, he was ok."

"Lord he didn't take you out after he'd hit you did he?" The stranger asked. Avion nodded.

"Made it worse when I passed out, and the paramedic said I got concussion. He disappeared for the weekend, left me on my own."

She had no idea why it felt right to pour her heart out about what had happened, but it felt like a weight had been lifted off her.

"You're staying here until you're better." Mrs Parker decided and her tone determined she got no argument, at least not from the stranger.

"No Mrs P, I only came in to work so you wouldn't have to worry about me. I can't stay you know I can't." Avion pleaded.

"You're staying young lady, and that no good boyfriend is welcome to come here, I'm sure Ceaser will be glad to meet him."

Avion was about to object when she felt a hand upon her shoulder, the fingers giving her a gentle squeeze.

"I'm Kristine by the way, the only granddaughter." The young woman pulled up a chair beside Avion, taking her hand and rubbing it gently. "Your boyfriend won't be any trouble here I promise you. Avion nodded her thanks, then sniffed.

"Avion." She said by way of introduction.

"Arh, so you're the young lady I keep hearing so much about. Granny adores you." Kristine exclaimed. Avion looked up at Mrs Parker, who just smiled kindly like grannies do.

"So you're the one studying business law?" Avion remembered. Kristine laughed lightly.

"Yea that's me."

She was beautiful, in a goddess kind of way, which made Avion wonder what the boys looked like, if their sister was so stunning.

"Who's Ceaser?" Avion asked thinking this maybe another grandchild Mrs P had forgotten to mention.

"He's my very nasty guard dog." Kristine said grinning, then she called him. A large Dobermann walked elegantly into the room, his ears pricked up. Avion cringed away from him.

"Don't worry Avion, he is very, very stupid. I was just kidding about him being nasty. He looks the part though doesn't he?" Ceaser nudged his snout under Avion's wrist making her hand flop onto his head. She obliged him by rubbing his ears, which made Ceaser moan in doggy satisfied tones. Instantly Avion felt better, more human than she had felt in ages.

"If your dog is so soft, he can't protect us from my boyfriend."

"Ceaser has a special gift, in that he can see right through people. Let him decide what your man is like, if he turns up." Kristine suggested.

"I think we could do with a cuppa tea, Kristine can you handle that?"

"Gracious no!" Avion tried to vacate her chair.

"Avion please sit down." Kristine asked. "I really can make tea, it's about the only thing I can do next to sandwiches."

"Bah! You're not good at sandwiches my dear." Mrs Parker leaned over to Avion "She makes them like worn out steps, thin in the middle, huge on the outside. Lord only knows how she manages it."

Avion laughed.

"Tea it is then, Avion?" Kristine tipped her head to one side just like Mrs Parker did, it was then that Avion could see the similarity between the women. She nodded sheepishly.

"I suppose you're wondering why Kristine is here at all. I'm dog sitting this week, see she's off on a holiday and cannot take Ceaser with her, so he is staying with his granny." Her voice had melted into the tone that adults use on children, as she looked lovingly into the soppy mutts dark eyes. He panted.

"That's Ceaser equivalent of a smile" Mrs Parker explained.

"How do you know where he is?" Avion asked.

"Mrs Parker frowned, then smiled, was I looking him in the eyes?"

Avion nodded, and said yes, making the old lady laugh. "Spooky isn't it when a blind person does that? Pure fluke on my part I promise."

When Kristine delivered the tea tray and had settled beside Avion, they passed some time chatting about life before Kristine returned to the subject of Avion.

"You don't have to go back to him you know." She said watching Avion's reaction.

"I do. He will never give up trying to get me back, and then he will really lay into me for leaving at all. Been there, done that, failed in the attempt." She gave a sad smile.

"Tsch." Mrs Parker said.

"If you want to leave this man altogether, we can help. You have so much to offer Avion, you deserve to have someone in your life who will care about you, put you first."

Avion wanted it more than anything, but she'd been failed before.

"Won't work. I was promised all that once before and then Damion found me, persuaded the shelter to let me go, promised to take anger management, promised to attend AA, promised all sorts, and they believed him. Soon as we got home, I got a beating."

"Give us a chance." Kristine begged.

"Why do you care?" Avion asked, truly perplexed.

"Granny loves you Avion and when granny takes someone to heart, she won't let go either! Honestly you're family now, and we believe that family sticks together."

Avion stayed quiet, she wanted so badly to think these kind people could help her, but Mrs P was old, and her kind of monster was not Damion. She had no idea what he could do.

"Wouldn't you like to take *your* wages and shop for *you*? To eat every day? To bathe in hot water? To have real friends? To date a decent man?" Kristine asked, and Avion had to admit, she painted a picture that was easy to love.

"It's a nice thought." She said sadly "but I am ruined. I have scars all over me, what man would want to look at those? I can't have children, most men want a family don't they? I have no qualifications, who wants a thick cow like me? I have nothing to give to a relationship, so no, I have no future in that sense." She pulled at a thread on her thin shirt.

"You could have a home of your own, we can help with that." Kristine insisted. Avion barked a laugh. "Yea from frying pan to fire. No offence but owing you is the same as owing Damion without the violence."

"Family don't owe each other." Mrs Parker growled.

"I'm sorry, I didn't mean to offend." Avion whispered as she slightly cringed, and relaxed when the expected slap never came.

"It's up to you. We have this week, let's see how things go eh? Just promise you won't dismiss the idea completely?" Kristine implored. Avion nodded and promised.
"Well forgive me for saying, but do you have a change of clothes?" Kristine asked. Avion shook her head.
"Mm. Look why don't you go upstairs, have a nice long soak in a hot bath, while I go make a phone call?"
When Avion looked at them both to protest, she could see how that wasn't going to be entertained, so she smiled gratefully and took herself up stairs.
"I don't have a change of clothes." She muttered more to herself than to anyone else, she might get clean in a bath but she would still be wearing her dirty clothes.
"I think one of my outfits might fit you, well drown you, actually, but you'll look good in it."
Avion's eyes widened. "I can't wear your clothes!" She gasped.
"Why not?" Kristine looked genuinely perplexed.
"Too good for me." Avion was going to say they would be too posh, but thought that might be insulting in some way.
"Tsch" Mrs Parker said again.

The bath was heaven. Avion stepped into the foamy tub and settled her aching body down, feeling the warmth of the water soak into her bones, soothing and relaxing. Heaven. The scent of the soap assaulted her nose, and she breathed in its aroma, smiling from the pleasure. She gently ran it over her skin, loving the silky texture, the sheer expensiveness of the experience. She picked the stinkiest shampoo she could find, and lathered it into her hair twice, scrubbing her head clean from over a year's worth of grime and grease. It felt so good. Heaven. Her bruises shone bright but for now only Avion had to see them. *This could be me every day.* She dared to imagine it, dared to think it could last. Dared herself to dream she could call these people family. Yet if they gave her all this, what could she give them back? Wasn't life about give and take? She sighed deeply, she was nothing, had nothing; so

what right did she have to take from people whom she could give nothing back to? A soft knock on the bathroom door brought her back to the present.
"I put some clothes on the bed out here ok?" Kristine's kind voice was muffled against the wood.
"Thanks." Avion shouted back, just happy the woman didn't have to see her battered state. Reluctantly she forced herself to part company with the bubbles, and she found herself somewhat horrified at the tide line between clean bath and dirty water. Wrapped in a huge bath towel, which was as soft as lamb's wool, she returned to the bedroom. Kristine had left her a pair of jeans, a t-shirt and a cardigan to hide her arms. Her other clothes had disappeared, but Avion didn't care, she was snuggled into the towel, and she would have stayed that way, except she was a guest here, and she had to put in an appearance downstairs. She sat on the bed, her bed for this week, a real bed with a bouncy mattress and feather pillows. She smiled and tears welled in her eyes. *I remember when I took such things for granted, how did I come to this*? She knew in that moment she would never go back to Damion and his slum. She began to rub her hair with the towel, then realised Mrs Parker wouldn't begrudge her the use of a hair dryer, especially as she found one lying on the bed, as though a polite reminder of the fact. It felt wonderful to feel warm air blow through her hair, to see it fly out in ribbons as she moved the dryer over her head. Avion smiled at such a luxury. She closed her eyes and imagined being in a sports car in summer, the feel of the warm breeze tugging her locks as she drove along. Heaven.

It was close to tea time when Avion reappeared in the back parlor, both women stopped talking to take in the visage that stood before them. "Wow." Kristine said and whistled. "Where is Avion and who are you?" She teased, making Avion blush.
"I can smell you from here." Mrs Parker smiled, holding out her hand to Avion. Those bony fingers missed nothing, every

slight rise of a bruise she saw it through her touch, she felt Avion's hair soft as silk threads.

"She's glowing granny, and her hair is brown with copper strands, so beautiful." Kristine said with genuine pride.

"Stop it, you're making me cry." Avion pleaded, but she was smiling and the tears were happy ones.

"And how do you feel?" Mrs Parker asked, her face filled with expectation.

"Wonderful." Avion replied truthfully. "Just wonderful." She wiped a stray tear from her eyes. "Sorry. I keep crying, it's just this is all a bit overwhelming. I'm just not used to it."

"Well we have a week to sell real life to you in, and frankly I can't wait." Kristine beamed.

Chapter 5

"I thought you were going on holiday?" Avion asked frowning.
"That was my phone call." Kristine smiled. "I was supposed to go on a university observation week, but I didn't want to go. My *family*," She sneered the word. "Refused to give me a get-out-of-jail card, but then you happened and I called my hubby who said I should stay and help you and granny. He has two policemen outside as well. If your Mr turns up and causes trouble, he will wish he hadn't." Kristine looked triumphant.
"Patrick, her husband, is high up in the police. More fingers in pies dear." Mrs Parker explained.
"I am sorry to be the cause of all this trouble." Avion muttered. "Won't missing your observation week cause problems for you?"
"Na." Kristine said airily. "The boys, those would be my brothers, but we always call them the boys, were being smart arses, and Patrick wouldn't listen to me, so I was destined to be sent on a terribly boring week away without my baby Ceaser."
Ceaser whined at the sound of his name, making Avion instinctively rub his ears.
"I'm sure your course is far more important than I am." Avion said factually.
"I'll agree the course is important, but not as important as girl time together. We have to go shopping, we have to make new friends for you, gosh I only have a week Avion; it's going to be amazing, and I am starting out with a haircut for you."
Avion frowned. "I like my hair."

"Yes but it could do with tidying up." Kristine looked bashful, which made Avion smile, besides she was right, her hair hadn't been cut or trimmed in over three years, so Avion agreed.

"Great. I have a friend who cuts for all the important peeps in life, and she needs a guinea pig, so you get a free haircut and she gets to practice."

A loud knock on the front door had them all freeze.

"Hi Mrs P, It's me Damion."

All the blood drained from Avion's face, and she began to tremble. Mrs Parker put her hand on Avion's and gave it a powerful squeeze, reminding Avion, she wasn't as frail as she appeared.

"In here." Mrs Parker called back, and a moment later Damion stood in the doorway. He stared at Avion, not quite able to recognise the woman before him. He also gave Kristine a sour look, he hadn't expected a witness to be here.

"Arh thank God." He said smiling. "I have been looking everywhere for you Avi. You had me so worried, what with your concussion an all. Thanks Mrs P for looking after her, I hope she ain't been too much trouble."

"No trouble at all." Mrs Parker replied calmly.

"Where's your clothes Avi?" He asked puzzled.

"In the bin." Avi answered softly.

"Shit Avi, whose are those? You didn't steal again did ya?" He looked concerned.

"No I gave them to her." The stranger said. Damion turned his gaze to Kristine.

"Who are you?" He asked trying to keep the sneer from his voice.

"I'm the granddaughter of Mrs Parker."

"An what right have you to decide what my girlfriend wears?"

"I have the right to expect my mother's cleaner to look respectable, as her boyfriend I'd have thought you would want the same?" Kristine said firmly.

Damion smiled, he had ruffled the bitch's feathers.

"Ain't none of your business what I want my girl to look like. So kindly keep your nose out of my business."

"Damion I'll thank you not to speak to my granddaughter like that in my house. I think you should leave." Mrs Parker looked straight at him, her glare seemed to see right through him, which was creepy.

"Come on Avi, ain't staying where we ain't wanted." He glared at Avi, who stayed firmly in her chair.

"*You* ain't welcome. I'm staying Damion. I don't want to go back to your slum and I never will. It is over between us." Avion's voice wobbled slightly, but her gaze said what her voice feared to, and Damion's expression changed to thunder.

"Get off your fucking lazy arse right now bitch." He growled, caring not for his act any more.

"Time to go Damion, Avion has told you what she wants, please respect her." Mrs Parker told him.

"Like I said Mrs P. I'll go only when Avion stops behaving like a spoilt brat. Avion, you think these people care about you? They don't. You ain't nothing to them, just a charity case. They will dump you soon as they get bored of you. So stop this shit and come home." He took a step forward. Mrs Parker stood up, hands resting on the table cloth.

"You do not have the right to seize her." A low growl erupted from under the table, followed by a long snout and tall pointed ears. Avion wanted to laugh, how clever of Kristine to call her dog that. Damion stepped back, glaring at the Dobermann.

"Call it off." He said calmly, backing into the door frame. Ceaser curled his lip showing off white sharp canines.

"You have out stayed your welcome Damion, now kindly leave and do not ever return." Mrs Parker said with an authority Damion loathed.

"You fucking witch" He snarled as he backed up down the hallway, Ceaser stepping forward with each back step

Damion took. "This ain't over Avi, you'll fucking pay for this."

Ceaser barked, snapping his jaws as saliva dribbled from his jowls. Damion turned and legged it to the front door, as he opened it, he was met by two policemen.

"Damion Smallman you are under arrest for attempted burglary." They spun him round and slapped cuffs on him.

The three women listened as he shouted expletives whilst being taken away.

"Well done Avion." Mrs Parker turned to face her. Avion stood up trembling from head to foot. Mrs Parker gave her a bear hug, again demonstrating a strength a woman her age had no right to.

"Don't think for a moment he will stop, he won't. He'll be back every day in any way he can. In his mind he owns me." Avion sobbed allowing herself to let go of the fear she had held back. Mrs Parker rubbed her back comfortingly.

"Of course he will. Men like him don't take kindly to being over ruled by a woman let alone three of us."

A phone began to ring, and Kristine answered it.

"Hey honey. … Good timing. Really? …. Oh that's great. I love you. … Bye." She put her phone back in her bag. "Patrick says they are holding Damion for seven days for attempted burglary, which means we have seven days to have some fun in." She grinned like a Cheshire cat. Avion's eyes went wide. Seven days of freedom, of not looking over her shoulder, of not being afraid. She sobbed again from relief.

***

It had been a long day. Avion sat on the edge of her bed, *when I woke up this morning I couldn't have dreamed I would be taking a bath, wearing clean clothes and sleeping in a real bed, what a difference a day makes.* She smiled. Her hand traced over the duvet cover, and she inhaled its scent. Clean. She even smiled at the night shirt Krissy had left for her. *I am blessed.* She thought, pulling back the covers and climbing inside. She lay for a while marveling at her change of fortune, and praying Damion was wrong, and this would last, she drifted into a deep sleep, in the arms of a stranger, who smelt divine.

***

"This ain't no cop shop. Where am I?" Damion shouted as he was dragged into a dark room and forced to sit in a chair. He was still handcuffed but his hands were in front of him now. He was left alone in the dark, shouting and swearing, demanding a solicitor, a phone call, to have his rights respected. He was left for several hours until he could be heard sobbing. He needed a fix, a smoke, a piss, but got neither. He'd screamed himself hoarse and now wanted a drink, but that didn't come, nor did salvation. He was pretty sure he was going to die here, even though he had no idea why. Fuck Avion, she would so pay when he got free, *if* he got free. Fuck that old woman, blind bitch, Avion had gotten her wrapped round her little finger, and who the fuck was that rich bitch? Granddaughter, bet this was something to do with her. Damion seethed, his leg jiggled violently in his nervousness. Fuck em all, he'd get revenge, make em pay.

A door opened and a bright light came on, making Damion squint. He heard footsteps and then a chair scraped over the concrete, and someone sat down.
"Bet you could do with a drink?" A deep voice asked calmly. Damion squinted at him, and nodded. A freezing cold cup of water was thrown at him, making him gasp.
"Ooops. Let's try that again shall we?" The voice said with humour. Another freezing cold glass of water washed over Damion. He shivered violently.
"Now that you have expelled some of that anger, perhaps we can have a chat?" The man paused and after some seconds of nothing, Damion supposed he should respond, so he nodded his head.

"Good. You're a nasty piece of work aren't you Smallman?"
Damion had no idea what the idiot was saying, so he shrugged.
"I didn't think you would need reminding, seems I was wrong."
A violent pain erupted in Damion's eye and the side of his face. He was thrown off the chair. He lay on the floor moaning.
"Tut tut. Surely you saw that coming? I mean you expect Avion to know when she has pissed you off."
So that is what this was about. How did this bloke know about him and Avion? Had to be the rich bitch.
"Smallman, get up and stop being a baby." A boot kicked his foot, and Damion struggled to stand. A pair of hands undid his handcuffs.
"I believe in fair chances, so feel free to defend yourself at any point."
Damion shielded his eyes, but couldn't make out his attacker. He was forced to sit back down in the chair again.
"Let's try again. You are a nasty piece of work are you not?"
"No I ain't, an you got no right to hold me here." Damion shouted back.
"You don't have any right to hit a woman, especially someone you call a girlfriend. So we are even for now. You would agree hitting a girlfriend is really cowardly?"
Damion remained quiet, he was on a losing wicket whatever he said.
"That requires an answer by the way." The voice remained controlled. Damion remained silent. Another violent flash of pain erupted on his lower jaw, again sending him flying.
"How does it feel to be a woman?" The voice asked. "They have no idea when a punch is coming either."
Damion snarled.
"I quite like being the man in this relationship. I can see how it makes you feel. You look pathetic to me now, it's a

disappointment. I want you to fight back but you won't, which makes me want to hit you again."

Damion squinted in the bright light, trying to search for where the voice might be, but it changed all the time.

"See being you, Smallman, I don't really need a reason to be pissed off, the sight of your pathetic form is enough to set me off." Another punch landed on his nose this time, snapping his head back so hard he thought they'd broken it for him. Blood gushed down his front and Damion moaned in misery.

"Alright. I'm sorry. You can stop now ok?" He was hoarse and scared, more scared than he had been in his whole life.

"This is how Avion feels when you punch her."

Damion doubted it, but wasn't going to argue.

"She wants you to stop but you don't do you?"

"Yea I do." Damion panicked, he knew what was coming this time, and he tried to defend himself, putting his arms up against his head. The fist smashed into his puny thin arm, snapping the bone audibly. Damion screamed.

"Please." He begged, tears closing up his already swelling eye.

"Well seeing as you asked so nicely." The voice said. The light went out, the feet walked away, a door shut and Damion was left alone in the dark once more. He curled up in a ball on the floor and cried.

Chapter 6

Avion woke with a feeling of excitement, it was the first time in a long time that she had something to look forward to; she washed and dressed again in Kristine's borrowed clothes, and then arrived in the back parlor.
"Arh Avion, I just spoke to my hairdressing friend, she has a day off today, so is on her way round." Kristine sounded as excited as Avion felt.
"I can't remember the last time I had my hair cut or trimmed." Avion admitted. It was starting to feel good, being pampered, so she decided to enjoy it while it lasted and face the cost later. The rest of the day they would be shopping for clothes.
"I don't have any money for clothes. Damion drank it all last Friday." Avion admitted.
"A loan. I'll pay for your clothes today and we will decide later how much you pay me back?" Mrs Parker suggested.
"That's very kind." Avion began, but her employer cut her off.
"Good, that's settled then." Her tone brooked no argument, so Avion cowed and thanked her nervously.

When Cassidy the hairdresser arrived, she was overjoyed that Avion gave her free reign to assault her fine hair anyway she wanted. She cut and feathered the hair to fit and sit around Avion's face, the back was bobbed to give it volume and make it easier for Avion to care for, when done Avion hardly recognised herself.
"I look so different." She observed, smiling.
"You look adorable." Kristine said.
Mrs Parker held her hands out and Avion moved into them, allowing the blind granny to feel the difference.

"Cassidy, you have done us proud." Mrs P concluded.

"Thank you so much." Avion said sincerely, she had never looked so pretty in all her life. *Who'd have thought a haircut could make that much difference!* She also noted how Cassidy never looked at her bruises or commented about her thin state, something else she was grateful for.

"Krissy, it's Ally Cats birthday on Friday, we are going for drinks and a meal, you are both coming I hope?" Cassidy asked.

"Ooo, are we having a meal at the Delhi?" Krissy asked, her eyes lighting up. Cassidy nodded and spoke her confirmation for Mrs Parker's sake.

"Yes Gods count us in!" Krissy insisted.

"Umm. Not me if you don't mind." Avion said, suddenly self-conscious about her looks.

"No no, Avion you have to come, it's amazing hun, honestly." Krissy begged. "The Delhi has the most drop dead fantastic, sexy, waiters you ever clapped your eyes on. They have amazing looks, so macho and so *not* worthy of being waiters, Chippendales perhaps, but not waiters! Tight shirts that leave nothing to the imagination, all muscle and biceps, and smiles that melt yer knickers! You have to see them, oh you just have to." Krissy cooed.

"Kristine Gilmore you are a married woman." Mrs Parker reminded her granddaughter.

"Oh granny, you think Patrick doesn't know I behave badly around gorgeous men?"

"Well those you're not related to at any rate." Cassidy put in.

"Have you met her brothers yet?" She leaned towards Avion conspiratorially. Avion shook her head. Cassidy wafted her hand in front of her face, "Named after angels, look like fucking angels."

"Cassidy!" Mrs Parker shouted in alarm, but she was smiling. Cassidy apologized.

"Ignore her, are you coming or not?" Krissy gave her a pleading look and Avion caved.

"You think I want to be seen looking like this? Having people think I am anorexic or worse, seeing me covered in bruises?"
"We will hide those, cosmetics Avion, and the waiters don't care, they will pamper you because you need feeding!" Kristine insisted, so Avion smiled, shaking her head, not believing she was agreeing to this madness. *Out of the frying pan Avion*, said a voice in her head.

Having fed Mrs Parker her lunch, both Avion and Kristine headed on out, Ceaser padded along beside them, ears pricking in all directions, ever alert to dangers.
"Do you take him everywhere?" Avion asked.
"He's my guard dog, he has to come everywhere, wouldn't be much point having him otherwise." Kristine said as they reached her car, and Ceaser jumped into the back seat immediately.
"Where are we going to shop?" Avion wondered as Kristine pulled away into traffic.
"First things first, lunch. Cannot shop on an empty stomach."
They arrived at the large shopping Mall, four levels of shops with a food mall on the top floor. Aromas of food drifted in the air, making Avion feel really hungry. Pastry and coffee mixed with pizzas and chicken, burgers, chips and bacon all met her nose with an enticing seduction to her stomach, to come and try them. They sat at a table overlooking the floors below, and the melee of humanity that wove around each other like so many ants in a nest.
"So how did you meet Damion, or is that too painful?" Krissy asked as she sat down. Avion shrugged.
"My friend wanted me to go with her on a date, and her boyfriend brought his mate along, Damion."
"Love at first sight?"
Avion laughed. "I was naive, gullible. I still am really. Damion was good looking, sure of himself and a bit of a bad boy, I suppose he was exciting."
"So what went wrong?"

"I don't really know. He used to smoke cannabis now and then, but over time he smoked it more and more, and his temper got worse. He saw demons in everyone. He said a woman's place in life was to keep the home clean, and be a whore in bed. I could do the house clean thing, but I could never be a whore for him, he made me into that. I hated his kind of sex, and hated myself more for allowing it, but then if I didn't obey, I got punched."

"That's such a shame. I bet you hate the idea of being with a man?" Krissy's face was a picture of sympathy. Avion blushed.

"Pretty sure there are nice men out there, but I'm not looking for anyone, not after him. I don't trust me."

"Avion, I know it's all pretty raw right now, but most men are not Damion. You have to learn that you got unlucky, but unlucky once isn't forever, look; smile and let men compliment you, you deserve it, ok?" Kristy looked at her earnestly, squeezed her hand and smiled encouragingly. Avion nodded.

"It might be easier when I don't have a body covered in bruises."

"If you're a part of this family now, then compliments are something you're going to have to get used to, not to mention flirting. My brothers are notorious for it."

Avion smiled. "So is what Cassidy said about them true?"

"Yea, more's the pity, and they all know they look like demi gods!"

"So who do they take after, mother or father?" Avion asked.

"Well dad I suppose. See we never knew our paternal grandfather, he died when dad was a boy. When granny remarried, my dad didn't take his name, he kept his own name because granny had used his father's name on his birth certificate, and it was too much hoo ha to change everything. So my dad is Nathen De Luca, and according to granny, his father looked like a demi god, so I think that's where they get their looks and sadly their dark side." Kristine informed her.

"People keep hinting at a dark side, how dark do they get?" Avion asked intrigued. Kristy sighed. "They make Damion look like a pussy cat."

Wow. That was hard to imagine.

"Our family is well known for underhanded practices and none of the boys are adverse to violence. I'm sure granny told you about Cuthbert's nickname?"

"Yea. Cut?" Avion asked raising her eye brows slightly. "He doesn't sound too friendly."

"Arh! Now that's where you're wrong. With a name like Cut, I agree he should be a moody bastard, but actually Cut is one of the nicest people you'll ever meet. They all are really, it's just if you cross them, it comes at a cost."

A clock nearby chimed the hour of two, and Kristy sighed. "Are we done here? We haven't brought a stitch yet!"

Avion smirked, and both women got up to go shopping, yet Avion worried. The men of this family were violent, hadn't she had enough of violent men in her life? Then it occurred to her that Damion might not have been arrested. Avion stopped dead in the middle of the Mall.

"Where is Damion?" She asked. Kristine stopped and looked at her. "I don't know, why?"

"You said your brothers are not adverse to violence, so was Damion really arrested?" She was trembling now, and Kristine noticed immediately.

"Yes he was arrested, and I am sure he is in custody." She tried to sound soothing but Avion wasn't convinced.

"I want to see him." She burst out, not quite sure why except she wanted to know he was safe. Kristine looked confused. "Why?"

"I want to know your brother's aren't beating him up."

Kristine frowned, clearly she hadn't expected this.

"Avion I'm sure Damion is fine, he is being held on charges of attempted burglary, to give you a week of being free of him."

Avion could feel the tension in the air, Kristine wasn't being truthful.

"I know Damion is a bad person, but I wouldn't want him to suffer what I have, I wouldn't wish that on anyone, even him. So I want to see him please."

Kristine hesitated, her confident air had cracked.

"I'll make a phone call. Why don't you start looking in that shop see if you can find anything you like?"

Avion didn't move, she didn't want this family's charity, and especially she didn't want to be in any deeper debt to Mrs Parker. Instead she found a nearby bench and went and sat on it while Kristine made her phone call. It seemed entirely wrong of Avion to be out and about spending other people's money on herself, laughing and joking while Damion was tied up somewhere having the holy hell beaten out of him, whatever she thought of Damion, he didn't deserve this. What right had these brothers got to judge him, when they didn't know the first thing about him? Suddenly Avion didn't feel so safe anymore, hadn't Mrs Parker and now Kristine confirmed these men were so much nastier than Damion, more dangerous? Avion felt eyes on her from everywhere. *It's a panic attack*, she told herself as she trembled violently. She only had Mrs Parker's and Kristine's words to tell her she was safe, these men didn't hit women, but who could she trust, really? Her palms were sweaty, her skin pasty and she jumped visibly when Kristine came and sat beside her.

"Avion. I don't know what has upset you so much, but I think it is a bad idea to see Damion."

Avion turned to her, livid. "Why, have you hurt him?"

Kristine hung her head. "He is learning how he makes you feel." She said softly. Avion stiffened.

"You have no right. You said he was under arrest. You lied."

"It's more complicated than you realise. Please Avion, I'll take you home, we can talk about things there."

The journey home was made in silence, Avion wringing her hands in her lap, hoping Damion was alive. She paused in the short driveway outside Mrs Parker's home, if she went in, would she ever come out again?

"I promise no harm will come to you." Kristine said kindly as though she had read Avion's mind. In the back parlor Mrs Parker sat waiting.

"Avion sit down please." Her voice was strained. Avion remained standing making Mrs Parker thin her lips with annoyance. It was suddenly clear to Avion who the monster was in this family. Mrs Parker wasn't the sweet old blind lady Avion had always thought she was, without those rose tinted glasses, she could see the power the old woman oozed, this was the head of the family, there sat the power. It was all Avion could do to stay there and not bolt for the door.

"Suit yourself." Mrs Parker said in a strained voice, she wasn't used to disobedience. "I was hoping I wouldn't have to have this conversation for some weeks yet, but it seems you have been spooked in some way. Damion is a bad man. He is also a dead man walking."

Avion sucked in her breath.

Mrs Parker raised a bony finger. "Here me out." She warned. "Damion is a crack and cocaine addict. Six months ago he lost his job as a laborer paid under the table. He was sacked because of his cannabis habit, it made him unpredictable and unreliable. He went to Danny Baker for help and Danny had him selling cocaine, which worked out fine for a month or two, but then Damion got curious and stole a customer's order to try for himself. That's how he got addicted. Nobody noticed that Damion was stealing the goods, as he also brought his own crack and cocaine, but then Danny realised too many of his customers were beginning to complain their packages were not being delivered. He called Damion to account, and demanded he pay for the stolen drugs. Damion couldn't that was why he beat you for not having the money he needed to pay Danny back. He hadn't borrowed money from him, he'd stolen drugs, and his debt runs into thousands Avion, so your wages wouldn't have started to cover what is owed. If we let Damion go, he will be picked up by Danny and almost certainly killed, forced overdose is the usual method for Danny Baker, we have no use for Damion, he is never going to change; right now he is angry. He is filled with hatred for you, because you are always the reason for his problems in life. It will be dangerous for you to see him, but it is your choice. Whatever you think of his treatment, he is a nasty narcissist, and he will kill you as soon as you both get home. You don't need me to tell you that, your own knowledge of him has already warned you, your time is running out." Mrs Parker stopped talking. Avion stared at her in horror. Damion was no hard drug addict, she had never seen him snort cocaine or smoke crack, though he did suffer nose bleeds sometimes, and his eyes were always blood shot, though she was sure that had been the alcohol he consumed. They were both rake thin but that was more because they couldn't afford to eat, *surely*? She *knew* Damion. This was a lie, but why would these people lie? Avion wasn't anyone to them, nor Damion for that matter. Avion rubbed her forehead, this was impossible, unbelievable. She'd lived with Damion for three years, how could she not have seen what he was doing.

"How do you know all this?" She asked, accusingly. Mrs Parker smiled sadly. "I had him watched from the first time I felt your skinny arms and bruises. I had some of our people ask questions."

God, this woman could see more blind than most people could with sight.

"A car is waiting for you outside, Kristine can go with you if you wish?"

Avion wasn't entirely sure having Kristine along was a good idea, but then again being on her own with a complete stranger wasn't comforting either, so she nodded and Kristine told her grandmother she would be going with her.

Chapter 7

The drive to the holding place was about half an hour, and quite the longest half an hour Avion had ever suffered. Nobody spoke making the journey stretch even longer. The driver was a big man, biceps that could crush skulls, she was sure of it. Buildings became industrial estates and they in turn became fields, before the SUV turned off into a small village whereupon stood a farm with suitable out buildings. The SUV parked outside the front door of the farm house and all passengers went inside. It was dark and without furniture, but towards the back of the building, was a large country kitchen complete with Aga. Avion was diverted towards a small off room.
"He is doing cold turkey Avion, he won't look well at all." Kristine warned her. At the nod of her head, a body guard opened the door. Damion lay curled up with his back to them, shaking. Avion stepped into the bright room. "Damion?" She asked softly, appalled by the sight of him, reduced to a shivering mess, just as she had been many times at his hands. Tears welled in her eyes as she carefully approached him, she squatted down beside him and reached out to lay her hand on his shoulder. He turned his head, terror in his swollen eyes. His nose was flat and bloody, his blond hair had flecks of blood in it, and on his arm he wore a splint, just as he fixed for her a few times. When he recognised her his terror turned to rage, his lip curled in contempt and he batted her hand away.
"So they dumped you already did they? Told yer so. Serves you right Avi. Or did yer come here to gloat? Take a good

fucking look cos you done this." He snarled at her. "You fucking bitch, you done this to me."
"Damion did you take drugs?" She asked desperately.
"Fuck off. This is all your fault you fucking miserable slag."
Avion felt a wave of anger wash over her. She knew Mrs Parker had told her the truth after all. Damion couldn't admit it to her, it was always easier for him to lie. Her boyfriend, the man she lived with, had taken drugs and she hadn't known, but a blind old stranger had. How stupid had she been? So caught up in her own misery, she hadn't noticed how desperate Damion's life had become.
"Why didn't you tell me?" She whispered. Damion spat at her. His skin looked waxy, grey and sweaty, but for all his appearance was dreadful, he maintained a healthy hatred towards Avion. Damion tried to laugh, but it came out as a weak huff.
"Always the fucking same Avi, always trying to be a smart arse, telling me what is fucking best. What do you know?" He screamed the last at her, making her stand up quickly. He turned over and glared at her.
"You pathetic cow, what the fuck do you know about anything? Look at you, standing there crying like the fucking baby you are." He turned his head away and curled up even tighter as a wave of pain shot through him.
"I'm fucking dying here, and what are you doing? Feeling sorry for me again. I don't want your sympathy, why don't you just fuck off Avi, go back to your fucking rich friends."
Avion watched him for a few seconds, numb. Mrs Parker's grandsons had punched Damion and withheld drugs he needed, they had no right to treat him this way. Almost twenty four hours had passed since he was "arrested", and he was a mess. She couldn't go to the police, Kristine's husband was someone important in the police force, and they wouldn't help her. Damion needed a doctor, a proper clinic to get him straight, yet hadn't he told her to leave him alone? He'd never thanked her for trying to help him, so why did she bother?

She stared down at his broken body, and tears ran freely down her face.

"I'm sorry Damion." She said softly. Helpless, she turned and walked back to the door, which opened for her immediately. Kristine didn't say a word as she walked back to the SUV with Avion, her heels being the only sound as her shoes clicked on the concrete floor. All the way back to the house, Avion replayed her life with Damion, and she still couldn't see where he had chosen drugs over life.

***

The SUV didn't return to Mrs Parker's home, but stopped at the flats where Avion and Damion lived. It was a relief to be back where she belonged, and away from the people she had come to fear. Kristine didn't say a word to her, nor make any physical effort to restrain her from leaving. Avion didn't look back as she ran towards the block she lived in, the block she vowed not to return to. The flat stank even worse than it had two days ago, and Avion went straight to the bedroom to open a window, that she realised wasn't there, just the board the council had put up. The place was still in darkness, but now she could light the candles they had stored up. She collapsed onto the mattress on the floor and cried her heart out. She didn't care that it was self-pity, everyone was allowed to feel that from time to time, especially when their whole world had come crashing down. Her parents had turned their back on her, her boyfriend had made sure all her friends had no contact with her, even her employer wasn't who she seemed to be. As far as Avion knew, there wasn't anyone in the world she could trust any more. She couldn't leave, she had no money for starters, and where would she go? She was trapped, and scared. How long would it be before she was being punished? For not cleaning properly, or paying her debt back, how long before Mrs Parker's boys started on her?

The following day, Avion stayed at home. She sat by her bedroom window, straining with the light that seeped through the grime at the edges, with her embroidery in her hands. Her book of life laid open to all the memories she had sewn into it. She finished the picture of the Victorian bath with its lion feet and slightly higher head end, it was a luxury picture. She smiled. Thoughts of Damion curled up in a beaten mess, and the truth of his life, all crowded her mind. Why on earth should she waste her time feeling sorry for a moron like him? She hadn't been the one to introduce him to cocaine, nor had she been the one who lost him his job, and after her visit, where he could have asked for her help, but didn't, why should she care what happened to him. Avion sighed deeply. *I don't care.* She realised, not any more. Let the De Luca men beat him to death, it wasn't her problem it never had been, he'd made it abundantly clear he hadn't wanted her help, he never had. *I deserve my life.* She thought. But what of her life? Did she still have a job anymore? Was she safe going anywhere near that family? Avion looked at her book of memories. The cake for Mrs Parker's 90th birthday, a happy day. She couldn't deny that when she thought of Mrs Parker she felt happy, and safe. Alone she felt vulnerable. Avion shivered and looked around the slum she called home. *I can't stay here. Danny knows we live here, he's bound to come calling wanting to know where Damion is, who will pay his debt now? Me, who else?* She felt a cold terror slide down her spine. How long before Danny came after her? Her fingers traced themselves over the bath tub, soft fine hair like silk against her skin. She had taken Mrs Parker's hair from her hairbrush, the white was perfect for the bath. Safe, Avion thought. Did it matter that Mrs Parker wasn't what she seemed? Perhaps she was only trying to save Avion, and who better to protect a vulnerable woman like her than five men, all of whom could have made an appearance at any time over the last year, but never had, because they had never needed to. That had all changed when Damion wanted Avion back. Avion snorted.

Five filthy rich men, why would they be interested in a nothing like me? They have no reason to beat me, nor did Damion, but that hadn't stopped him. Yet Damion was driven mad by the drugs he'd taken, and Avion was pretty sure the De Luca men wouldn't be drug addicts. She had no idea what would happen to Damion at the end of the week. Mrs Parker had made it clear they had no use for him, which indicated that her grandsons had only interfered because Damion would come looking for Avion. They were protecting their grandmother, and Mrs Parker was protecting Avion. So what to do now? Avion couldn't go back to her job, Mrs Parker was still at risk. Danny was still a problem she had no right to inflict upon anyone, maybe the police would help but how could they he hadn't done anything yet, no crime had been committed, no threat had been made. Avion was stuck with no money and nowhere to run to, and she was hungry, having not eaten since lunchtime the day before, there was no hope for it, she either went back to Mrs Parker or go hungry. Avion never got to make a choice because the door got smashed in. She hurriedly hid her tapestry book back in the bag, and pushed herself back up against the bedroom wall, just in time to see two well-honed men step into the bedroom. They looked thoroughly disappointed there was no furniture to smash up, so stood waving baseball bats menacingly. Avion shifted slightly, pushing her bag behind her, listening to the sound of splintered wood being brushed aside with a foot, then the appearance of another man, dressed in black trousers, black shirt open to his chest, short stubbled hair and stubble face. He looked about him with a sneer of disgust. Then he turned to face Avion.

"Sorry about the mess. Well actually no I ain't. Where is your lover, boyfriend, partner whatever?" He asked conversationally. Avion tried to answer but her throat had ceased up, and nothing came out, so she did a reasonable impersonation of a gold fish.

"I take it you're Avy on?" He asked.

"Avion." She corrected, swallowing hard. He grinned.
"Well my name is Danny Baker and your bloke owes me a lot of money, so where is he?"
Avion shook her head. "I don't know."
One of the thugs smashed his baseball bat down in front of her, making her jump a mile.
"He, he got arrested." Avion said tears spilling down her cheeks. Danny Baker thought about this.
"Did he now." It wasn't a question. "Funny thing is one of my own also got arrested Monday night, but is now back wiv me, and he says Damion weren't in the nick. So where is he?" Danny yelled the last bit in her face. Avion sobbed. "They took him out of town." She blurted.
"Whooo?" Danny asked, still in her face.
"Us." Came a new voice from the doorway. Danny Baker spun round, his eyes went wide as saucers.
"Fuck me, it's true then." He said softly. Avion leaned over to see who the new person was. He was taller than Danny, and wore a very expensive looking suit, apart from that Avion couldn't make out his features, but his voice was as smooth as silk and really calm.
"I don't think you have any business here." The new man said.
"Arh but I do sir." Danny said carefully. The new man waited. "See her bloke, owes me a lot of dosh, and you have him locked up somewhere safe, no doubt, but thing is, I need to collect. You know how it goes." Danny smiled. The new man sighed.
"Kristine take the young lady out of here, she doesn't need to see men's business."
Avion was surprised as hell to see Kristine step out from somewhere in the hallway.
"Come on Avi, it's ok. I promise."
Avion stood on shaky legs and moved slowly towards Kristine, no body moved.
"Now Mr Cut sir, that ain't fair. I got no beef with you."

Did he just say Cut? Avion was about level with the tall stranger now, so she glanced up into a tanned face that had short hair which was wavy, and shaved at the sides of his head. His eyes were a bright hypnotic blue, lined with dark long lashes, chiseled cheek bones and thin lips. *Fucking Demi God.* He winked at her and a soft smirk thinned his lips even more. Avion blushed. So this was Cuthbert, and obviously not about to behave like any saint.

"You have no beef with her either." Cut said as a matter of fact.

"She owes, she is Damion's woman, so the debt falls to her. I have rights." Danny protested in kind.

"Mr Baker, she is no longer Smallman's woman, so I reiterate, you have no business or rights to her."

Kristine and Avion had made it to the smashed-to-bits front door.

"You don't want to test me sir, we are three against one." Danny pointed out, hopeful that the rumours about Cut De Luca were wrong.

"I am going to be really pissed to mess up this suit, but if you're going to insist, I will oblige." Cut replied and Avion would swear he was smiling, for all she couldn't see him.

"Always best to let the men get on with business." Kristine said encouragingly. Avion followed her outside.

***

"You really shouldn't na taken her away like that sir." Danny said through his teeth "Now I am going to ruin your suit."

Cut had enough time to undo his jacket button before one of the thugs launched at him, baseball bat swinging, Cut stepped into the assault, grabbing the forearm of the thug and snapping it loudly, the man screamed as he crumpled onto the floor. The second thug had already started to move, his bat came down hard on Cut's back as his companion screamed. Cut stuck out his leg linking it around the second man's leg and pulled him off balance, as the thug began to fall, Cut swung his fist into the man's face breaking his nose and cheek. He paused when no one else came for him, looking over at Danny Baker, he now saw he sported a knuckle duster and flick knife.

"Excuse me." Cut said as he carefully removed his jacket, undid his tie and wrapped it about his knuckles. Danny was watching mesmerized, this legend was living up to all the hype he'd heard about him, and now he faced Cut De Luca on his own. Sweat beaded on his top lip. Danny swung a false attack which failed to draw Cut out, instead the bigger man smiled thinly at him. Danny lunged with his knife and then punched with his knuckle dusters, landing a blow on Cut's forearm Cut's other arm was quick to land a ringing blow of its own on the side of Danny's head, he saw stars and had a ringing in his ears. Cut brought up his fist and planted it in Danny's diaphragm knocking the wind out of him. Danny curled up coughing, desperate to get air back into his lungs. Finally Cut brought his elbow down hard on Danny's back, making him crumple to the floor.

"If you want to survive this, you might want to stay down." He advised in a voice that was calm and without a single indication of breathlessness. Danny made no sound, save for his wheezing to get air into his lungs, so Cut turned to leave, he retrieved his jacket, fished in the pocket for his phone and called the emergency services. He then walked calmly down to the car

Chapter 8

Cut slipped into the front passenger seat, put on his seat belt as the driver pulled smoothly from the curb.
"That's a new shirt you owe me Krissy." He said as he reclined his seat, so he could stretch out. "I'm Cuthbert, by the way." He had twisted in his seat to look at Avion, who still looked bug eyed at him. "Avion, but you know that already." She managed
"Granny owes you too." Kristine complained.
"So do I." Avion added.
"You owe me nothing Avion. My sister and grandmother asked me to step in here, so at their request I did, therefore it is they who owe me a shirt."
"I caused the problem because I wanted to see Damion and didn't trust Mrs Parker anymore."
"Avion." Cut leveled his blue eyes on her, holding her attention.
"Our grandmother wanted to protect you and forgot to respect your free will. She neglected to explain that the best way to help your boyfriend was to let him go cold turkey. It isn't a pretty sight, and she wanted to save you that. She was afraid you would want to help Damion and he would sweet talk his way into letting you, luckily he didn't choose that option. They asked me to keep an eye on you, Danny Baker was always going to find you at that flat."
Avion got it, but she wasn't sure she could trust Mrs Parker, for all she loved her dearly.
"Damion is an ex now, thought you knew that?" She pointed out.
Cut shrugged and grinned.

***

"Gracie Parker you owe me an explanation as to why you had me do a task so menial?" Cut shouted as he marched down Mrs Parker's hallway.
"Is she safe Cut?" Mrs Parker shouted back.
"Are you trying to offend me?" Cut barked.
"I'm fine." Avion shouted as she hurried after Cuthbert. Mrs Parker sighed with relief and let go of the table cloth she'd been wringing to death.
"Raphael has chicken pox and is a pretty poorly boy. Uriel was too far away and Gabriel is overseas, completing a deal with Gordon. You were all I could call upon."
Cut bent down and embraced his grandmother in a huge loving hug.
"Raph's got chicken pox?" Kristine asked.
"Well that's what he said he had, I hope it isn't anything worse, you know how he is at not wanting me to know things." Mrs Parker sounded worried.
"So we got the deal with Gordon? Good old Gabriel, wish I knew his secret." Cut said smiling. Avion had to guess that whatever deal Gabriel had secured must be very beneficial to the family, given the smiles of delight or pride, or maybe they were both.
"Avion you didn't get hurt did you dear?" Mrs Parker looked worriedly around the room.
"No Cuthbert and Kristine arrived in time, thanks."
"You owe Cut a new shirt granny."
"You both owe me a new shirt." Cut corrected his sister. Kristine opened his jacket to reveal his shirt front slightly splattered in blood.
"Something wrong with the cleaners Cut?" Krissy asked looking his shirt up and down. It hugged his torso hiding nothing at all. Avion felt her pulse race.
"It is ruined." Cut growled at her. Kristine sighed. "And what's it going to cost me?"

"Eighty pounds."

"*How much?*" Both Mrs Parker and Kristine shouted an octave higher than normal.

"Who the bloody hell wears a shirt *that* expensive? It's a *shirt!*" Krissy asked.

"It's a *dress.*" Cut replied.

"Oh no you don't." Krissy snapped playfully. "A woman should never wear the same outfit as another woman, it isn't done." She jabbed a finger into his muscular chest. Avion was grinning, trying to suppress giggles.

"Same with men, it's an *expensive* shirt for that reason."

"A new shirt it is." Mrs Parker intervened, and Avion let go on the giggles.

***

By Friday, Avion felt at home. She and Kristine had shopped, shadowed by two guards of Cuthbert's and one Ceaser dog, she felt safe and happier than she could remember. She felt nervous at meeting Kristine's friends, especially Alley Cat, who was so named for her wildness when drunk. It transpired she and Cut had once had a thing going on, but it had run its course according to Cut, though Kristine said Alley Cat hadn't stopped being in love with her brother. Cut like his brothers didn't encourage long term relationships. Alley was fun for a time, but that was all she was to Cut. Avion made a mental note to never fall for any of the brothers, given women were for fun not life, though she wondered many times what would love look like to Cut? What might a wife be in Cut's world? It was a silly notion but the man was in his mid-thirties, surely he would want to settle down soon? He was handsome beyond measure, and it would be easy to fall for him. Avion realised a tiny part of her already had, but wasn't that born from him saving her? Cut was a monster, unafraid of men like Danny or Damion, perhaps it was the monster within them all that kept them from finding happiness. It said something about Cut and his brothers, that they seemed to want to keep their darkness away from their lives, yet they didn't shy away from telling people they had it, it was confusing in some ways.

    She studied her skinny body in the mirror, a sari no less. The dress code for the Delhi required men and women to dress in Indian clothes, they insisted it helped the customer to feel more involved with the Indian culture. Avion wore a short top with long sleeves, its colour was a mid-blue, over which was wrapped a long piece of material tucked into trousers and pleated around her, with soft gold embroidery making a thick hem. It was beautiful without being ostentatious. She hated how thin her arms were, all bone and no muscle at all, her hands the same. Still she looked passable, her hair was beautiful and changed her face from thin and gaunt to pretty. Make up hid the bruising around her eye, at least the swelling had gone down now. Avion cautiously stepped into the back parlor, to the smiles of Cut and Kristine.

"Are you coming to?" Avion asked Cut as he stood dressed in his own Indian attire, black trousers and a thigh long tunic with an embossed pattern on it, grandfather collar in black and black buttons. He looked amazing, like a model on steroids, full muscles pressed against the fabric, nothing left to imagine as far as Avion was concerned.

"I will be nearby. I know what Alley Cat is like, but I am not party to your party." He grinned broadly, showing immaculate white teeth. Avion blushed slightly, she had no idea why.

"Good let's get going then." Kristine urged and all three left Mrs Parker doggy sitting Ceaser.

***

    The Delhi had once upon a time, been a library. It sported floor to ceiling long windows which were narrow, the

floor was parquet herringbone design, and the walls were painted a majestic blue. The ceiling was a dome of glass, which would have allowed the stars to shine in had the light pollution not flooded them out. On the opposite wall to the windows lay a huge tiger, so realistic, Avion had to look twice to be sure it was just a painting. Huge crystal chandeliers hung from iron beams and a balcony skirted the dining area. Tables scattered the room, but Avion could see where they were meant to be, a set of tables had been pushed together to accommodate fifteen women, all in their mid to late twenties. They were drinking and laughing loudly to the annoyance of some guests. Avion and Kristine were met by a waiter wearing a tight fitting long black tunic, double breasted with short sleeves and a thin red piping around the edges, and along the buttoned front. The tunic was tailored to fit and the man wearing it was exceptionally so. All the waiters were exactly as Cassidy had promised, and Avion was glad for the low lighting, given her face was on fire from blushing. She noticed that Cut was nowhere to be seen, though he was around somewhere, which demonstrated how the De Luca's could blend in regardless of their looks.
"Krissy, how wonderful to see you, did you bring Cut?" Alley Cat was a tall slim woman, celebrating her 27th birthday, according to the balloons, who had dyed blond hair, which hung loose around her shoulders. She wore a golden sari with plenty of head decoration, gold chains that hung over her forehead, earrings that tickled her shoulders. Her lips were bright red, as though she had kissed a vampire, her long nails matched. Avion wondered how on earth a man as calm as Cut had managed an affair with one so vivid and wild, still opposites attract they say.
"Hey Alley, this is Avion, she is new to the family."
All the women were eyeing Avion up now, and she felt the scrutiny like needles on her skin. She smiled nervously, and took her seat as the waiter offered her to sit. He leaned in close as he asked her which wine she would like, red or white,

she chose white, it wouldn't show up as badly as red if she spilt it. The waiter smelt heavenly, and the warmth from his body seeped into Avion's arm, making her skin erupt in goose bumps.

"You look very beautiful." Another waiter said in her other ear. He was also adorable, perfect brown skin, vivid blue eyes, longer hair that touched his shoulders, and when Avion turned to face him, found herself almost kissing his full lips.

"Uriel! Oh my God, what are you doing here?" Krissy was wild with excitement at seeing another brother. Avion stared stunned. Uriel looked around Avion to see Kristine sitting on the other side of her. He grinned broadly, the same brilliant white smile Cut had, and Avion had to remember to breathe.

"Keeping an eye on our new family member." Uriel replied, then winked at Avion, who looked down instantly, like a shy child.

"You lucky bitch." Alley shouted from the head of the table. "You get to live amongst demi gods. I am sooo jealous. Have you met them yet?"

Avion shook her head, this was awful. She wanted to blend in not be the centre of attention, it was like a night out with Damion and his friends, only these people noticed her, at least Damion's friends ignored her.

"Naw she only knows Cut and now Uriel. Raph has chicken pox and Gabe is overseas." Kristine filled in.

"I bet he ain't got chicken pox, some other kind of pox more like." Alley shouted down to them. Kristine laughed, but there was anger in her eyes.

"Raphael is a womanizer, you watch that one. As for Gabe keep the fuck away from him, he is the really nasty one of them all." Another woman said as quietly as she was able considering the noise. Avion looked at her, she was slim, with a long face, sad eyes that drooped downwards, small lips and rather large teeth.

"Just about every damn woman falls in love with one or more of the De Luca men, All but Gabe will entertain them.

Gabriel is a different kind of monster, he has no emotions. Although," she looked Avion up and down, "I don't think you have to worry, he likes women with power and money, and I'm guessing you don't have either, so you will be safe, but not from Raphael, anything in a skirt with tits will do him."

Avion snorted trying not to lose the mouthful of wine she'd just taken. She swallowed hard.

"Then I think I can safely rule out Raphael too, I got no tits." She grinned broadly. The woman beside her burst out laughing.

"Abigail Merchant." She introduced herself.

"Avion Chaplin." Both women laughed.

"So which one broke your heart?" Avion asked. Abigail snorted.

"Thankfully I am not demi god material, so have remained unscathed, however most all of these have dated or hanker to date, a brother, Cut or Uriel usually, don't get me wrong, any one of them would kill to be Gabriel's date ever, but the only woman I know who adores Gabriel is his secretary, Ashley. She is one vicious bitch, and has broken up at least three of his relationships that I know off. I heard he got so mad with her about the last bust up, he threatened to sack her."

Avion wasn't sure if Abigail was joking or not. "How is threatening to sack her going to keep her in line?"

"Loves her boss, sacked, won't see her boss."

"Arh" Avion nodded her understanding.

"Your food lovely ladies." Uriel purred in Avion's direction. He served her Korma curry, with chapati bread, then he served Abigail.

"Can I get you anything Avion? More wine, water?" His face was so close to hers, she could only shake her head at him. "If you can't cope here, wave me over, I will get you out of here in the blink of an eye. I am here for you. Ok?" His voice soothed her ragged nerves, made her skin shiver in a delicious way, she nodded her head.

"Uriel likes you." Abigail noted, nudging Avion's elbow gently.

"He's only just met me, and he is only trying to make me feel a part of the family." Avion reminded her.

"Well the woman opposite you is called Anna-Mae, and she has had the hots for Uriel for several months now, and he isn't, apparently, interested. Can't think why not, she's beautiful, has a figure and wealth, everything De Luca men normally go for. No offence Avi, but you're hardly in the same league as her, and Uriel is all over you like a rash. She is giving you death stares."

Anna-Mae was indeed very beautiful, Asian by her features, perfect almond eyes outlined with kohl liner, heart shaped lips and flawless skin. Avion had to wonder what was not to like about her, she could see how Anna-Mae would look good with Uriel, yet he was avoiding her.

"Do you know the De Lucas very well?" Avion asked hoping to get off the subject of admiring women.

"I did a tech deal with Raphael's company last year, which put me in the circle if you like, but whilst I see them at social functions, I have no inside info on them. I hear the gossip though, and Lordy, there is a mountain of that!" Abigail rolled her eyes.

"Let me guess, all about their love lives?" Avion asked.

"Mostly. Anything you hear about Raph is about his sex life. Uriel will be both, that's business and sex life, Cuthbert will be rumour and none of it nice. He has a bad reputation, but nothing compared to Gabriel's. Gabriel is a man most women hold in awe, you can never really know if what you hear is truth or fiction, though I suspect it's a mix of both. I must confess Gabriel hasn't dated much since he turned thirty five, and now he's nearly forty he seems even less inclined, but he was seen with some woman at a charity dinner a couple of years ago, so you might be safe from him. I suppose the woman Cut dates is the most protected of any, he's the violent side, nothing he loves more than a good fight just about everyone on the darker side of life avoid crossing Cut but Gabriel is the secret side. He is a brilliant business man, but he is also ruthless. There is no escaping Gabriel if you cross him, you're never seen again. That is the truth, because I have known of two associates who have disappeared and have never been found. Michael lives overseas so we never hear much about him, though I know he has his own enterprises and family." Abigail did the quotation finger wiggle for family. So why are you so special to them?"

Avion shrugged. "I look after Mrs Parker, but I had a toxic relationship which she saved me from. My ex got into drugs and owed a debt, Cuthbert saved me from the guy collecting it."

Abigail was frowning at her. "That it? You look after granny and you get adopted?"

Avion nodded, there wasn't anything else as far as she knew. "Shit. Who'd have thought?" Then Abigail laughed, and laughed.

"You know how hard these sad cows work to keep themselves beautiful, so that they can nab a hot guy like one of the De Luca men? And apparently all they had to do to get noticed was care for granny Parker, and have a toxic relationship with a junky." Abigail clutched her stomach she laughed so much. Avion stared at her for a moment, then looked at her food, pushing it away with the sudden loss of appetite. Uriel was at her side without her even knowing it.

"Everything ok?" he asked, his voice smooth as satin, as he squatted down beside Avion, looking up into her tear filled eyes. Everyone had stopped talking and all the women were now looking at Avion. Abigail stopped laughing.

"I think I need some air." Avion muttered. Uriel stood and glared bloody murder at Abigail, who paled visibly. She reached out her hand to touch Avion's arm. "Avi, I'm sor." She watched as Avion stood and turned away from her. Uriel put a protective arm about her waist and she was glad of the support.

Outside, he held her gently. They were in a private back yard, alone. Cuthbert arrived. "I'll deal with her." He said in a low menacing tone. Avion shook her head. "It's ok. I just wasn't prepared for it. She doesn't understand what my life has been like. It's not her fault."

Cuthbert disappeared like a spectre in the night.

"What did she say?" Uriel asked softly, so Avion told him. He enveloped her in strong arms, holding her close to a tight muscular chest which was warm and seductive. She let silent tears seep from her eyes into that tunic top, which was far thinner than she had supposed. *Why do these men care so much about me, for me? I am nothing to them.* She wondered.

***

Two waiters arrived at the table. "Would you come with us please?" They asked of Abigail. She shook her head violently. "N no. I said I was sorry, please I didn't mean to upset her."

One of the waiters leaned down to her ear. "We wouldn't want a scene madam would we?" He asked kindly touching Abigail's elbow. She stood on shaky legs and followed them out. Alley Cat stared after her.

"What the fuck did Abby say?" She asked of no one. Kristine got up and followed the route Uriel had taken, when she got outside, she found Avion in the close embrace of her brother. She waited at the doorway.

"Avion, the party isn't over. If you want to go home, I will take you. If you want to stay, Krissy can redo your make up and we will go onto the night club. What would you like to do?" He put his hands on her upper arms and rubbed them gently, looking down at her.

"What about Abigail?" Avion asked sheepishly.

"She's been taken home." Kristine said with a strained voice. Avion nodded. "I'm sorry I ruined this evening."
"Oh Avion, you didn't ruin anything. That lot are jealous of you and there are always going to be women who are jealous of you from now on. You have the monopoly on my brothers, who isn't going to be envious of that?" She smiled kindly. "You just gotta pity them. Look, you know the boys are super protective of you, so what say we go and dance the night away? Bet Uri would love a dance wouldn't you?"
Avion looked up at Uriel, who grinned his beautiful smile down at her. "I can jive, or smooch." He winked at her, and she couldn't help the smirk that touched her lips.

Chapter 9

The two waiters escorted Abigail out of the Delhi and into the company of Cuthbert. He stood with his hands in his pockets, leaning casually against a black SUV.
"I didn't mean to upset her." Abigail wailed.
"So what did you say that was so damn funny it put her off her food?"
Abigail sobbed. "I was laughing cos she has no idea how hard most women work to make themselves attractive to men like you. All she had to do was get punched by a junky boyfriend."
"You forgot the bit about my grandmother." He sneered at her.
"Oh fuck."
Abigail had forgotten the De Luca men could all lip read. Granny Parker had insisted they learn such things, never knew when it might save your life.
"I'm sorry. I never meant no disrespect to Mrs Parker. Avion is a nice person she just has no idea how lucky she is."
Cut opened the boot of the SUV. "Put your bag in there." He said gently.
"Why?"
"Because I asked you nicely." His eyes were hard as glass, but his expression remained placid. Hands shaking, Abigail placed her bag in the boot. Cut then took her elbow and escorted her to the passenger door, helping her into the seat, he told her to put her seat belt on. He then walked calmly round to the driver door and got in.
"Where are you taking me?"
"I want you to understand something." He said softly. Abigail began to panic. As they drove in silence, she realised why he had told her to put her bag in the boot, he didn't want her trying to call for help. After half an hour, he pulled up at the

remote farm. He got out, walked round to her side of the vehicle, offered his hand to help her out, she noted it was warm and dry, whereas hers was warm and sweating.

"Cut please don't hurt me. You aren't going to hurt me are you?" She was shaking.

"I am not going to hurt you. I don't hit women, nor do my brothers." He escorted her into the building and walked her through to the back room where Damion was still being held. "You said the way to get noticed by me and my brothers is to have a toxic relationship with a junky; that was all. So, in there is the ex-toxic boyfriend of Avion's. He has just spent a week going cold turkey to get him out of addiction mode, so he's pretty screwed up right now. I want you to understand just how easy Avion had it when she got noticed by us."

Before Abigail could answer him, he opened the door and pushed her in, then followed her.

"Damion. This is Abigail, she is really eager to know how easy it is to be your girlfriend, and what that might entail. I'm sure you can fulfill her wishes."

Cut stepped out of the room, and locked the door behind him. Abigail screamed, ran to the door and began banging it as hard as she could, screaming for Cut to open it. After several minutes, Abigail gave up sobbing.

"Hi Abigail. What the fuck you wearing? Do you know how much I hate bitches like you?"

Damion was sitting against the wall, studying her with cold hatred. He was pretty beaten up, but his eyes were clear, even if the rest of him was black and blue. He stood up. Abigail screamed.

"Why'd you keep screaming?" He asked, it hurt his head.

"Don't hit me." Abby begged, turning to bang on the door again. Damion smirked.

"Is that what he told ya? I'd smack ya about a bit?"

Abigail stared at him wide eyed.

"I admit I hit Avi, she was a parasite, always taking stuff, like food and wanting stuff like money for bills, when she knew I had to av it for the rent. Selfish bitch. She got too demanding, so course I had to put her in her place. That's wot a man has a right to do, ain't it?" Abigail stared back at him, terror still etched onto her face.

"Ain't it?" He yelled. Abby flinched then nodded. Damion kicked the wall.

"Glad someone agrees wiv me." He sulked. He turned to look at the woman wearing a sari and looking ridiculous.

"You know how stupid you look?" He asked again, sneering. Abby clutched her arm over her chest.

"She used to be a good fuck when I first knew her, but then she got boring, always going on about how it hurt an all, never stopped her moaning though, so I knew she was lying, she liked it too much. A good woman should be a slut in bed, that's wot some actor said years ago." Damion grinned, showing yellow teeth, one was bad, two were missing. Abigail cringed and whimpered. She was getting it, Damion wasn't nice, and she wondered how long Avion had suffered at his hands.

"I ain't a bad bloke." He said as if he'd read her mind. "I know that shit out there likely told ya I was, but I ain't." Damion stared at the door fiercely.

"I'm the fucking victim ere. I took Avi out for the night, an she went and passed out on me, then she goes an tells her employer how hard done to she is, and that I hit her. I never did, she told the fucking paramedic she walked into a wall, bitch. She can't remember what she is doing. I tried to get her out of the house but she wouldn't leave and the old bag set a fucking guard dog on me, and the coppers were waiting at the front door for me, false arrest, claiming I was a burglar. Fucking bitch set me up and then turns up here and wants me to forgive her, fucking begged me she did." He kicked the wall again, harder, making Abby jump.

"I fucking hate her. She ain't no fucking victim, I am. I'm the one got beat up by her boyfriends. Fucking slag." He kicked the wall again, then punched at it for good measure

***

The night club was heaving with the hot sweaty bodies of youth, all bouncing to the music, and heavy thump of the base, that pounded into Avion's body like a punch bag. Lights darted over the crowd, highlighting heads and waving arms. Alley Cat and her party were all at the bar, waiting for drinks. Uriel had left Avion and Kristine at a table while he disappeared to get their drinks, arriving back several minutes before the others did.

"You can bloody get ours next round." Alley Cat shouted over the music to Uriel. He grinned at her. The women all got up and headed for the dance floor, leaving Avion and Anna-Mae behind. It was an uncomfortable situation for Avion, having the other woman stare at her long and hard. Uriel held out his hand to Avion, which she took gladly. He wove through the throng of humanity onto the dance floor, and held both of Avion's hands as he began to dance, a little swaying, and a lot of foot stomping. He smiled at her, encouraging her to let herself have fun. Slowly Avion began to let go, smiling shyly at Uriel, then laughing when he winked at her, and finally she found herself swaying and moving to the music, still holding his hands. He twirled her around, pushed and pulled her, and they laughed. He embraced her and released her, he placed his hands on her waist and encouraged her to swing her hips, which looked very sexy in a sari. Eventually Avion needed to rest, she indicated needing a drink, so Uriel held her hand and led her to the bar. Drinks arrived as soon as he waved at one of the many bar tenders, then they moved back to the table to join the rest of the party. Uriel sat beside her this time, and Kristine came and sat on his other side. Uriel put his arms across the back of the seats, effectively embracing both women. Anna-Mae looked into her glass.

Eventually Avion grew more and more tired, so that she longed to go home, she needed to sleep, but Uriel was nowhere to be found, so she left the club on her own, and embraced the cool night air, with relish.

"Are you and Uriel a thing?"

Avion jumped out of her skin at the sound of Anna-Mae's voice.

"No."

"Didn't look that way." Anna-Mae accused.

"It's none of your business Anna-Mae." Kristine said firmly. Avion was grateful for her arrival. Anna-Mae glared at Kristine.

"I only just met Uriel, honestly. He was just making me feel safe."

"Well he certainly did that didn't he?" Anna-Mae sulked, screwing up her eyes as she looked at Avion. At that moment the SUV arrived and Uriel got out, opened the door for Avion and Kristine to get in and then looked at Anna-Mae, he stepped over to her and spoke a few words, which must have upset her, given the tears that slipped down her face, as Uriel got into the driving seat. *I seem to be making a lot of enemies from these women, just by being in the presence of any De Luca male.* Avion observed with sadness.

***

Mrs Parker listened with her lips pressed firmly together. When Avion had finished telling her about the night out, she nodded her head slowly.

"Silly me." She said softly. "I let Kristine's enthusiasm get the better of me. You got thrown in the deep end after all your isolation, and somehow no woman was going to be jealous of you. Silly me. I should've seen that one coming."

"It's not your fault." Avion said quickly.

"You are not prepared for the women my grandchildren mix with, and of course they would be jealous of you. My grandchildren get their looks from their father's line, that isn't to say Catherine isn't beautiful, she is, but they have always

had each other for support, something Nathen never had, he was an only child." She explained. "You are an only child and Damion has kept you away from socializing, I should've seen how intimidating things would be for you. At least Uriel was there to support you." There was a long silence as Avion wondered what she should say, but Mrs Parker spoke first.
"How have you enjoyed your week regardless of last night?"
"It has been wonderful, and words cannot express my gratitude to you all." Avion smiled. Mrs Parker was smiling too.
"So what would like to do with your life?" She tipped her head to one side. Avion hadn't a clue.
I honestly have no idea." She said sadly. "I don't even have a home anymore."
"Tscht. You can stay here as long as you need to, sort yourself out, decide where you're going, then I can help you get there if necessary." Mrs Parker's eyes almost looked straight at her. Avion could see the sincerity in them, so agreed.
"You might benefit from some guidance from Alley Cat and Kristine on how to deal with jealous women." Mrs P smiled. Avion didn't relish that idea, but she had grown an extra skin when it came to Damion's friends, so she could do it, would *have* to do it, if she were to survive in this family, so she agreed to that as well.

***

It was a month later when Mrs Parker told Avion she should have a place of her own.
"I think you're ready." She enthused. Avion had gained a little weight, had become reasonably confident and was holding her own admirably according to the grandchildren.
"You don't want to be living with an old crony like me. You need your own space, which means your own place, so I want you to go out and find somewhere to your liking, take

Kristine if you like, or Raphael, he is good at property negotiations."

Avion hadn't met Raphael, so she opted for Kristine, who jumped at the chance of flat hunting. It was a tedious affair, looking at potential properties, viewing them and then discarding all of them because Avion couldn't love anything brand new or converted into open living, with echoing interiors and complete lack of character. It was the end of their first week of property viewing, and Avion and Kristine were about to embark upon another pointless viewing, pointless to Avion because she'd let Krissy talk her into looking at a warehouse conversion, which was another open space living area, characterless.

"Coffee before we head off? We have time." Avion suggested, and knowing Krissy loved her coffee, she was glad to be right.

"Great idea, we can go and sit in the park to drink it."

Avion smiled, she loved the park, and this day was warm and sunny and the park just screamed at them. The queue in the café was long, which made Avion glad of the fan she was standing beneath, cool air teased at her feathery hair, which in turn tickled her face. Eventually her turn arrived and she ordered two cappuccinos. Having paid for them, she turned and bumped into a solid block of humanity. The coffee flew forwards and sideways, covering a white shirt and the floor. The owner of the shirt swore and quickly tore the soiled item from him, ripping the buttons off in the process. Avion was aghast, unable to help with her hands full of now almost empty coffee cups. The man began dabbing his completely toned torso, leaving Avion staring at it in dumb struck homage. His skin was red from the scolding coffee, but otherwise he was a perfect male specimen of gym addiction.

"Oh God, I'm s so sorry." Avion flustered, unable to unglue her eyes from his perfection.

"That's a new shirt you owe me." His voice was soft and remarkably calm for someone who'd just got scalded.

"That's a bit de ja vu." Avion said, her eyes now wandering up the perfect six pack to perfect pecks, taught dark nipples and a strong clavicle with cricket ball shoulder joints, a strong neck, square jaw, with a hint of stubble. The soft full lips and almost sharp cheek bones, straight nose and amber eyes, dark eyebrows and dark scruffy hair, short at the sides, longer on top. "Which one are you?" She asked near breathlessly.
"Gabriel"
Oh .... Fuck.
She rolled her eyes. "Just my luck."
"Apparently not mine." He answered flatly. "Now I will have to go home and change. Thank you."
Avion blushed, and found herself looking into his beautiful eyes, with such long lashes. He was older than Uriel and Cut, she could see how they would age, in this brother, who was still infinitely handsome, and judging from his torso, remarkably fit.
"I am sorry, …. Again." She said unable to disengage from his eyes, and she noticed he wasn't disengaging either.
"Are you?" he asked, his voice soft now, so that it only applied to her. *What kind of a question is that?*
"Of course I am." She replied equally softly. They stood saying nothing, just staring into each other's eyes, like dumb kids on a first date. Gabriel clutching his ruined shirt, Avion clutching two fast growing cold coffees. After several long seconds, or perhaps they were minutes, she couldn't tell, she thought of something.
"Um, are your shirts very expensive?"
The worry in Avion's eyes amused Gabriel, and he wondered if she could see that reflected in his own.
"Extremely." He replied in the same flat tone. She let out a small high whine, and he almost lost his cool by laughing, but he managed to control himself, admiring his determination as he did. He watched the strands of fine hair dance around her face, and without thinking he lifted his hand slowly and carefully moved the annoying strands away, letting his fingers

trail softly and seductively down her skin. Avion shivered. His eyes roamed over her head, drinking in the copper glints that shone in the sunshine, then he lowered his hand and stepped back from her.

"Goodbye Avion." He said, still softly, still flat, then turned and walked out of the shop. Avion stared after him, like she'd been hypnotized and the spell hadn't worn off yet. If his front had been mesmerizing, his back was no less disappointing, full muscle rippled when he moved his arms, a thin waist with tight fitting trousers that made his backside look adorable, pinchable, grabbable and heaven forbid, *bitable*. Avion swallowed hard. She'd never needed a chair so badly, so she rushed out of the café and over to the park on shaky legs.

"What took you so long?" Krissy asked as Avion collapsed down onto the grass, spilling the left overs of coffee. She flopped onto her back, hands over her face.

"Oh man, how embarrassing."

"What happened?"

"I um. I kinda bumped into, um. I met Gabriel."

"Oh! I didn't know he was back in town." Krissy said surprised.

"Oh yea, he's back in town." Avion confirmed nodding her head like a demented oil donkey.

"So where is he?" Krissy looked about her.

"He, erm, he had to go home." Avion nodded, covering her eyes like that would eliminate her embarrassment. When Krissy didn't speak, Avion chanced a glance at her, she moaned at the quizzical look.

"Just go on line, you're bound to find a few up loaded witness accounts by now."

Krissy did, and Avion watched as her eyes went wide as saucers and then her lips smirked. Then she watched it again, and then again, before laughing.

"Mmm, I can see your humiliation. Do you owe him a shirt by any chance?" There was the briefest of pauses before Krissy laughed till tears wet her lashes.

"If his bloody shirts are anything like as expensive as Cut's, I'll be paying him back forever."
"Didn't you ask?"
"Course I did, and yes they are!"
Krissy fell about laughing, wiping her eyes. "He does like to make an entrance does our Gabe."
"No kidding?!" Avion moaned.
"I think you could sue him for mental distress, stripping like that in a public space. You looked pretty disturbed." Krissy laughed.
"Not funny, and I still haven't had any coffee."
"I'll go this time, heaven only knows who you might encounter if you go." Krissy said getting up.
"Blessed be for understanding friends." Avion replied as she watched Krissy head off.

Chapter 10

Gabriel swung the clean shirt about him slipping his arms into the sleeves as he strode across the office floor, flinging himself into the large leather chair, grabbing his phone from the desk top, he accessed the web and watched the many versions of the coffee affair. The beauty of doing what he had done, was that he now had many varying angles of this moment, all uncut. He watched with delight the expression on Avion's face as the shock unfolded, how her beautiful eyes widened, long lashes almost kissing her eyebrows. Her lips slightly parted, full lips that promised softness, and looked so seductive when he zoomed in. The video operators had not been close enough to capture the subtle gasp she had let out, but on every version, he heard the very audible gasps of the operators, and people nearby when he removed his shirt. Gabriel smiled. *Still got it,* he thought with satisfaction. A satisfaction that only deepened when he saw how Avion's eyes roamed over his chiseled body. He paused the video at the point their eyes met, hers were brown, dark orbs of alluring desire, with flecks of copper that matched those in her hair. She had held his gaze throughout their exchange, unable to break away, but what bothered Gabriel was that he'd been equally mesmerized. He'd been almost speechless looking into her eyes, almost wordless as he took in her fly away hair, and the copper glints in it, and he had no recollection of moving his hand to brush those stands away, but he remembered with painful clarity the feel of her skin against his fingers, the softness of it, and the scent of her, roses in full bloom. He closed his eyes, reveling in the memory. Blessed Gracie and her insistence the boys learn to use all their senses to the full. He could smell Avion even now, feel her skin, even now, and he ached for her. Gabriel opened his eyes. He *ached* for *her*. The realization was startling. He'd never ached for anyone in his whole life, but this unassuming plain woman had him *aching* for her. How the fuck did that happen?

"Coffee Mr DeLuca" Ashly swept into his realization like a hurricane down a high street. He felt a sudden surge of rage at the intrusion, but it wasn't her fault, so he clamped down at snapping at her. He watched impartially as she put down the silver tray, and organized his coffee, pouring the dark liquid into his cup and then adding the milk and sugar, then stirring before straightening up. "Can I get you anything else?"

A cold flannel. A bucket of ice water. Instead he looked up at her, Ashly in her cream jacket, tight pencil skirt which showed off her backside to maximum effect, and no effect on Gabriel, because he knew she dressed to get his attention, and it failed every time. Her cream blouse seductively open at the neck, and her perfume thick and choking, though probably not to her nose, but certainly to Gabriel's.

"No that's fine." He said in his flat tone, and Ash smiled her warm professional smile, before clicking her way across the wooden floor in stilettoes Gabriel admired her for coping with.

Avion. He closed his eyes and immediately saw her face, all innocence and as open as any book. Had his heart just missed a beat? This was Avion, the all bone, no shape woman who'd been beaten more times than Gabriel cared to know. Yet now she had shape, filled out nicely in all the right places, had not a bruise on her, and her skin was beautiful, pale cream in colour and smooth as porcelain. She was simple, yet perfect. Her innocence real not faked, and where once he thought he preferred a smart woman, a self-assured well turned out woman, he realised he had long ago woken up to the reality of such women, they had an agenda and men like him were it, but all the women Gabriel had known were superficial, fake in many ways, trained to eat little, train hard without gaining muscle, expensive hair styles, and makeup, subtle but hiding flaws, or obsessed with bust enhancements, liposuction and Botox. That was the society he moved in, and the women he avoided. But Avion, she was far beneath his radar, living in a world he'd walked in, worked in but never socialized in. Avion, whom he had seen from the first day she started working for his grandmother, and up until today could have walked past her on any street and never seen her. Unassuming Avion, yet he had been mesmerized by her. *Thank God she owes me a shirt.*

***

Avion barely saw the old Victorian house that had been converted to flats some years past. Her head was filled with images of Gabriel, mostly his smoldering eyes. She wondered if he had the ability to read her mind, because it sure felt that way. She had to force herself to push images of that De Luca to the back of her mind, she was house hunting. The warehouse conversion they were booked to see had fallen through and the estate agent had come up with this instead. They walked through the front door, which was a wooden double door painted blue. In the hallway stood the stairs and two front doors facing each other. Beside the stairs was an access to the back garden. On the second floor the layout was the same, two doors facing each other for the two flats on that level, then the last set of stairs led to a single front door, which was modern and white. The estate agent opened it up to reveal an open space with cupboards in the far left of the space, and a sink for washing up. There was a door on the far right of the space which he explained led to a bedroom, and the door nearest to them was the bathroom. Avion wandered over the room. It wasn't huge and nor did it echo like the other large spaces she had viewed. By the kitchen area was a French door, with glass panels that led to a small roof garden, complete with artificial grass, room for tubs and a small out door sofa. Avion could picture herself out there sewing her book of memories, it was perfect. The bedroom was larger than she had imagined, allowing for a king size bed. It had a built in wardrobe with drawers, so the whole space was compact yet spacious. Likewise the bathroom was modern, a wet room with gravity shower; it was luxury beyond her wildest dreams. The down side to the perfect property, was the distance it was from Mrs P's place, but Krissy assured her a fifteen minute train ride was nothing, so Avion accepted. Her first home, *her* home.

***

It was evening by the time they got back to Mrs P's, and Avion was starving. She and Krissy barged into the back parlor to find Gabriel sitting at the dinner table along with Mrs Parker. Avion came to a sudden halt at the sight of him, sipping tea from a china cup, in hands far too large for such a dainty thing. She almost laughed but her throat clamped up.
"Arh Avion, meet Gabriel, my second oldest grandson."
Without looking up, Gabriel replied "We've met."
"Oh" The disappointment was obvious in Mrs Parker's voice.
"They had a bit of a run in at the café this morning." Krissy smirked, the laughter in her words clear to Mrs P.
"I'm owed a shirt." Gabriel added in his smooth quiet tone. Mrs Parker's eye brows raised. "It's becoming a bit of a habit these days, owing shirts."
"Arh granny you should've seen him! Stripped in the café in front of everyone!" Krissy laughed. Mrs P smiled.
"The coffee was scalding." Gabriel added, still sipping his tea, and not caring to look up. Mrs Parker listened carefully, she knew her grandson wouldn't have been so careless, so he had meant to be scalded, and all to meet Avion? She wondered what was really going on.
"Did you find anything suitable Avion?"

"Yes, I did and we signed the papers." Avion couldn't keep the grin off her face. Gabriel looked up at her, such a raw innocence that shone from her, smile as wide as a Cheshire cat, he couldn't take his eyes off her.

"Do you need a second opinion on the details?" He asked Krissy, watching her with a stern look.

"Um, no. It was all pretty straight forward." She pulled up a chair and began to tell her grandmother about the flat. Avion sat beside her, acutely aware of Gabriel's fixed attention. She found it hard to breathe in his presence, and she wondered why he was affecting her so. This was the one brother she had been warned to steer clear of, and yet he was the one scrutinizing her.

"You'll need furniture next." Mrs Parker was saying.

"I can get it as I save." Avion insisted.

"You need a bed dear." Mrs Parker insisted.

"I only need a mattress really for now." Avion said, then bit her lower lip, and looked at the table. "I'm sorry, I didn't mean .." She trailed off because she didn't know what she didn't mean, except that she and Damion had only ever had a mattress to sleep on.

"Dinner is served." Came a cheerful voice from the kitchen, and Uriel emerged with plates piled high with food.

"You cook?" Avion asked surprised.

"All my grandchildren cook." Mrs Parker replied. "Although most can't be bothered." She looked in Gabriel's general direction. He ignored her.

"I clean as well, granny insisted we be domesticated men." Uriel smiled, and Avion blushed at the warmth in it, which didn't go unnoticed by Gabriel.

"So how long have you been back for?" Krissy demanded.

"Two days." Gabriel replied.

"And *now* you say hi?" Krissy asked. Gabriel paused in his eating and appraised his younger sister.

"And now I choose to say hi." He admitted and resumed eating.

"How is Mr Gordon?" Uriel asked as he pulled up a chair to join the diners.

"He is well." Gabriel informed him.

"Did you see his daughter? What's her name?"

"Henrietta and no I did not." Gabriel continued to eat.

"Um about your shirt?" Avion ventured, Gabriel paused and turned his amber eyes to her, making her catch her breath.

"What about it?" He asked, his gaze intent on her. Avion gazed back at him, hypnotized, tongue tied, and flustered. No one had ever made her feel so strange, he wasn't intimidating, but she could easily see how he could be. She could hardly blink under his gaze, and she felt inadequate in his presence.

"I um, I could perhaps pay in installments?" She asked sheepishly. Gabriel didn't know what to say to that, so he kept looking at her, her innocence was intoxicating, and he felt as though he might be drowning.

"You could" He managed, and cursed himself for being so vague. "However, you have some expense ahead of you, so we can leave it for now." His eyes fixed on hers, and he drowned in their darkness. Avion nodded and tore her eyes away.

"Ok." She muttered, and both resumed eating. Mrs Parker smiled softly.

After the meal, they all piled into the front living room, Avion chose to sit in a corner and Gabriel by the door. Uriel and Krissy sat beside Mrs Parker on the sofa. They talked of family things and Avion listened, and stared at the floor, aware of those amber eyes watching her. Of all the warnings she'd had about Gabriel, his intense gaze hadn't been mentioned, yet it seemed unlikely any one could miss it, if it were his normal behavior, so if it wasn't, why did she cause him to stare at her so? Perhaps she was not approved of, and he was waiting for her to slip up? Each time she checked, he was still watching her, so she would smile shyly, and lower her eyes again. It was unnerving but also intensely flattering she realised. It wasn't as though his stare was hostile, in fact it seemed curious more than anything else, like he had a thousand questions and yet none at all. His voice was soft and reassuring, and he was definitely a man of few words. Avion got up and headed for the kitchen, she needed a glass of water, to cool herself down. The kitchen was a mess, so she started to pile dishes into the dishwasher, and did not hear Gabriel silently arrive, so she jumped visibly when she stood up and saw him standing just a few feet away from her, his proximity had her spiraling into hot flushes, as he stood, tie undone, shirt buttons open to reveal a hint of that exquisite chest she'd got the full Monty of that morning. His gaze was hypnotic, and her mouth dried up all over again. "Can I get you anything?" She asked huskily, then wondered where her voice had gone. He stepped closer and she swore her heart stopped. Amber eyes burned into hers, and that hand came from nowhere to brush her fly away strands into place, Avion sucked in a breath, he was so close, she could smell his cologne, musky and sexy. Heat rolled off him, she closed her eyes as his fingers trailed down the side of her face, soft pads of seduction, which caressed her skin, trailed along her jaw line, her lips parted involuntarily, she could feel his breath, a warm gentle touch that lit up every nerve in her being. His thumb traced her lips which trembled at his touch, she was beautiful, vulnerable in a way he had never seen, yet she trusted him, and he knew she had been warned, women were always warned about him, not that he cared, but he had been at the Delhi when Cut had taken Abigail away, he knew she had warned Avion against him. His eyes drank in her lips, so soft, and tender, he yearned to place his own upon them, and she would let him too. There she was, laid bare to his affections, open to his attentions like a helpless creature about to die.

"No." He said barely above a whisper, his eyes still drinking her in, his body aching for more. Gabriel was a man who appreciated torture, and this was torture. His senses were screaming, his nerves on fire, she was intoxicating, even now the scent of roses wafted towards him, calling to his instincts, inviting him to explore her more, and he wanted to but he needed this torture, he craved this denial. She likely had no idea just how alluring she was. He moved closer still, his mouth close to her ear.

"I am more than the rumours Avion, much more." He forced himself back so he could watch her reaction, the way her eyes flashed, the colour that traced up her neck. He let his fingers trace that neck, her beautiful soft neck, a neck that deserved kisses, not bruises. Then with a determined effort he forced himself to walk away, yearning to turn around, but not wishing to destroy the agony he was so enjoying, his agony, his denial, his torture. His hunger, an endless aching need.

***

Avion couldn't sleep that night. Images of Gabriel were too vivid in her mind, so she sat in a large comfy chair in her room at Mrs Parker's, with the floor light leaning over her shoulder, her embroidered diary on her lap. She looked through it, at the new images she had sewn, all happy memories now, not things she'd had to think of, but events that happened all the time. Krissy with her long blond hair so often scraped into a tight bun, always dressed in a suit, like her brothers. Uriel, in his Indian outfit, tanned skin and clean shaven, sharp cheek bones and adorable smile. Cuthbert solid and strong, his wavy hair gave him such a sexy look, and now she was about to embark on Gabriel, but his most striking attributes were his eyes, yet she had no hair colour as amber as his eyes were, so she decided to stitch him in his half naked form, as he'd been that morning at the café. She began to stitch, multiple strands for depth and shadow, fewer strands for detail, and soon lost all track of time.

***

The weeks passed and Gabriel kept himself away from Avion. He'd always intended to meet her and then move on, his grandmother insisted on nothing less, and he had no reason to think of this woman as anything other than a pet project to keep his grandmother amused. He hadn't banked on the affect Avion was having on him, it made him short tempered, not seeing her, and as time passed it got harder to hide, but he refused to give in to his desires. Gabriel was not a man who demonstrated emotions, nothing had mattered enough to him up till now, he realised, yet he could not stop reliving Avion's responses to him, and every time he did, his body reacted as well. He found he had become quite addicted to her, had even fantasied about her. He had a tail on her, so he knew her every move, and he had the videos of his first encounter with her, which still had him hot and horny. Unfortunately there was another reason for his absence from her life, and if he were being honest with himself, it suited him to have the distraction. Information had come to him that Mr Gordon's product had flaws, and now Gabriel sat in his board room, surrounded by employees, all heads of various departments. His fingers tapped his phone impatiently, a deep longing to get another fix on that video, his eyes watching them all, watching him.
"We are sure this information is accurate beyond all doubt?" He asked in his quiet unassuming voice.
"Absolutely." A young man replied from further down the long table.
"And is Gordon aware?" Gabriel asked.
"We don't know sir." The same young man answered. Gabriel drummed his impatient fingers on his phone, with his other hand he used one finger to tap his lips, noting as he did, Ashly licking her lips, at the far end of the room. He picked up the photos and the written report in front of him. Barry Gordon had been a long standing friend of his father's, so when Gordon's business started to lose money, Nathan had offered to buy him out. That had been five years ago, and

Gordon had stubbornly hung on, even when Nathan had asked Raphael and then Uriel to try and persuade him, Gordon had refused to sell up, which was why Gabriel had been brought in, and Gordon wasn't going to refuse him, because nobody refused Gabriel. Now it seemed sabotage was at large, because Gabriel had inspected the merchandise carefully before making any offers, and the minute the company was sold, defective merchandise had been discovered.

"Bring Gordon in, he has the right to defend himself or at least be notified." Gabriel decided, he couldn't imagine Barry Gordon knowing anything about this, but then crazy things happened sometimes.

"Also put a man on the inside." He added. The young man nodded, and then Gabriel dismissed them, turning away from the room, he focused on the view from his large window. *Where are you Avion?* How he wished he could just text her, but then she would get scared. Gabriel was an obsessive man, it was a trait he'd never mastered, and he feared in Avion's case such obsessiveness would have her running for the hills so he fretted, it was a bad idea to get involved with her, she was fragile and innocent, he was not. She'd just escaped from one monster, she really didn't need another, yet as he thought these things with a sensible mind, his emotions knew he wasn't listening. It was a battle he was losing so he sent a text to his man on watch. The reply was instant, she was shopping with Krissy.

Chapter 11

Avion loved the tug of autumn breeze in her hair, which blew all over the place. She smiled at how much this would annoy Gabriel. Gabriel who hadn't put in an appearance since that first day, and at first Avion had wondered if it had all been a joke on her, it wasn't very nice if that were so, but then the ever attuned Mrs Parker, had mentioned a few weeks past, that Gabriel was very busy, problems needed sorting out. Avion had wondered why she had felt the need to tell *her* of all people, but she was glad she had, though she refused to dwell on how those problems would be sorted, some things she just didn't want to know the details about. She had been buying things for her flat, a junk shop here, an auction there, a charity shop or a boot sale, it was all coming together and costing very little. Mrs Parker was storing her things in a warehouse the family were not currently using, so Avion saved on storage as well. It was still a strange sense of freedom to be able to walk along a street without having to fear being late, or Damion finding out she'd been out spending money he considered his. She wondered what had become of him, but never dared to ask, fearing she might not like the answer. She knew eventually she would ask, she'd have to, if only to be able to finally put that past to rest, for now Avion walked down a street, the wind tugging at her hair, listening to love songs on her ear phones.

Mrs Parker was waving a large envelope when Avion got home, and she gasped when she discovered it was the deeds to her flat.

"I'm sure the boys will help you move in." She said enthusiastically.

"Which boys?" Avion asked warily.
"Well Cuthbert and Uriel for certain, and Raphael if he is free, but don't worry, Gabriel isn't into furniture moving, not his thing."
Avion felt a little deflated, a part of her had hoped he might help, but then again, she couldn't quite envisage him lugging a sofa up two flights of stairs.

***

Gabriel watched from a safe distance, he was multi-tasking from the office. Waiting for Barry Gordon and watching Avion move into her new home, courtesy of his tail filming her on his phone live. A part of him wished he could have been there, but moving furniture was something others did, not him, but he felt the jealousy when Avion posed for pictures with Uriel and Cuthbert. He scrutinized her face and theirs, seeking any kind of indication she was showing an interest in them, but he detected nothing but friendship, much to his relief. Jealousy was a whole new experience for Gabriel, he had never wanted anything that anyone else had, so he'd never known how paranoid it made people. He enjoyed the notion of cutting his brother's throats for flirting with Avion, but he hated how she seemed so relaxed with them, smiled with them, damn it laughed with them. He wanted it to be *him*, but how could it be, if he kept himself away from her like he had? He savored the new emotion learning its taste and effect, like a new food or wine. Gabriel was a control freak, which is what made him so efficient, the ability to take over someone's life and control them, it was also why his relationships were so shallow and ended so soon, normally on his terms. So feeling left out, which is how he felt right now, was a new experience, and he didn't much care for it. A knock at his door tore his attention away, and a moment later Barry Gordon entered the office and Gabriel reluctantly turned his phone over, so he couldn't be

distracted. He waited until Mr Gordon stood in front of him.
"What's going on Gabriel?" The older man asked.
"Please sit Barry." Gabriel indicated the chair Gordon stood beside. He watched as the man sat cautiously down. Gabriel pushed the incriminating papers towards Mr Gordon, who took them with a frown. Gabriel waited, all the time itching to know what was going on at Avion's flat. He wasn't normally impatient, but his jealousy was eating at him, and he had to close his eyes momentarily to regain control. Her face swam into his mind and he resisted a soft smile, had to fight the memory of her skin on his fingers, the smell of roses in her hair ..
"I don't understand." Mr Gordon saved him. "Is this why we were losing money?"
"I don't think so. I checked your merchandise, and I found no faults. This, I believe is recent." Gabriel leveled his gaze onto Mr Gordon.
"But why?"
Gabriel made no answer, but waited for Gordon to work it out for him. The silence stretched out and Gordon stared at the paperwork, shaking his head slowly. Gabriel drifted back to Avion, his fingers inched towards the phone then he stopped them, thinning his lips in his determination to abstain.
"I swear I didn't know Gabriel."
Another long silence.
"Nesbitt and Son always wanted my business, Abe was not happy when I sold to you. Do you think it could be Nigel?" Gordon looked up hopefully at Gabriel, whose steady eyes gave nothing away.
"Nesbitt would've broken the company up and pocketed the profits." Gabriel said in his flat tone and quiet voice, as though he too were thinking it out.
"Exactly." Barry Gordon said, equally unemotionally. "Yet this doesn't fit the Nigel I know."
"You knew he was a mole for his father right?" Gabriel asked.

"Well yes, your father told me that, and it was your father who insisted I keep him on. Arh! Were you about to sack him?" Gordon asked hoping he had hit the nail on the head.
"No." Came the answer in typical Gabriel style.
"Then I don't understand?"
"Nor me." Gabriel concluded. Another pause that eeked out too long for Gabriel.
"Really this has nothing to do with me anymore, you are the boss now." Gordon said and sighed heavily. Gabriel managed a small quirk of his lips.
"You are a silent investor still as per your conditions of sale, therefore it is still your business. You know who might be seeking to destroy "Gordons""
Mr Gordon wiped a hand over his balding head that shone under the bright office lighting.
"That's the thing, I don't know. If it is Nigel Nesbitt then he is doing himself no favours, he can't buy you out can he?"
Mr Gordon looked across at Gabriel's hypnotic stare. He felt trapped. Gabriel De Luca was the last person he'd wanted to do business with, but it was his own fault for refusing to deal with Uriel or Raphael.
"If this had not been discovered, an accident was inevitable, depending on the seriousness and loss of life, would depend upon the options available to me. Nesbitt could have brought me out and broken the company up, that would work well in his favour, however I don't think that was his plan, I think he intended to discredit me."
Gordon swallowed hard. "Then why did you keep him on?" He growled softly, and immediately regretted it, because he *knew* why. Gabriel didn't move, didn't even blink.
"I'm sorry, that's my fault. I insisted you keep the employees on." Gordon looked down at the desk, and washed his face with his hands. "Bloody hell." He said tiredly, a sentiment echoed by Gabriel for entirely different reasons, he thought of his phone, *what is going on now?* And this idiot was stopping him from knowing.

"What can I do?" Gordon asked.

"Nothing." Gabriel replied as though that told Gordon everything. After another long staring session, Gordon licked his lips.

"Then why did you bring me here? I am only a silent investor, and I don't actually invest any longer."

"I wanted to see if you knew anything." Gabriel stated.

"Well I don't." Gordon fidgeted when the silence drew out. "Are we done then?"

Gabriel waited. He wasn't sure why, but he liked the uncomfortable vibes rolling off Barry Gordon, he didn't thank himself for the extra time away from watching Avion. "Yes we are." He said eventually, and watched as Gordon rose from the chair and headed for the door as fast as was good manners to do so. Gabriel reached for his phone and made a call, then resumed watching.

***

Avion rose the first morning in her new home, sunshine pouring through the window; that had yet to have blinds fitted, she was excited to be traveling to work like she used to do, excited at being her own person for the first time in her life. She showered and dressed in loose trousers and a long tunic top with an open neckline, and light jacket, then she set off to the tube station, carrying her small shoulder bag that contained her keys, her purse with money in it, another first, and her embroidery. She stood on the platform as the train came in, the wind from the tunnel blowing her hair all over the place. She got on board along with a tide of humanity all heading off to various locations. It was packed so for her, standing room only, she grabbed the hand rail as the train jolted into motion and rattled as it picked up speed. Avion listened to her music and glanced lazily around the carriage, then her eyes went wide as she met the steady gaze of Gabriel

De Luca. He stood at the other end of the carriage, with a clear view of her over the seated passengers.

What the hell? Why was Gabriel on a tube train? It looked so wrong! Come to that why was Gabriel on *her* tube train? As far as Avion could tell, none of them took trains or buses, they had their own transport. Then she realised that he was only on that train for her. It didn't matter why, it just mattered that he was, and he wanted her to know it. Avion smiled slowly. Gabriel was transfixed. She smiled at him. A beautiful, warm, honest smile, and his heart flipped, his blood raced, his grip tightened on the rail and he wished he was closer. His own lips curled seductively at the corners, and Avion felt her own heart flip. He had to know how sexy he looked when he did that. *Course he does.* And she smiled wider, holding his gaze completely. *So he does like me after all,* she thought, and it felt nice, no it felt warm and cosy. Yet this was dangerous, wasn't he the worst De Luca son? Wasn't he the one who had no feelings? So was he playing with her? Avion wished she could ask Krissy or Mrs P, but then they would tease her, and she didn't want that either. She felt like the mouse the cat was about to pounce upon, knowing there was danger about but not sure if she was really afraid of it, so she looked away but she could *feel* those eyes upon her, she relented and looked back at him, he let a slight twitch cross his sexy lips, and Avion blushed. He knew he had her snared and that slightly annoyed her, but it was also flattering, after all, he was the one on a train he never would've chosen to take.

A couple of women had started taking pics of Gabriel and one followed his gaze to Avion, she smiled when she saw Avion grinning back at him. She nudged her friend and nodded from one to the other, and then they started filming. Avion didn't care, the sexiest man ever was looking at her, smiling at her, or at least his version of a smile, and she was the only person on that train as far as he was concerned. She felt like a pop star. Gabriel didn't care either, he had Avion's attention and she had realised why he was suffering this uncomfortable closeness to humanity, and she approved by the radiant smile she gave him. How she had grown in a couple of months, from terrified mouse to confident woman, and what a woman! She had amazing curves, and a tender face, with dark hypnotic eyes, she dressed well and from what he had observed, mostly from second hand shops or charity shops. She had proved that you didn't need designer labels to look stunning, and Gabriel liked that in her. She radiated vitality and he found himself admiring her ability to shine so brightly after the life she had so recently led. The comprehension of that took his breath away, she was so unlike any woman he had ever met or known, and he liked her, his whole body was beginning to like her, it was embarrassing to be on a train packed with people and his nether regions were getting hard at the feelings Avion evoked. He wondered what she felt about him, and that was another first. He'd never cared what any woman thought about him, he always hung around long enough to get what he wanted, then ended things, now he actually wanted to know what the woman at the other end of the carriage *thought* about him.

  The train lurched to a stop at a station and Avion tumbled forward, Gabriel yearned to be the one to steady her, but he was a carriage away. His gaze intensified momentarily, until she was standing straight again. She glanced back over to him, and broke out in that dazzling smile, as though she were telling him, she was ok really. When the train arrived at her stop, she stepped out with a tide of humanity, all vacating at the same time. She strained to find Gabriel amongst them all, but she failed to see him, she spun around and just as the train doors closed and it pulled away, she caught him staring at her from inside, her disappointment was evident, and not lost on him, but the satisfaction it gave him was a new kind of high, she had wanted him to get off with her, she was interested in him, and he felt warm and important in ways he couldn't put into words. Avion walked slowly up to the surface, following the wave of humans all heading the same way, she had hoped he would accompany her to work, so why did he take the train? Surely he didn't want to just ogle her from the far side of the carriage? The thought made her smile, *Idiot*.

"How was your journey?" Mrs Parker asked as soon as Avion arrived.
"It was fun and Gabriel was on the train." She said as she hung her jacket over a chair. Mrs Parker's eyebrows raised, and she smiled.
"Gracious" was all she could manage. Gabriel never took the train, this intrigued Mrs Parker no end.
"Did he talk to you?" She ventured keeping her voice vaguely interested.
"Um no, he was at the other end of the carriage." Avion said as she entered the kitchen to make coffee, so she missed the frown on Mrs P's face.

***

Gabriel arrived at his office a little flustered from being packed tightly into a tube train, but he had a new momentum in his stride, joy. He couldn't remember feeling this kind of joy, the school boy first love kind of joy, probably because when he was a school boy, he was also being trained to fight, to hurt, to survive being hurt, and to kill. His love, if that was what he had known back then, was the love of pain, and how to control it. He loved inflicting it, and he loved surviving it, as macabre as that was. He never felt joy with any of his dates, they were just dates; women who wanted to be in his bed and he liked bringing them pleasure, but Avion, was joy. She was happiness that made his world brighter, rainy days warm, and now she had told him that she liked him. Gabriel was grinning.
"Wow Mr De Luca." Ashley gasped. She had never seen Gabriel so much as grin, let alone smile. His smile vanished

instantly, she had to ruin it for him didn't she? He stormed into his office chastising himself for being lost to a moment, he'd be certain not to let his guard slip again. *Damn Avion*!

"Coffee." He ordered snappily. He sat at his desk and checked his emails, then his phone messages. He noted the one from his grandmother. "*A train?*" He smiled again, turning his back to the door in case Ashley came in and caught him for a second time.

"*News travels fast.*" He replied and put the phone down. She could ask and ask, but he would say no more and Gracie knew it.

"Coffee sir." Ashley announced as she entered his office. Today she wore another tight pencil skirt with an even lower top allowing the full mounds of her enhanced bosom to bounce seductively before him. He deduced the reason for this being she had seen the social media videos of his meeting with Avion. He concluded that jealousy made people blind. *Had* Ashley *noticed* Avion, she would now have toned her dress sense down, and her makeup, but instead she saught to make herself even more desirable. It didn't work. He made no acknowledgement to her as he opened his emails. He deleted all the uninteresting ones, and opened one from his inside spy at Gordons. He read with interest, there was indeed some bad feelings going around, and rumours as to his intentions. If one day on the job brought this news to him so quickly, things must be bad. He picked up his phone and made the call.

"Well *find him.*" He snarled into the phone. He made another call to his friendly traffic officer, and left him to do his thing. Friendly traffic officers were very useful to have in pocket, as they had access to the city's traffic cameras, and there were few places anyone could go that were camera free. He knew Avion was with his grandmother, but he still wished he could text her, ask her what she was doing, not because he didn't trust her and not because he wanted to control her, but because he just needed that contact. He waited, sorting other mail and reading contracts, often staring out of the window, thinking of Avion and that smile, God, that smile.

Gabriel was listening to his favourite song when he got the call from his traffic friend. He thanked him, the man would find a generous bonus in his pay packet this month. Gabriel made another call, and ordered that Nigel Nesbitt be observed until the morning, it was getting on for home time for Avion, not that Gabriel was going to suffer the train ride back to her place, one suffocating journey was enough for him, but he needed to check on Damion who had been released from the farm house, no longer a junky, though Gabriel had few expectations the idiot would remain off the crack for long, especially as Danny was out of hospital, broken jaw mended, internal injuries healed and a new hearing aid fitted. He wasn't foolish enough to imagine those two didn't hold an almighty grudge against his brothers, and being out classed by the De Luca men, two vengeful pricks would go for the only common link, Avion, so Gabriel drove over to the council estate where Damion lived and watched. Damion had taken up with a new girl, one who had yet to discover his monstrous side, given she still looked fairly healthy. It had pleased Gabriel that Damion had respected Abigail, though he had managed to demonstrate that a monster did not always need fists to live up to his name, and she had been truly terrified of the idiot. He had filled out a bit, but he still sported a sickly look, which made Gabriel suspect he was back on something addictive. Perhaps if Damion had a new interest, he would let Avion go, but it was Danny that concerned him most, because Damion owed a debt to the gang boss, and he had to pay. Gabriel watched but there was no sign of Danny, not this evening at any rate, Damion seemed happy enough taking his new girl to the pub he frequented with Avion, and for her part, the new girl seemed to like having her breasts groped in the car park before entering said establishment, so Gabriel drove back home, again setting a watch on Danny Baker.

His phone rang, and he put it on speaker, the news was interesting. Nigel Nesbitt had a date with one of Gabriel's ex's. If it were information he was after, she wouldn't have any to give, Gabriel never discussed business with any date. However, he smirked at the idea she would be comparing Nesbitt to him in bed, and he let loose a soft chuckle as to which one of them might win.

Chapter 12

Avion stood on the station platform searching the crowd for Gabriel. She couldn't help the overwhelming disappointment that he wasn't there to see her home. *Perhaps trains are a bit much for someone like him, but then that just shows his commitment if he is willing to suffer a train even once.* She tried to convince herself. *Then again may be he is just playing games.* If that were true, then she wished she knew the rules so she could step up and try to play along. She lost herself in her music that played into her ear phones from her phone. At home she sat in the roof top garden, stitching her latest memory, Gabriel on the tube, when she grew too tired to sew any more, she put her secret back into the bag, she knew she ought to replace it, buy herself something new, but that bag had kept her secret safe for three years, and she trusted it would go on doing so. She couldn't sleep. Visions of Gabriel's soft up turned lips had her heart racing, she could definitely cope with him on her train every day, even if it was only in the mornings, so when morning came, she couldn't wait to get to the tube station. She scanned the mass of people on the platform, but couldn't find any hint of him, and as the train swept into the station, with its accompanying whoosh of warm air that flung her hair all over the place, she still had not found him. Once again she found herself standing by the door, holding onto the vertical hand rail. The train lurched forward and every one stumbled, Avion found herself stepping on a foot and leaning against a solid wall of masculinity. She turn quickly, with an apology already on her lips, only to find Gabriel at her back. The train jolted, and she was forced into his torso, her hands on his chest, warm and solid, had her heart racing. Her eyes locked onto his, intense and sensual. His eyes burned into hers, then he leaned down towards her parted lips.

"Good morning Avion." He said in a voice laced with sexual tones. He watched her response, the way her eyes shone back at him, dark and alluring. Avion let go of his shirt and opened up his jacket so she could inspect it, he watched with intrigue, wondering why she wanted to inspect his shirt. He watched as she brushed it over with her fingers, sending sparks of heated desire racing through him, and to his alarm, to his groin. *Jeezus stop it Avion.* He pleaded mentally. She looked back up at his molten lava gaze, then stood on tip toe to talk into his ear over the loud rattling of the train.

"I didn't want to ruin another shirt." She explained sheepishly, her eye lashes blinked, caressing his face, and he inhaled deeply to keep his control. He was speechless, fighting all manner of emotions and responses. He felt like a teenager again, and the uncomfortable memory of his first sexual encounter flashed into his mind.

Nathen De Luca had insisted that by the time his boys reached legal adulthood, they would be mature men in every sense of the word, which meant learning about life from an early age, things like manners, fighting, and learning about sex. Gabriel had never wanted to know how his father had engaged a top prostitute to teach his boys the ways of women, or how he knew her. His first lesson at fifteen had not started out well. He had lost the plot the minute he'd seen her naked, messing his boxer shorts, and as if that hadn't been humiliating enough, she'd laughed at him. He felt that same lack of control now with Avion, and he was almost forty.

"Why are you taking the train when you don't get off at my stop?" Avion asked, her breath again warm on his neck, sending fire to his nether regions. The train jolted as it turned a corner, and Avion lost her balance. Gabriel's hand was on her hips, fingers splayed to support her, she could feel the light pressure against her thin trouser material, her hands were back on his chest, gripping the material tightly. Gabriel looked down at her and got an eyeful of her cleavage. He had no doubt she had no idea how revealing her top could be at such close quarters, and as a gentleman, he ought to not ogle, but gentleman be damned, he couldn't stop himself, and his groin responded with eagerness. He closed his eyes and silently prayed she wouldn't notice. Of all the god damned places to get a hard on, a train wasn't one of them. Nor could he answer her question, why did he stay on the train?, it was a good question, he had no reason to, he realised he could easily walk her to work and be picked up by a driver outside his grandmother's home. The train slowed as it came into the station, and once again Avion was forced against Gabriel's chest, and as the doors opened, he caught the aroma of roses from her hair, his eyes closed as he inhaled slowly and deeply. Avion felt his chest expand steadily and his heart beat strong against her palm. He had an intoxicating aroma of his own, spice and soap, and her own heart beat hard in response. She longed to slip her arms about his waist, to push herself against him just to be closer, nearer, merged. The carriage emptied and instantly refilled like a mechanical lung breathing out and then in. Avion smiled as she got pushed against Gabriel, had she looked up she would have found him smiling too. The train rumbled on and suddenly it was slowing again and this time it would be her who had to leave. Everyone piled out of the doors but Avion and Gabriel didn't move, she couldn't and he couldn't bring himself to be the one to part them. The seconds ticked by and eventually Avion pushed herself away from him.

"I have to go." She said sadly, and stepped off the train just in time as the doors were closing. She turned and watched the train disappear into the tunnel, the warm air blowing her hair as it left. Her feet felt heavy, and her heart ached, it hurt being away from Gabriel. *This is madness, how can he mean so much to me when we've hardly spent any time together?* She trudged along the platform and onto the escalator to the ground level. All the way to Mrs Parker's house she wondered about his hand on her hip, how he hadn't wanted to let her go, it felt nice to think he wanted her to stay with him, and he felt good, *he felt so good.*

"Is everything alright?" Mrs Parker asked as Avion entered the back parlor.
"Yea, I think so. Why?" Avion asked as she plonked down in the spare chair.
"You sound depressed." Mrs P informed her.
"No not really, how'd you know?"
Mrs Parker smiled kindly. "You sounded like a drunken elephant, stomping down the hallway just now."
"Oh sorry. I didn't mean to." Avion apologized.
"Did you see Gabriel?"
"Yea, I saw Gabriel. We …stood together." Avion bit her lower lip, she couldn't really tell her any more this was her grandson after all.
"Mmm. I like Gabriel, he's like a thick lamp post to lean against." Mrs Parker said smiling, and Avion laughed.
"Well you got that right." She giggled. Mrs Parker smiled, happy she had lightened Avion's mood, but also thrilled that Gabriel was smitten. It was about time he learned real emotions, he'd lived in a false world for far too long.

***

Gabriel stood on the train, his arousal subsiding to his relief, though he ached because of it. He hated the proximity of people hemming him into a corner, then he felt a hand slip into his pocket, he immediately put his own hand into the same pocket. The intruding hand tried to escape, but Gabriel grabbed it tightly. He turned his body pulling the intruder towards him, so that the young man fell onto the floor beside him. Gabriel leaned down with his other hand and grabbed the youths hair, making him yell loudly, and stand up. His thief was hardly twenty, and scruffily dressed, wearing a hoodie and torn jeans. Some people stared at

Gabriel wondering what was going on, but Gabriel ignored them, and leaned over to the young lad.

"People who try to steal from me, pay the price." The lad pulled at his arm trying to get free, but Gabriel squeezed harder, bones crunched, and the lad screamed. Gabriel squeezed harder still, the hand was fairly skinny so the bones were easy to snap, and snap them he did. All of them. The lad passed out.

"Is he alright?" Some man asked. Gabriel smiled charmingly and indicated his pocket where two arms were currently in occupation.

"He is trying to steal my wallet." Gabriel informed the stranger, who looked at him nervously, then smiled.

"You got it in hand then?" He grinned, and a few folks laughed. When the train pulled into the station, Gabriel waited until new people had boarded, then released the thief's hand and left him crumpled on the floor, he walked calmly off the train and mingled with the mass of people all heading for the exit.

After the train left, a distant scream echoed from deep inside the tunnel.

***

Gabriel entered his office in his usual way, nodding his morning greeting to Ashley, then closing the door behind him, he headed for his private closet and changed his shirt. He had no intention of giving Ashley anything to question him about, and Avion had screwed his shirt up so that it looked like he had slept in it. Besides it had her scent, and he inhaled deeply before he put it in the linen box. Donning a clean shirt, he stopped to check his composure in the mirror, he placed his hands either side of it on the wall, and lowered his head. *Avion*. God but he was coming undone. He groaned softly, he felt frustrated and alive and for the first time ever, jealous. He couldn't bare being apart from her, and being with her just made him want to rip her clothes off. He washed his hands through his hair. This pain was becoming unbearable, he had to spend more time with her, but would she want him once she discovered what he was? Hearing a thing wasn't the same as knowing it or seeing it. She'd had a violent relationship, she didn't deserve to be involved with another violent man, but Gabriel knew that didn't matter to him, he just wanted *her*, and he'd settle for no one else. Then there was Ashley. He looked up into the mirror. She was going to be a headache any day now. He knew that Ashley scrolled the internet looking for any hints of what he did away from the office, and he knew very well that she had seen the video of the day he first met Avion, and the pictures and video of the two of them on the tube. He also knew from her silence, that she was biding her time, looking for more information about Avion no doubt. He'd warned her after the last relationship she brought to an early end, but if she dared interfere with him and Avion, he knew he'd be hard pressed not to kill her, and with that vile thought at the forefront of his mind, he returned to his desk, just as Ashley entered with a tray full of coffee. Gabriel was staring out of his window his mind far away.

***

"Mr Nesbitt is here sir." Ashley announced in her sexiest voice that grated on Gabriel's nerves.
"Show him in."
Nigel Nesbitt entered Gabriel's office slightly crumpled and disheveled. He walked over to Gabriel's desk.
"I bet Barry Gordon didn't get hauled in here by the scruff of his neck." He grumbled. Gabriel looked up at him and let his eyes roam momentarily over the man before him, in truth he looked like Gabriel had, once he'd stepped off the tube, shirt creased and jacket upset.

"Please take a seat Mr Nesbitt." Gabriel nodded to the seat opposite him, and watched as Nesbitt sat down. Again Gabriel studied the man before him. Nesbitt was calm, for all he'd been slightly man handled. He was a thin man but not without some toning, especially in his arms. He had thick brown hair and some stubble on his cheeks, thin lips and his eyes were hazel in colour. The silence dragged on, Nesbitt seemingly unwilling to say anything, so Gabriel would have to. "You have been uncontactable."

Nesbitt smiled briefly.

"I've been doing my job." He replied. Gabriel considered this, as his eyes watched Nesbitt.

"A CEO who does his job with his phone switched off." He considered this as well, without changing expression or tone. The silence filled the room. Nesbitt wasn't playing ball and this annoyed Gabriel, so he cracked his fingers loudly. Nesbitt smiled, taking a small victory. Gabriel smiled, taking it back, as Nesbitt paled slightly.

"Read the papers please." Gabriel pushed the report towards Nesbitt.

"I don't need to. You have finally cottoned onto what is going on. Congratulations." He began to clap slowly.

"Please be careful Mr Nesbitt, I dislike smart arses."

Nesbitt smiled again.

"Is that a threat Gabriel?" He tilted his head to one side and then straightened it. They stared at each other. Eventually Nesbitt started to lose his patience, it was one thing to know about the way Gabriel De Luca did business, and something quite uncomfortable being a part of it.

"I suppose you think I am the saboteur?" His voice not so cool now, a little edge to it.

"Are you?"

"I heard you spoke to Gordon. I suppose this is his doing? Blame the spy."

Nesbitt remained comfortable in his chair, despite the slight edge to his voice.

"Are you to blame?" Gabriel asked in his flat tone. Nesbitt studied him again, and Gabriel kept his composure indifferent. After a long time, Nesbitt sighed.

"Fine. I can see you have no idea what's going on. So I'll tell you, if you really are as open minded as you claim, then you'll listen, but I doubt anything I am going to tell you is going to remove the blind fold you're wearing. So fuck you De Luca, bury me in the foundations of your next project, but then who will you blame when you're ruined. Won't be me eh." He smirked and chuckled. Gabriel just watched.

"Let us go back five years. Gordon's business was failing, not making the profits he needed it to make. He didn't want to evolve into the twenty first century, he liked things done the old fashioned way, but you know that. Your old man tried talking to him, offered him shit loads of money to help him up date, but Gordon just used it to pay his debts, and his worker's wages. This pissed your old man. He got Raphael to try and persuade Gordon to sell up, but Gordon refused. You'd think your smart old man would wonder why, wouldn't you?" Nesbitt cocked an eyebrow at Gabriel, who remained impassive. Nesbitt continued.

"My old man questioned it, and that was why he persuaded Gordon to employ me. He wanted me to get close to the man to know his secrets. It didn't take long. First Christmas, Gordon has the board dinner at his place, you've been there, as friends of his. You, your dad and your brothers. All important men for Gordon to be seen with. You still ain't twigged have you?" Nesbitt could tell, and he grinned.

"Gordon has a daughter, Henrietta. From the age of fifteen that spoilt brat has had a thing for Cut."

Now Gabriel was interested, not that it showed.

"Either Cut never noticed, and I fail to see how he could've been that blind, or she really was too young for him, he'd have been what 24, 25? Anyhows, your dad just thought Raphael wasn't putting enough pressure on Gordon, so he left things for a while. Henrietta is growing up and not out of her love for Cut, in fact she is getting more into him." Nesbitt laughed softly.

"Gordon then sees an opportunity. If Cut marries his daughter, he can merge the company. Gordon and Son. He keeps his business and it is linked to your family, so he would have access to all the funds he needs to keep going. So he takes a gamble with your dad, saying he's thinking of selling up after all. Now Gordon is putting all his bets on Cut, more experience, an all that, so imagine his shock when Uriel turns up. He hadn't considered what your old man would do if Raphael didn't get the deal. He had promised his daughter she could have Cut, your old man was bound to send him, but he sent Uriel instead. Henrietta is furious with him, and Gordon is stuck with Uriel. Plan backfired." Nigel Nesbitt paused so Gabriel could mentally catch up.

"You'd think at this point your old man would twig something from his bestie, but no! So Gordon messes with Uriel's plans, to buy himself time, and starts looking for another way out. Enter yours truly. Gordon thinks he is doing my old man a favour, taking on his no good son, training me up blah de blah. Secretly Gordon is hoping to distract Henrietta, at the same time putting pressure on Nathan to get Cut involved. He asks me what I think of her, and could I date her, little extra in the wages if I do. Lucky for me, she ain't interested, besides I know Gordon can't afford to pay me as it is, let alone extra for dating his spoilt brat. Turns out Gordy needs an ear to bend, so we go out and he gets drunk, pouring his heart out to me." Nesbitt fidgeted in his chair and then continued.

"Your dad is pissed when Uriel fails to get through to Gordon, and he is just about to turn his back on his old friend, when he gets wind my old man is interested in the assets. The assets are worth more than the damned business, so debts paid off and plenty over. Your old man knows what'll happen, and he still has hope for Gordon, besides he's invested a lot of time and his own money in the man, so he isn't about to lose out. In desperation he brings in the top gun." Nesbitt smiled generously at Gabriel, who felt quite honoured at the compliment. The silence floated down like a feather on a still breeze, and the smile started to fade from Nesbitt's lips.

"Is that it?" Gabriel asked eventually. Nigel Nesbitt looked at him blankly as if it should all be perfectly clear, except he could see from Gabriel's lack of expression, it wasn't. Nesbitt sighed.

"I thought the De Luca's were smart?" He sighed and leaned forward. "Henrietta has disowned her father, and her father has lost both her and his business. What's he got to lose man? I was hoping to be able to provide proof that he is the one sabotaging the business, but he got to you first." Once more the silence weighed heavy. It hadn't been Barry Gordon who'd informed him of the sabotage. Gabriel didn't imagine Nesbitt could've thought all that up overnight, and so precisely. It gave Gordon a reason to discredit the De Luca name, though he had no idea Henrietta had a thing for Cut, and he was fairly sure Cut had no idea he was the object of her desires.

"Gordon could've asked for Cut as a negotiator." Gabriel pointed out.

"I never said I had all the answers. You'd have to ask him that yourself."

Gabriel intended to.

"What is your interest in Juliet?"

"That's private." Nesbitt replied, his lips thinned.

"She's out of your league, so what's your interest?" Gabriel pressed. Nesbitt sighed. "I heard she was flaunting herself a bit after her latest break up. No harm in trying." He grinned, shrugging his shoulders.

Gabriel eyed him suspiciously.

"I slept on the sofa." Nesbitt admitted, annoyance clear in his voice. "And if it makes your day, it cost me a bloody fortune for the privilege."

Gabriel smiled inwardly, he knew the cost well.

Chapter 13

Avion sat in the roof top garden stitching, when the doorbell rang. Her heart sped up with a cold fear. She wasn't expecting any visitors. She suddenly wondered if it was Damion, could he have found her? He'd found her before. She took out her phone, and got ready to speed dial Kristine in case it was him. The doorbell rang again, and Avion walked carefully to the door, peeking through the spy hole, and seeing a tall woman, wearing a smart cream suit, and a seductively low cut blouse. She had red hair which sat on her shoulders, pale skin and subtle makeup. She didn't look like a threat, dressed like that, so Avion opened the door.
"Hey. My name is Ashley, can I come in?" She pushed passed Avion before Avion could answer her.
"You probably haven't heard of me, but I'm Gabriel's secretary." As she spoke, her eyes appraised the living space.
Avion felt intimidated immediately.
"Why are you here?" She asked cautiously.
"To warn you, so you don't get hurt. I saw that video of you spilling coffee all over him, and you have the same reaction that most women have when they first meet him." Ashley looked down her nose at Avion.
"I also saw the video of you on the train. Really? Have you any idea what an idiot you're making of yourself, and so publicly as well, you are embarrassing him."
Avion felt her hackles go up, so this was the famous Ashley who broke up Gabriel's relationships. Clearly this was jealousy; the woman reeked of it.
"Would you like a drink? I'm afraid I don't have any alcohol, but I can offer you tea or some coffee perhaps?"

Ashley glared at her, so when she gave no answer, Avion walked over to the kitchenette and put the jug on, intending to make tea for herself at least.

"He will break your heart, I mean you are so out of his league, and clearly you know nothing about him."

Nor you it seems, but Avion kept that to herself. She poured the hot water into a tea pot, and then turned to face Ashley, leaning against the counter for support.

"I know about Gabriel, I've already been warned, thanks."

"He's playing with you. He never stays long in a relationship because he doesn't care about women, and emotions. He is a hard man, a cold man, and you honey are making yourself a laughing stock." Ashley walked to the table and sat down.

Avion put the tea pot on the table and a couple of mugs.

"I am new to the De Luca family, and the men are very protective of me. Gabriel isn't the only one who flirts."

"Which is why you need to stay away from him. He will hurt you Avion, and I'd have thought you've been hurt enough already." Avion poured the tea.

"I appreciate your warning me and risking your job to do so, but I am not in the market for a relationship, and they all know it." Avion sipped her tea, watching Ashley watch her back.

"What do you know about my job?" Ashley growled.

"I know if you step into this you will lose him forever." Avion's voice was so soft, it was hard for Ashley to hate her.

"Then make it worth the loss and stay away from him." Ashley reached out for Avion's hand and squeezed it earnestly. Avion looked at it, how could she explain the feelings she had?

"I am flattered that you care so much, but Gabriel and his brothers have been so loving to me, something I have never had and I love them all for it. Yes I like Gabriel, but no I don't love him." She hoped.

"You might not love him now, but I can see you will. I know the guy and I can see the naivety in you Avion. You're a new concept to him, and he is going to crush you." Ashley was almost pleading her.

"If you're right, then I am the only one who will pay for my stupidity, and you and others will be justified in your feelings towards me. I'd say that is fair. You have warned me, so now let me learn." Avion smiled softly, tipping her head on one side. She patted Ashley's hand then sipped her tea. Ashley leaned back in her chair. Avion was a good negotiator, and she found she quite liked her.

"Well I can see why he likes you." She mused. Avion smiled.

"Nice place you have got here." Ashley observed.

"Do you want to see if he has moved in yet?" Avion grinned, as Ashley snapped her head back ready to snap at Avion, but stopped at her grin.

"He wouldn't live here. You'll see why when you see his pad." She smiled back. Avion's eyes glittered with mischief.

"So tell me what his pad is like?" She stood and began showing Ashley her own place. They walked out onto the roof garden, which Ashley adored.

"His place is huge, also in a loft, low windows and really expensive furniture." Ashley walked over to the garden wall and peered over, then stepped back, paling visibly.

"Oh fuck. He's here." She gasped. Avion stepped up beside her and peered over the wall. She could see the dark SUV but no driver.

"Don't worry Ashley, I won't let him sack you, if he won't believe me, he will not argue with his grandmother."

"You know her?" Ashley looked surprised.

"I work for her. I thought you'd know that?"

"No. I just thought you were some poor cow who spilt her coffee over him." Ashley said, then when she saw Avion laughing, she smiled and joined in. They were still laughing when Avion opened the front door and found Gabriel standing in front of it.

***

Of all the situations Gabriel had imagined on his way over to Avion's flat, this wasn't one of them. He was only momentarily struck dumb though.

"Ashley" He growled. She paled at the rage in his eyes.

"I hope I get to see you again Ash, it was kind of you to pop round." Avion said with determination, her eyes leveled on Gabriel.

"Won't you come in Gabriel?" He did and Ashley escaped unscathed. As soon as the door was closed Gabriel spun round and glared at Avion, fixing her with such a violent glare, she physically shriveled, making him curse himself, and try to calm down.

"I know what you're thinking." Avion began.

"Do you?" He growled, his eyes blazing. Avion swallowed.

"I know you think she is interfering in something, but she isn't. I mean, she was, but she isn't now." Avion bit her lower lip, which did strange things to Gabriel's guts and blood pressure.

"Care to try again?" He asked in a voice that was so deep Avion thought the floor would rumble

"She came to warn me about you, but you knew that. I knew that too. I told her we are just friends, and you are just looking out for me, like your brothers are." Avion looked away, pulling strange faces with her lips. Gabriel stared at her. He felt her words like daggers to his heart, yet she could not know how he felt, he *had* only been like his brothers, only Ashley would see what his behaviour really was.

"And will you heed her?" His eyes had mellowed to curiosity now, his question catching Avion unexpectedly, she looked back up at him and shrugged.

"I, I don't know." She replied softly, injecting an overdose of hope into him without even knowing it. He stepped closer.

"Are you afraid of me or the rumours about me?" His voice was deep and smooth, sending goose bumps racing over her skin. Avion blinked and looked into his smoldering eyes.

"I have no reason to fear you, but," She paused, searching his eyes for the words she needed.

"But?" He whispered, hypnotized by her eyes, her worried expression.

"But I fear one day I might." The silence was deafening, and hung heavy between them. Gabriel imagined Damion beating her, he could understand her fear of somehow upsetting him, yet he was not Damion, perhaps worse, but hit her he never could, never would. He lifted his hand gently and stroked the side of her face tracing his thumb along her jawline, watching as she closed her eyes, parting her sensual lips. He smiled inwardly. She might be afraid of upsetting him, but she wasn't able to stop responding to his touch, to his words.

"I am so much more than the rumours Avion. I can be dangerous in more ways than one." He reminded her, his lips were at her ear, his breath softly brushing her hair, tickling her skin.

"I think in truth, you are afraid of yourself. Afraid to dream, afraid to live. Afraid of your heart." His lips touched her ear lobe, warm and soft. Avion nearly passed out from the sensual touch, she gasped softly, making Gabriel close his eyes in ecstasy, glad she couldn't see him. He inhaled her scent, he let his lips remember her soft skin; he relished her slight shudder, the blush that coloured her neck.

"Teach me." She breathed so softly she hadn't realised she had spoken out loud. Gabriel withdrew his closeness, his eyes dark orbs of sexiness and desire, a soft smirk touched his lips.

"Good night Avion." He said in that deep voice that melted her knees.

Avion lay on her bed unable to believe that encounter had happened. Had she *really* spoken out loud, and how fateful were those words going to be. She smiled. Everyone had an idea something was going on between them, Ashley was ready to risk her job and Gabriel was ready to sack her for visiting, Avion smiled again, it was making her face ache and that made her heart soar, because for the first time in her life, she meant something. He was dangerous in more ways than one, and now Avion wanted to discover what that meant, yearned for it.

***

Once more she searched for Gabriel on the train station platform, but if he embarked from her station, she couldn't find him in the tide of humanity that swarmed there. It was only ever, once she was on board that he seemed to solidify from thin air, and always behind her, so close it was intoxicating.
"Good morning Avion." His deep voice crooned into her ear. She smiled and turned to face him, but he blocked her, pulling her instead to his chest, so that her back rested against him. Some people around them stared, it was hard not to when there was scarcely room to blink between commuters. Most were of course, immersed in their music, audio books or watching phone screens, but Gabriel had his arm around her waist, his hold was gentle. She wondered why he wanted to travel like this, but as she obeyed she realised she had a close encounter with his masculinity, his scent, spice and soap. She closed her eyes and he felt her relax and breathe deeply. He also inhaled, for him the scent of roses, and a hint of lavender on her second hand trouser suit. If he glanced down, and he did, he had a near perfect view of her cleavage, the gentle swell of her breasts as she breathed in and out. As the train rock and rolled its way to the next platform, so his fingers

pressed and released against her body, holding her firmly, keeping her safe. Avion began to feel frustrated. She had no way of touching him, every time she tried to turn around, he prevented her doing so, and she couldn't talk to him either, he seemed to just want her, without anything else, so she lifted her arm and placed it over his, feeling the strong muscles contract instantly. Gabriel held still as Avion rested her head against his shoulder, her neck so close to his lips he could taste her. *Avion*, his mind screamed. He angled his head around and placed a soft kiss upon her jaw, she instantly stiffened, then sighed. He smiled at the extra swell of her chest, and just as Avion began to wonder if she'd imagined it, his deep whisper came against her ear.

"Did you enjoy that?" He teased, leaving another right where he'd left the first. Avion was weakening at the knees, her breathing had intensified, she was drowning in hormonal over load, if this is what he meant by dangerous, she was dying, and to hell with who watched it. The train began to slow, the screech of breaks sending everyone standing, lurching forwards and sideways. Gabriel increased his hold and Avion dug her fingertips into his jacket sleeve, he hissed from the pleasure, and the instant warmth in his groin, putting his head back so she didn't hear him over the noise of the train. People poured out of the doors, allowing a moment for fresh air to swoop in, cool air that soothed the heated bodies, especially of the two pressed so close together. More passengers squeezed into the carriage, and Avion relished once more, the pressure of being pushed against such a solid body. As the train moved forward, so everyone stumbled, treading on each other's feet and apologizing.

"Perhaps I should add a pair of shoes to the shirt you already owe me." He said sexily into her ear. Avion smiled, but she hoped he was joking, she really didn't know him well enough to know what a joke was to him. She turned her head to speak but found herself staring at his neck, a strong and powerful neck, which held an intelligent and very smart head and a jaw line a model would envy. Whatever she was going to say was lost in her overwhelming desire to stroke that jaw as intimately as he had done hers. Yet she could not, he simply would not let her near him. Instead she blew softly at his exposed skin, and smiled as he snatched his breath in deeply. *I can play this game too.* She thought to him. When she did it again, he turned his face towards her, their lips mere centimeters apart.

"Don't." He growled, making her shiver, God how she wanted his lips on hers, she almost whimpered. The train jolted its way into her station and Avion wanted to cry at the thought he would not get off with her, she lingered against him until the last passenger had left, and then she pulled free of him and disembarked, unable to turn around to look at him, she let the train go, knowing his eyes were gouging holes in her back.

***

Mrs Parker had never saught to know how her grandsons dated, and certainly they would never have shared their opinions of any woman with her, so it came as something of an insight when Avion finally poured out the train journey to her. By the time Avion had finished, poor Mrs P was fanning her face and grinning like she was a young girl again.

"My, that boy likes his games." She said breathlessly.

"Is that what I am to him?" Avion snapped, suddenly annoyed as hell that she was being made fun of.

"No dear. You are not the game. *He* is." Mrs P smiled warmly. "Gabriel is not an emotional man, none of them were raised to embrace emotions, but Gabriel is the least feeling of all of them. I think you have opened a Pandora's Box where he is concerned, and now he is testing himself." Mrs P nodded as she agreed with her own hypothesis.

"So what do I do?" Avion asked confused.

"Arh. Good question. I think you play him along, let him state the rules. I think he wants you to test him a little, like when you blew on him, and he told you not to, that was naughty but he enjoyed it."

"How'd you know?" Avi pushed. Mrs P tapped her lips for several painful minutes.

"I know." She stated and would say no more.

"It would help if he said more, but when he talks he talks in riddles." Avion complained as she dusted around the room. Mrs P did not bite, just listened.

"He even turned up at my flat last night cos Ashley paid me a visit." Mrs P stiffened at that news. Avion smiled at the reaction, and then told Mrs P what had happened and how Gabriel had behaved.

"I so hope he doesn't sack her." Avion said. "I like her."

"Mmm and she is in love with him."

"How can you know that?" Avion asked.

"An old woman knows many things. Few of us get to be old without learning something about life. Besides Gabriel has often complained about her dress sense, which is the most obvious indication of her adoration. Plenty of secretaries or PA's as they like to be known as these days, have a secret crush on the boss."

"So why doesn't he date her, she is really beautiful."

"Beauty is in the eye of the beholder don't they say?" Mrs P offered. Avion scrunched up her nose.

"You're starting to sound like him now." She complained, making Mrs P smile.

Chapter 14

"Gordon's has a problem." Gabriel stated. "I have two choices, sell it or sort it." There was a murmur of shock at the choice to sell.

"You can't sell it." Barry Gordon demanded. Gabriel turned his cold gaze upon the man. Gordon squirmed.

"It's my lifes work." He said apologetically, then looked around the room for support, but got none.

"Interesting how you jump to that rather than sorting?" Gabriel queried, his tone flat and quiet. Gordon fidgeted.

"You never talked about selling before." He said quietly. Gabriel's gaze never moved from Gordon, who began to sweat on his shiny pate.

"You never thought to be honest with me either." He said softly.

"What do you mean? I kept nothing from you."

Silence fell as the two men stared at each other. Eventually Gabriel spoke.

"Why didn't you ask for Cuthbert to negotiate with?"

Gordon's eyes widened by the slightest amount.

"Why would I ask for him?"

"Because of Henrietta."

Gordon's eyes did widen then.

"This has nothing to do with her." Gordon snapped, flushing with anger, he really didn't want his dirty laundry out in the open like this. Gabriel knew guilt when he saw it, so Nesbitt had been right.

"Did you think I wouldn't find out?"

"I don't know what you've been told, but it's a lie." Gordon shouted. Everyone looked at him now wondering what was going on.

"So who's the saboteur?"

"How should I know? You're the one looking into it." Gordon shouted in desperation. Gabriel smiled thinly at him. "And I did, and I found you wanting." His voice was ice, calm and in control.

"It isn't me." Gordon was frantic. "For God's sake Gabriel, damage my own goods, risk my good name, years of work? Are you insane?" *Quite probably.* Gabriel thought of Avion and pressed his lips into a thin line to hide the smirk that threatened. *Quite probably indeed.*

"If this were about you, then no, but it isn't about you or your company, is it? It's everything to do with your daughter and my brother."

The room gasped collectively. Gordon was shaking his head. "No. You've got it all wrong. You're talking about Henrietta's crush on Cut." He laughed nervously. "That was years ago." He laughed again, waved his arms about casually. "That candle blew out long ago." He smiled unconvincingly. Gabriel never took his eyes off him, and again the silence fell.

"Could someone explain what is going on here?" An older man asked frowning. Gabriel leaned back in his chair and opened his arms.

"Please do Barry." He said warmly. Everyone turned to Barry Gordon, who looked back at them despairingly.

"I. I don't know what he thinks he knows. Whatever it is, has nothing to do with the sabotage of the product we make."

"You were broke?" Gabriel offered, and Gordon nodded. "Hardly a secret." He said almost proudly.

"What did you do?" Gabriel asked, his features neutral.

"What do you mean, what did I do? I turned to my dearest friend, *your* father." Gordon said exasperated.

"And what did my father do?"

"What the hell is this? He offered to help me, so what?"

"He gave you money right?"

"What if he did?"

"What did you do with that money?"

Gordon looked baffled. "I spent it." He said loudly, looking bewildered.
Gabriel nodded. "What on?"
"None of your fucking business."
Gabriel glared at the man, but Gordon refused to say any more, so Gabriel let the silence hang, heavy and dangerous. Suddenly he slammed his hand down hard on the table top, making just about all the board members jump out of their skins.
"Tell them what you did with the money Gordon." Gabriel shouted. The whole room was on edge now, because Gabriel De Luca never raised his voice. Gordon shook, sweat trickled down the side of his face.
"I spent it on wages and debt." He said softly, shame in his tone.
"Thank you. So my father gave you money not for the purposes you used it for, but to improve the factory, bring it up to date. Wasn't that what he wanted you to do?" Gabriel's voice was back to being glacial.
Gordon nodded.
"Then what happened?" Gabriel asked softly.
"Nothing."
"Something happened, because you didn't make any profits did you?"
Gordon shook his head.
"So what happened?"
"I lost more money. I had to sell up."
"Arh now it gets interesting. Keep going." Gabriel tapped the pad of his finger on the table.
"I offered the business to your father."
"No. Before that you offered it to Nesbitt didn't you? You had a plan." Gabriel tipped his head to one side. Gordon sighed.
"It was foolish." He pleaded
"What plan?" The older man who had spoken before asked. Gordon waved his arms about.

"It was nothing. I thought I might sell to Nesbitt and train his kid up in the business, but I realised the boy was a spy, so pulled out of the negotiations. It was nothing." He pointed at Gabriel. "He's the one making it something."

"That isn't the whole of it though." Gabriel reminded him, levelling his gaze at Gordon.

"Yea it is." Gordon protested.

"According to Nesbitt, you wanted him and Henrietta to get married, then you could keep the company, making him a joint owner, Gordon and *Son*, with access to Nesbitt's funds." Gabriel cocked an eyebrow at Gordon, who paled.

"Son of a bitch." He whispered. "He remembered."

"Yea he remembered it all Barry. When Henrietta refused to play ball, she got to thinking it could work if she married Cut, and you realised what a smart move that'd be, unlimited access to the De Luca bank funds. Except Cut wasn't interested in her, and my father never sent him as negotiator."

The silence that fell was as thick as pea soup, and could be cut with a knife. The whole board looked at Gordon and Gabriel and each other, confused, betrayed and angry.

"So who's the saboteur?" The older man asked. All eyes moved to Gordon.

"It isn't me." He insisted. "I swear."

"Consider this." Gabriel offered to the whole room. "Here is a man unwilling to accept his losses. My father gave you funds that would have enabled you to modernize and improve the company, thus making you able to pay your debts, but you chose to take a different road. *I* set you up comfortably Gordon, and you still cannot let go. I have allowed you to remain a silent investor. I kept your name as the business. I kept your employees. Yet none of that has healed the wound that my family owns you and your business. What better motive have you got than to discredit my family's reputation through an act of sabotage?"

Gordon opened his mouth to speak, but Gabriel held up his finger.

"Not another word. I want the board to decide what happens to Gordons. I want the board to decide what we do with you. We will meet again in the morning."

Gabriel watched as the board members filed out of the room. He found himself reliving the train journey. The way he had managed to make Avion use her senses, to inhale his masculinity, and she had, melting into him. She had let herself go, let herself believe, and that was a step forward. He had longed to kiss her lips when she blew on his neck which was something he had not expected, nor the way she clutched at his arm, gripping with her fingertips, not her nails.

He was drawn from his contemplation by the sound of a throat clearing. Gabriel cast his eyes across the room to Ashley, who stood in her usual smart suit and low cut blouse, with her hands clutched in front of her. He cocked an eye brow as his eyes met hers.

"I, um, wanted to apologize about the other night." She said hesitantly.

"Accepted." He replied and looked away.

"No, I mean she is a nice person. Avion."

Gabriel looked back at his PA, then turned away picking up his phone. *Yes she is*, he thought as he opened up his social media and watched the video of his train journey that morning. A video he had paid to be made. Ashley took the hint and left him to it. The person who had taken the video had understood Gabriel's instructions well and the result pleased him immensely. After discovering Barry Gordon was not what he seemed, Gabriel was left feeling disappointed. He wasn't looking forward to telling his father how deceived he had been, still, that could wait, for now he had something pleasurable to do, study a woman who had gotten under his skin and was slowly taking him over. He had kept her back to him on purpose, and now he could watch her reactions to him, her frustration at being trapped, at having to let him be close without being able to interact with him, the clever way she had found to get to him. He shivered at the memory of her cool breath upon his skin, he felt again the ache it caused him, the sudden desperate need to kiss her, to hold her tighter. Avion was changing him without knowing it, and he wondered if this is what had happened to his own father when he met his mother, for their love was set in stone, anchored by a deep, soul bonded love. Gabriel had never imagined he had the ability to really feel emotions and he wondered, not for the first time, if this was a good thing or not.

***

Danny Baker looked at the heap of bloody flesh curled up on his office floor. He'd been beaten to crap by a De Luca in a posh suit. He now sported a hearing aid and he was pissed as hell *plus* he hadn't had a single penny back from the money Damion had stolen off him.
"Get up Smallman I want to know what you gunna do about the debt you owe me?" He sat down behind his fake wooden desk. Damion moaned and managed to get onto his hands and knees. Getting beaten up was becoming a life choice he hadn't exactly set out aiming for. He coughed and spat blood, not sure if he had a broken rib or just another bad tooth had been punched from his skull. His head ached almost as badly as it had went he went cold turkey back at the farm house.
"I can sell some stuff for yer." He croaked, his throat was on fire with dryness.
"You can't, you already tried that an look what happened. I'm seriously wondering what your fucking worth on his planet is." Baker snarled to the druggy on his hands and knees.
"I don't know what else I can do." Damion moaned pathetically.
"I got an idea." Baker said in a low voice. "I think you should kidnap that ex of yours. Them De Luca bastards should pay for what they done to me, an they did steal your gal, and they did lock you up and beat the crap out of ya. Reckon we both

could go some pay back?" Danny waited for the idea to take root. Damion shook his head.

"No way. The fuckers'll kill me for sure. No one can touch the bitch, she's under their protection." He said informatively. Danny threw something hard at Damion's head.

"An yer think I won't?" He yelled making Damion cringe. He was fucked whatever he did.

"They'll kill you too." Damion tried, then whimpered when one of the thugs kicked him. "Ok, I'll do it, but where am I gonna take her?" Danny Baker smiled and chuckled softly.

***

Avion was getting used to mornings on the train with Gabriel. Each day was a different kind of test for her to undergo and now she had started to look forward to them. Their fame had spread far and wide on the internet, and they had quite a few fans who longed to see the handsome man kiss the pretty woman he obviously adored, and as the tension mounted by the day, so the bets were being placed openly as to which day he might cave in. The down side to this fame was the extra humanity that took that tube on the off chance they would get a glimpse of the famous couple. Gabriel hated it, but he did love the fame he now had. Even his own parents had started following his romantic courting of Avion. His siblings watched with amusement as well, for the second eldest brother sworn to bachelorhood, was making his feelings very public, yet he never did anything more than keep Avion close, than look at her with molten desire – a Krissy favourite – and he only held her with hands on her hips, an arm around her waist or a hand on her back, yet it was provocative enough to have female fans cooing over him, wishing it were they he embraced. Mrs Parker had been astonished at his openness, Gabriel the heartless was fast becoming Gabriel the heart on sleeve. She held close to her own council on the worry she had about that, such behaviour brought consequences, especially from rivals, and Gabriel had plenty of those, yet he was enjoying himself, and this was all new to him, so she watched and watched, and looked at the spaces between words for any clues that might bring sorrow.

***

Gabriel sat in the board room, watching the men and two women who sat with him. This was the day he would announce the fate of Gordon Barry. He had reported back to his father whose response had been to show no mercy to the man he had once called friend. Gabriel wasn't in the least surprised at this instruction. He had opted to let the man stew for a few days, so had delayed the following morning dead line, now he let the silence grow to absolute breaking point, before he finally decided they had sweated enough.
"Gordon's is to be sold." He said in his usual flat tone, his cold gaze fixed on Gordon.
"What of the employees?" Someone asked.
"Standard redundancy." There was a gasp to that.
"It's me you wish to punish, don't make them suffer." Barry said, trying to keep his ire in control. Gabriel ignored him, he nodded to Ashley who handed Gordon an A4 envelope.
"What's this?" The disgraced man asked.
"I'm suing you for destroying my company. Your house is being taken away from you as is your property in Italy, your cars, your savings and anything else you will need to sell to meet the bill." Gabriel almost sounded bored. Barry Gordon paled.
"I'll have nothing." He whispered. "What about my daughter?"
"You intended for me to have nothing, and who cares about your daughter?" There was a long silence as everyone looked bashful at the fate they had allowed Gabriel to dish out, once

Gabriel was sure his message had sunk into each of them, he dismissed the meeting. In truth he was eager to view that mornings train trip, he had become quite addicted himself to see what people filmed, so he arrived in his office and settled behind his desk, then flipped on his phone and watched. He smiled at the shameless commuters who openly held their phones at the couple, and watched as he nuzzled Avion's hair, *arh roses* he remembered, though her scent was etched into his memory regardless of the footage. He smiled appreciatively as the person filming sighed when he stroked Avion's jawline, when he moved her hair over her ear, so he could talk to her without anyone else hearing, he watched her smile seductively, heard the person beg him to kiss the woman. He watched as his lips brushed Avion's ear, and heard a loud cooing from the female passengers. He recalled how excited it all made him, how badly he ached to give in and kiss her. He had it all planned, and he knew it would have to be soon, for the suspense was crippling his groin every morning and the crush of humanity was killing his suits. At the end of the video he watched as Avion reluctantly departed the carriage, looking back at him with longing and disappointment. He was about to switch off when another video started to play. He watched as a familiar figure snuck up behind Avion, and when she turned how she stiffened. Gabriel scowled. He watched in helpless horror as she was escorted out of the station, he watched as Damion Smallman stood in front of her on the escalator, bent over her, and grabbed her jaw with one hand, pinching his fingers deeply into her cheeks. Gabriel watched as Damion filmed himself kissing her, leaving a trickle of blood to seep over her bottom lip. He was incensed. He noted how muscular the man had become, which meant he had to be on steroids. The last time he had observed Damion the man had still been rake thin, and he was pretty sure he had no appetite for the gym. He watched helplessly as Avion was bundled into a black SUV and driven away.

It took seconds for him to snap into action, calling his contact on the traffic cameras to follow the car. He called his grandmother, for if Avion had been kidnapped who was to say, Smallman wouldn't come after her. Mrs Parker answered the phone on the first ring.
"I am safe darling." She said softly, sadly. "Krissy and Ceaser are already here."
"You know?" He snarled.
"We tried to call you but your phone was switched off." Krissy shouted from some distance away. "Patrick has put undercover police up and down the road." She added. Gabriel hung up and called his brothers. Uriel was the only one who had not seen the footage, they all assured him they waited his instructions. Gabriel was lost. He turned and punched the window hard enough to crack it and make his knuckles bleed, leaving a single trail of blood to dribble down the pane like a solitary tear.

Chapter 15

It was all his fault. Had he not flaunted Avion in front of the world, she might now be safe. Gabriel had dared to imagine he could have what his brother Michael had, what his parents had, even what his grandmother had found in her second husband, that soul deep bond of completeness. Instead he had destroyed himself by destroying her. His phone pinged. A message from an unknown source. He knew who that was. He opened the message and saw Avion tied to a bed, her blouse cut open, her bra pushed up her breasts on full display.

£50,000 and you get her back untouched. Try to find her and I will send you live footage of every man that fucks her. You have until five pm to respond.

Gabriel stared at the message, and closed Pandora's Box of emotions. He was being told to pay of Smallman's debt, he felt his anger rising. If this was the cost of caring for someone, then he could not allow his heart to feel, the consequences of not protecting Avion enough were plain to see. She would never trust him or his brothers ever again, if she survived, if she lived. For now he had a choice to make, and he'd be damned before he gave that arse wipe a single penny.

His phone rang. Gabriel swore, all he wanted was some time alone to think, why couldn't they leave him alone to do that? He was about to ignore the call when he noticed it was his father. No son of Nathen De Luca, ignored his father and lived, so Gabriel answered. He didn't have to speak.

"Take the deal." His father's voice was a razor against Gabriel's skin. How did he know?

"No." The silence dropped like a concrete block. He heard his father suck in a breath.

"Then she will die at his hands. Do you want her blood on yours?"

Gabriel looked down at his fist coagulating but still oozing blood. *I already have*, he thought but did not voice that to his father.

"I'll not give that shit a fucking penny." He said in his own deep soft voice that flowed down the phone like molten lava. Again silence.

"Take the deal. My money." His father hung up without even asking what the ransom amount was. Gabriel bent his head, grit his teeth and roared, slowly lifting his head and tilting it backwards. He roared till his neck corded. He roared as he fisted his hands so tightly, the wounds reopened and bled afresh. He roared till he thought his lungs would burst from the strain. He roared until his temples pounded from pain and a headache burst into his brain. How dare his father take from him the right to choose. How dare Damion Smallman take the woman he cared about and debase her like he had. He would kill him. He would kill him slowly, carve her name into his body with one of Cuthbert's knives. Or maybe he would spar with the man. Gabriel felt a cold hunger for the pain of punches being rained down upon him, he felt a desperate need to suffer more than Avion; he felt an old yearning for the pleasure of being beaten. Steroids gave muscle tone but they did not make you strong, and Damion had never been strong, the fight would be a match in Gabriel's favour, but for all that he would allow the bastard to punish him for his slackness. He reached for his phone and sent the text.

Deal.

***

Ashley sat in her reception area, sobbing down the phone to Krissy. The sound of glass breaking had her gasping and weeping louder. The silence was worse. She was just about to see if she could peek into the room, when the roaring started. Ashley wailed into the phone, she had never been so terrified in all her life.

Mrs Parker sat beside her granddaughter listening on speaker phone to the torment her beloved grandson was going through. She heard the glass smash, she heard his roaring, a howl more lamenting than any wolf, a promise of bloody murder to come. They did not see the message Gabriel had seen, they did not know what had triggered such a response, but Mrs Parker knew something bad had happened other than Avion's kidnapping, she knew something bad had been seen by Gabriel only, for him to have responded as he had. She blamed herself. Hadn't she *wanted* him to care for Avion? If she hadn't stepped in to protect the girl, none of this would've happened. Avion would most likely already be dead, but Gabriel wouldn't be broken, and her other boys wouldn't be angry. *Arh, Damion, you've no idea what you have done.* She let the tears fall freely down her ashen wrinkled face. *There's a storm coming, so you'd better run.*

***

Avion's wrists ached and bled where the plastic ties cut into her skin. She could do nothing to stop Damion touching her exposed breasts, and laughing as he did so. She shut her eyes and let herself remember what real affection felt like, the soft breath that whispered through her hair, the lips like petals that caressed her skin, and the scent of him, of the man she had fallen in love with, had wanted in her life. She knew that wasn't true anymore. He had failed to keep her safe. She had trusted him and he had let this happen. She had played with fire, dared to dream, dared to hope that finally she had found happiness. How easy it was to burst a bubble so fragile, so thin. She knew he would think her a slut now, after the picture Damion had taken, could see the scars he'd left her with, *well this is what I am*, she thought sadly, *he could never have loved this body, so flawed, so damaged.* It was a small solace that she had been spared his shock and revulsion, still she could not stop the aching heart that lay shattered in her rib cage, nor could she stop the tears that bled from her eyes. Had it been love, or just a dangerous silly game he'd played? It was easier to think so. *"I am so much more than the rumours Avion"*. He'd warned her, yet she had not heard it, choosing instead to interpret it as interest. Truth showed her now he *was* so much more dangerous than she could've dreamed. She just couldn't decide which monster was worse, the Damion beat monster or the Gabriel seductive mind game monster. *Foolish me.*

"Looks like your boyfriend is gonna do the right thing after all." Damion said as he sauntered into the tiny room where Avion was being held.

"He'll kill you. Him and his brothers." She spoke softly, defiantly.

"I'm already fucking dead you stupid whore. Look at me?" He flexed his bicep, making the vein stand proud. "He can fucking try killing me, but I'm fucking superman these days." Damion laughed but there was no joy in the sound. "I didn't want to do this. I had no fucking choice. Danny made me do it, or he'd cut off the drug supply. I ain't going cold fucking turkey again." He looked at Avi, then reached out and fondled her, making her want to gag. He slapped her face. "Thought you liked men with muscles?" He sneered. "Oh, I see, it's men with muscles and loads of fucking money eh? Well soon enough, we can be rich." At that, Avion barked a laugh.

"You'll never be rich Damion, you'd spend it all on drugs." He slapped her again.

"Fucking bitch."

***

If Danny Baker had thought the whole kidnapping thing had gone a bit too easy, he forgot to notice so glad was he to have that much money in his bank. It actually took two whole days and several missing thugs before it occurred to him what the consequences might be. He tried to escape by taking a flight out of the country, but found himself barred. Strangely he wasn't arrested either, but he eventually discovered that Nathen De Luca liked hunting, especially people who had pissed him off, and so Danny found himself on the run. He had dumped Damion as soon as the transaction had taken place, and the idiot had been caught on the second day, which was when Danny realised he was walking dead. Now he was a week into his dodge-the-goon life, and he was exhausted, hungry and destitute. He was discovering that having £50.000 was of no benefit at all if he couldn't spend it, and he *couldn't* spend it. Every time he tried to buy so much as a bar of chocolate, his money was refused and his card was blocked. He should've known playing with the big noises was not smart, but he wanted his money back. He was owed. He had no money for fuel or a roof over his head, and he had been unable to change his clothes. In truth, had he been able to check his bank account, he'd have found it empty. There never had been a deposit of any kind, it had all been carefully orchestrated by Nathen De Luca, who had taken all of Danny Bakers funds as compensation for Avion more than himself.

Danny found himself outside a super market. He watched carefully as customers walked in and out. He checked the car park for suspicious vehicles, and only then did he enter, walking around his stomach grumbled at all the food on offer. He stuffed an apple into his pocket, then another. He grabbed a carrot or two and then slipped a bread bun into the same pocket. He headed towards the exit and just as he reached the doors the alarms went off. It couldn't have been him, apples and carrots didn't have bar codes, yet he found himself surrounded by three security guards. They took him to the office upstairs and he had to hand over the food he had stolen. He was retained with no one explaining why, he guessed he was going to be finally arrested for theft, but when the door next opened it wasn't the local constabulary that walked in. It was Gabriel.

"Are you enjoying this game?" He asked in his flat expressionless tone. Danny rolled his eyes.

"You must be Gabriel. I already met the others. Another beating?" He said, as each time he had been cornered, that is what he got, from one brother or another, only to be left for dead and the whole on the run thing, to start again. Gabriel stared at him with cold amber eyes.

"Is that what you want?"

"No the fuck it isn't." The silence settled as a thick blanket. Eventually Danny could stand the staring no longer.

"Didn't your mother teach you that staring is rude?" He goaded.

"Didn't yours teach you not to steal?"

Danny shifted his position, waiting for the punch or slap that signaled the start of his beating, but it never came.

"What do you want De Luca?" Danny's skin was prickling, he had a bead of sweat trickling down his back.

"I'll happily give the fucking money back." He was a bit surprised to see Gabriel almost smirk at that.

"You never had the money, it was a ruse." That made Danny raise his eyebrows and his mouth to drop open.

"Ain't possible." He said, believing it a truth. Gabriel shrugged, what did he care what this moron thought.

"I am here to offer you a choice." Again the silence dropped.

"Yea?" Danny prompted.

"To continue as you are, until you die in some alley from wounds and starvation, or to fight me." Gabriel rested his cold gaze on Danny's eyes, burning into his soul. He watched Danny's dark eyes stare into his own wondering what the catch was.

"Well I'd like to say it was a fair fight, but you got the upper hand ain't ya?"
Gabriel conceded that point.
"I believe in fair fights, so you will be fed."
Danny nodded. This was the brother who had been dating Avion, he'd be pretty pissed and ripe for a good fight, but with some food inside him, Danny was up for fights, especially as they had conned him out of his money after all. He did hate liars, especially when it was him being lied to and not telling the lie.
"I'll sweeten the deal. You can use your knuckle duster." Gabriel offered as he nonchalantly inspected his finger nails.
Danny grinned, this was going to be really bloody.
"Deal." He grinned, showing beautiful white teeth, and a few gaps where Cut had knocked some out, back when he'd saved Avion.

***

The room was devoid of decorations, it was clinical though not a hospital, just a place for the damaged to go to be healed, or at least that's how Avion viewed her new home. According to the manager who'd welcomed her, this clinic was owned by Raphael De Luca, the only brother Avion had not met and hoped never to. She'd had enough of this family and it's fakeness to last her a life time. She held no interest in the manicured gardens or the friendly open spaces where clients could take visitors, she had no particular interest in her room either, but none of this could she escape. The De Luca family had apparently decided she needed to be here, when in fact she needed to be as far away from them as she could get. The clinicians, as they liked to be called, though Avion preferred shrinks, were very kind and chatty, but she could read them all like a book. They had a job to do, sort her head out, make her see how the De Luca's were not really to blame, she was and they could help her move on with her life. They had attempted to engage her in talking about her early life, but the subject was too boring and obvious for Avion to be bothered playing the game, so she made it abundantly clear that her past was not up for dissecting. They were ok with that, presumably they hoped they could go back to it at some future date, but for now they were trying to dissect what Avion felt about her experience at being captive. She was tempted to remind them that she had been captive, a new word for imprisoned, for three years with Damion, and nothing her forty eight hours at being kidnapped, could hold a candle to his treatment of her, but it was too much effort to put into words, so she just stared at the councilor with pity in her eyes. When they got too monotonous she turned her thoughts to her secret, to the book that held her memories that were no longer as happy as they had been when she'd stitched them. It wasn't safe to look at the book here, too many hidden cameras, so she stewed. She ought to unstitch the memories of Gabriel, but to do so was to erase the special lesson they held. "Beauty is in the eye of the beholder." Mrs Parker had said once, and Avion could see now how a wolf in sheep's clothing also worked. She had seen them all as beautiful, especially Gabriel. She had fallen for his charms, for his ability to seduce her in public, all to make himself important, desired. She wondered now if it hadn't all been something of a mid-life crises for him. She had heard that men in their forties and fifties could go off the rails, get a younger woman, and escape an older wife. Have numerous affairs. Buy a sports car and blow the savings. People did crazy things when they realised their lives were creeping closer to old rather than young.

  Whatever these clinicians thought they were achieving, Avion knew that life was the best teacher, and learning from it was supposed to prevent it from repeating. There were many forms of monster it seemed, and she'd had only Damion's version to learn from, at least now she knew of another form, no less painful and harder to identify. She also knew that anything she said was being fed straight back to the family, and she had stopped caring what they thought of her, she would never walk in their world again, she'd had enough of being a sacrificial lamb for their entertainment. All Avion wanted was a way to pay Gabriel back, to kill him in the way he had her, and for now she had no idea how to go about it.

Chapter 16

The arena, such as it was, was a small area in the back of a warehouse, it was lined with brutal men dressed in black, all wearing balaclavas. It was suitably cold, but a large water barrel stood to one side. Raphael, Uriel, and Cuthbert stood to one side of the arena, whilst Damion and three other men all stood facing them. Uriel removed his shirt, showing his impressive body muscle. One of Danny Baker's men was chosen to join him. The man was cut free of his ties, and he sneered at the prospect of a fight with a De Luca.
"Your body will be sent back to your family to remind them of the consequences of gangs." Uriel informed the man, who spat in response. The gang member lunged forward to punch, but changed to a kick, which Uriel caught in his hand, holding the man's leg in firm fingers, before kicking him back straight in the crown jewels. The man screamed and fell to the floor. He vacated his stomach and gasped lungful's of air. Uriel leaned into the man and lifted him off the ground with one strong arm, and his fingers round the gang member's neck. He placed him upright on shaky legs, then punched him in the jaw, sending a stream of blood across the floor space. Without pause, he landed punch after punch into the man's torso, each time saying. "For Avion." "For Avion." Until the man just lay on his back, his foot twitched for a moment, then went still. Someone began to clap slowly. Uriel turned and bowed to his brothers. Cut entered the ring, and another gang member was chosen to face him.
"My name is Cuthbert. Most people call me Cut." He smiled a beautiful smile, which was radiant against his dark skin and bright blue eyes. His opponent recognised the name and paled. Cut moved forward so fast, his opponent had no time

to react, as Cut's head smashed into his own. His nose broke, and blood poured like a river down his face. The man landed two good punches into Cut's ribs, to no avail. Cut was as meaty as his brothers, and the punches made nothing more than bruises. When the man stepped back, blood seeped from slices down his arms, he'd been cut without knowing it. He staggered towards Cut, but his arms no longer worked, Cut had severed the muscles and tendons. The man took a clumsy lunge at Cut.
"Cheat." He fell against the big man and Cut slipped a knife under his ribs and into his heart.
"Yup." He answered. As the gang member slid to the floor, Cut added softly.
"The last cut is for Avion."
One of the men dressed in black tipped some of the water barrel over the floor to wash the blood away.
Damion struggled in his ties.
"You fucking bastards." He screamed. Raphael punched him in the diaphragm.
"Shut up fuck wit, your turn is coming."
The third gang member was cut free, but he bolted for the exit, wherever he imagined that might be. Raphael rolled his eyes.
"Ceaser, din dins."
"Din dins?" Uriel cocked an eyebrow, Raph shrugged.
"Krissy says he likes raw meat." He sounded almost apologetic. There was only the sound of running feet, and Cut was about to ask if the dog hadn't already slouched off to find din dins, when a blood curdling scream came from the far side of the warehouse, followed by more screams, growls and then silence.
"And then there was one." Raphael said in a sing song voice. Damion trembled as he was cut free. He wondered which damn brother he was supposed to die at the hand of, and looked to Raphael, the only one who hadn't fought yet.
"Not me mate. I didn't know her."

A door closed somewhere, and footsteps could be heard making a leisurely stroll towards them.

"Well well. So glad you saved the best for me." Gabriel's smooth cold voice slithered over Damion's skin. It was a setback indeed. Damion knew Uriel and Cut's punches, they had helped him through his cold turkey and anger issues, as they liked to call it, but he'd never known Gabriel and they said he was worse than Cut, just because he didn't use a knife. Damion rubbed his wrists, his veins strained so hard Gabriel wondered they didn't just burst of their own accord. Slowly, Gabriel removed his jacket, revealing a white t-shirt and white trousers.

"I ain't replacing those." Uriel put in quickly. Gabriel smiled, it was the first smile he had given since Avion had been taken. Had the circumstances been different, Uriel would've welcomed it as a good sign, but as it was, it was anything but.

"My way." Gabriel said to his brothers, giving them a hard stare. All gave him a level gaze back, they knew what that was code for, and none of them liked it.

"Ain't yer gonna take that off?" Damion nodded to the white t-shirt.

"Nope."

Damion looked at Gabriel's exposed arms, the scars that covered them, and grinned manically. This was why he was the most dangerous brother, he took punishment, and Damion could guess that his body had as many scars again. If he was going to die, he was going to leave his mark on Gabriel. He lashed out catching Gabriel on the jaw, breaking his knuckle in the process. Gabriel's jaw was solid. When Gabriel didn't respond, not even to wipe the dribble of blood that seeped from his lip, Damion punched again, hitting his opponent in the cheek, cutting the skin enough to cause a dribble of blood. Then he launched into an attack of punches, all into Gabriel's torso, winding the man severely, and although Gabriel staggered and stumbled, he did not fall. Damion grinned.

"Are you having fun Smallman?" Gabriel asked, as he checked the blood from his mouth. Damion laughed and kicked at Gabriel's ribs and legs. Gabriel made no response but spat blood. He was taking internal injuries and that worried his brothers, who were honour bound not to interfere, no matter how bad it got. Gabriel had done this many times in his life, it was the love of pain he craved, the possibility he could lose that fed him, and a curious urge to suffer more that prevented him fighting back. This was the monster that Gracie Parker feared, why he was the worst brother of them all. Damion packed a lethal punch with his enhanced muscle, but he had little stamina for a long term altercation. Gabriel took blow after blow, he knew Damion had broken his arm, and he likely had a broken rib or two, but still he craved the pain. *For you Avion, I deserve this.* His tortured mind reminded him. The minutes ticked by and the white top was closer to red now, and still Gabriel did not fight back, but Damion was staggering as well. Sweat poured off him, and his breathing was laboured. Try as he might he couldn't knock the bloody De Luca over, all the man did was smile as if to say, *that the best you can do?* So Damion kept punching, though there were longer gaps between each punch now. He couldn't see if he was inflicting any damage, Gabriel De Luca wasn't giving any indication of pain. Just when Damion thought he would be the one to fall over from exhaustion, he found his latest punch stopped, a formidable force was crushing his knuckles even his broken knuckle was breaking again. He opened his mouth to scream but no sound came out. His legs buckled and he found himself being forced downwards, landing heavily on his knees.
"My turn." Gabriel said softly. He placed a hand on Damion's forehead, and pushed slowly making his head tilt backwards. Damion tried to make a scream, but his throat was too tight. He grabbed Gabriel's hand and tried to prize it off his head, but the man held fast. Damion could feel his muscles objection, his arteries were pounding blood to his brain and

his heart beat was deafening him. His eyes bulged and still Gabriel pushed, Damion's tongue bulged, and Still Gabriel pushed until finally Damion's neck snapped. The silence was all consuming. Gabriel stood in front of his victim, disappointed at how easy the death had come, *it should've been me.* He thought sadly. *I failed her.*

***

Avion had suffered weeks of sickly fake endearments, of people doing their best to get inside her head, but she had figured out that by being sickly cheerful herself, she was closer to the exit than by being herself. She sat by the window waiting for her discharge, when a nurse informed her she had a visitor. Immediately, she was filled with dread. *Surely he wouldn't visit me?* She hoped he wouldn't. In fact the nurse wheeled in Mrs Parker. Avion studied the old woman with some scepticism.
"Forgive me for arriving at the point of your leaving, and uninvited, but I wanted to apologise." Tears welled up in her pale eyes and spilled unashamedly down her cheeks. Avion watched the display without emotion. She moved to sit on the bed edge. *She waits till I'm leaving to do this? Too late old woman.* "It's all my fault. I should never have made a promise I couldn't keep. I am so sorry Avion, so deeply sorry for causing you such sorrow." Mrs Parker dabbed her eyes with a tissue, as Avion watched her, unimpressed. She might never forgive the woman for failing her, but deep down Avion had always known Damion would come for her, he always did, *and* she had told her that. In her peripheral vision she saw the nurse watching her keenly, and she felt a trap being set. If she didn't forgive Mrs Parker, she might never see the outside world again, but forgiving her wasn't something Avion could do, so she smiled broadly and told a lie.

"You didn't really think I believed you did you? Silly Mrs P. You told me yourself many times how busy your boys were, so how could they possibly keep me safe? I always knew Damion would come for me, he always does." She reached over and made herself pat Mrs Parker's hand reassuringly, smiling for the nurse.

"Well he will never do that ever again." Mrs P assured her. Avion had a sick feeling wash over her, those words could only mean that Damion was dead, still she had known it all along, but hearing it, still made her shiver. She said nothing, she didn't really care anymore. None of them had visited her, none had sent flowers, none of them had apologised up until now, what did she care how any of them felt? If killing Damion cleared their consciences then bully for them, it had no effect on Avion.

"There is something else." Mrs P said meekly. "I want to offer you your job back." Avion felt the trap snap. Still she had no job to go to, she had no qualifications to do much, and at least if she worked for Mrs Parker, she could keep her home, for she felt certain the De Luca's would find a way to take it off her if she didn't work for them anymore.

"That's very kind of you Mrs Parker. Though I want one condition only." Avion said calmly. Mrs Parker knew what it was, but Avion voiced it anyway.

"None of your family, and I mean none, visit you while I am there. If you want them to, then I have a day off."

Mrs Parker nodded vigorously. "Deal." She said with a weak smile that trembled on her lower lip. Avion nodded and the nurse wheeled Mrs P out of the room.

***

Avion stopped off to buy milk and bread on her way home, and as she walked down the street, she fought the itch to turn and see if she were being watched, she expected to be, she didn't trust the De Luca's not to tail her everywhere now, even though they didn't have a reason to, they had a point to make if only to themselves. She was relieved to enter her flat, to inhale the stale dusty atmosphere it had held for her. She set about sorting the kitchenette out, cleaning up the fridge and making herself a pot of tea, then she walked out onto the roof garden and reclined out in the sun. It was private, for anyone to see her, they would need a drone to fly above the roof wall. Avion dug deep into her bag and retrieved her book of memories, she immediately turned to the page of the dead baby in the old fashioned pram, she slowly stroked the fine raven hair that covered his head, traced her fingers over his soft face, each stitch so small as to be only seen as a stitch up close, She held the book close to her chest and let herself slip into a real and deep sleep, free from prying eyes, free from noise, and finally for the moment, free of De Luca's.

***

Once more the warehouse served as an arena for bloody sport, as Danny Baker stood in perfect health, muscles toned and adrenalin pumping. He had enjoyed his time as a prisoner of the De Luca men, eating steak every day, working out, it had been a pleasure most certainly, but the time had come to face Gabriel De Luca. The video of his fight with Damion had been shown to Danny, and Danny had watched in horror at the amount of punishment Gabriel had taken, he was under no illusions as to how this was going down, so he had eaten, prepared as best he could and now he stood in the arena surrounded by darkly dressed thugs and the other De Luca men. Once again, Gabriel made his entrance, a steady stroll to the fight, wearing white as he had before. Danny assumed this was for show, that he and others were to be impressed with the amount of blood Gabriel could let flow. Gabriel did not speak as he removed his white jacket, exposing a tight fitting white t-shirt with cuffs over his shoulders. He nodded to Cut, who stepped forward, addressing Danny.

"Your knuckle duster and knife." He said in a courteous voice. Danny smiled, trying on the knuckle duster and feeling solace at the snugness of fit. Cut gave his brother a worried glance, he knew Gabriel had a plan, he just didn't like not knowing it. Gabriel stood in front of Danny and silence fell. Danny wasn't sure what was meant to happen, so after a long wait he just threw a test punch. The fist with the knuckle duster hit Gabriel in the chest, knocking the air from him in a sudden oomph. Gabriel bent over with the blow, feeling the pain like a welcome lover. He unfurled slowly, allowing Danny the satisfaction of thinking he had scored a good hit, though all he had done was create a bruise. Danny stared at him, shocked that nothing happened, and shocked that everything on the damn video was for real, this bastard was a brick wall. He punched again, making to swipe for Gabriel's jaw, but he missed. Gabriel had moved his head, yet had not counter hit, so Danny aimed for a punch to Gabriel's arm whilst using his other hand to come under his cover and stab Gabriel in the gut. Gabriel used an arm to block the knife, saving any vital organs from harm, but the stab was deep and his blood flowed freely. Danny smiled. Gabriel breathed in deeply, absorbing the pain, relishing its viciousness. Danny struck again and managed to stab Gabriel's collar bone, the blade sinking into the flesh deeply, once more blood pumped from the wound. Danny was on a high, he kicked into Gabriel's thigh, but could not break the bone, he kicked into Gabriel's calf and knee but the man would only stagger. Danny launched himself at Gabriel wrapping his legs around the man's waist and he punched with the knuckle duster as hard as the close proximity would allow, blow after blow rained down into Gabriel's face, as Danny tried to get the knife into his neck, but consistently failed. Sweat poured from Danny as he delivered his blows, and then he was on the floor. Gabriel had taken all the blows he wanted to his head and had literally uncurled Danny's legs and dropped him. Danny scuttled backwards, panting heavily. What did it fucking take to kill this shit? He had never met anyone like him. He looked up at Gabriel who stood patiently, no sweat, no heavy breathing, just a steady flow of blood that had soaked his t-shirt. Danny got himself up and brushed himself down, he was covered in Gabriel's blood, none of his own. The man had simply allowed him to attack over and over.

"So that's yer game eh?" Danny suddenly got it. He'd almost stepped into the trap Damion had, by exhausting himself before Gabriel hit back. Danny stood still a safe distance away. Once his breathing had slowed, he walked up to Gabriel and waved his blade, smiling he cut a slow line down the torso of Gabriel's muscle toned chest. It was a bit of a gamble but Danny was sure Gabriel wouldn't prevent him.

"You like to be cut eh?" He said, understanding Gabriel's desire.

"You're one sick bastard, but you know that right?" Danny punched hard into Gabriel's ribs which snapped, making Gabriel wince.

"Did yer like that eh?" Danny goaded. He stepped back, turned and aimed a high kick at Gabriel's chest, but found his ankle caught in a tight grip. Danny hopped on one leg, looking at Gabriel smiling a bloody grin at him, then Gabriel yanked on the ankle, pulling Danny to him, he punched him in his knackers. Danny collapsed, gasping for air. Uriel stepped in and tipped a goodly amount of freezing water over both of them, then stepped back to the edge of the arena. Gabriel found the iciness refreshing, invigorating, but Danny fought for air again as the water stole what little he'd gained. Gabriel bent down and grabbed Danny by the forearm, heaving him up. He landed a punch of his own on Danny's nose, breaking it, pulverising it. Blood poured. The bastard knew how to pack a punch, and if Danny hadn't been the victim here, he'd have been impressed. Danny had trouble seeing through his tears, he frantically wiped his eyes with his arms, but missed the next blow to the side of his head which knocked his hearing aid out. Gabriel punched the other side of Danny's head puncturing his other ear drum, so the world became silent and scary. Danny couldn't hear a thing, had no idea how to fight deaf, he couldn't hear Gabriel's breathing, or any voices, he began to panic. The worst of it was not hearing the punches coming, it was blow after silent blow that gave him pain beyond measure, but the silence of it had him screaming in his desperation to hear himself. He felt his bones breaking, saw his blood flowing, but the silence, it was wrong, so wrong. Danny lost his knife and Gabriel had found it, he hadn't heard it fall, so hadn't realised he'd let go of it. Gabriel cut him then, carved into his torso, slashed lines down Danny's arms, and let go the anger of betrayal he felt for letting Avion be kidnapped. Gabriel kept the vision of her naked upper body in the forefront of his mind, remembered the lines of scars that covered her stomach as he slashed bloody murder at the man who'd caused it. At the man who had humiliated him. He saw Damion raining punches down on Avion's curled up body, he saw the bruises he had left on her; the scars on her hands from broken glass he'd thrown at her, and Gabriel punched and punched until he had no strength left inside him. Danny Baker lay staring at nothing above him, his blood pooled the warehouse floor, and Gabriel knelt beside him unfeeling, uncaring, and as dead as the man before him.

Yet it will never be enough. He thought with sorrow.

Chapter 17

It was early winter and Avion was getting tired of pretending to be a happy undamaged human being with her employer Mrs Parker. Monday to Friday she plastered a smile on her face and walked or cycled to work, she never took the tube any more, she was too afraid. The need to escape was burning a hole in her psyche, but she had to also find a way to get back at Gabriel, to hurt him like he'd hurt her. Whilst she waited for enlightenment to strike on that issue, she had at least gained an idea of what to do when she could escape. Avion had it all planned, she had plenty of funds in her bank, far more than she had before, apparently the De Luca's thought she was worth buying silence from, or maybe they wanted to compensate her, which added up to the same thing really. She didn't care, she was leaving in the New Year, she'd made up her mind regardless of the Gabriel issue; she simply couldn't stand to stay any longer. She had spoken to an estate agent who had agreed to sell her flat for her and give the monies to Mrs Parker, after all she had brought the flat for Avion. Having made up her mind, had lifted a huge weight from Avion's shoulders and she genuinely did feel happier these days. She would tour the UK, take her time and then settle down as far from the De Luca family as she could get. She was of no consequence to them anymore, and likely a thorn in their side. A permanent reminder of how they failed, which gave Avion a warm feeling, but they had become a thorn to her also, so she was ready to leave them behind, let them play their games on others.

It was on a Friday at the end of the day, Avion had just finished work, and was about to say her goodbye's to Mrs Parker, but stopped in the hallway because Mrs Parker was on the phone. Avion didn't like to intrude and couldn't hide in the living room that was locked up unless in use, so she decided to sit at the bottom of the stairs until Mrs P had finished. Her jacket was in that room as well, so Avion waited, catching Mrs P's end of the conversation, when the front door opened and Gabriel stepped inside. Avion was on her feet instantly. He filled the space and blocked her escape. He stood staring at her, as she was him, both like rabbits in headlights. He was taller than she remembered, broader than she remembered, and had gained two scars on his face, a small one by his eye and a longer one down his cheek. Avion's heart flipped and then twisted, how had he got scars? She shouldn't care, but she did. He was still handsome and powerful and she hated how her heart pounded, it was quite obvious from his expression that he hadn't expected her to be there.

"Is that you Avion?" Mrs Parker called out.

"No, it's me Gabriel." He stepped aside and continued down the hallway, allowing Avion her escape. When he arrived, his grandmother was standing.

"Gabriel you *promised*." She berated.

"I didn't know she would still be here." He grumbled, sitting down.

"She's left her jacket here." Mrs P informed him. Gabriel grabbed the jacket and headed for the front door, as he opened it, so Avion fell into his chest. His arms caught her immediately, making her blush.

"I. I left my jacket." She mumbled and all but snatched it out of his hands as he offered it to her. He watched as she ran back to the pavement and walked smartly down the road, swinging her arms into the sleeves as she went. *Stupid, stupid, stupid.* She admonished herself, *I bet he's pissing his pants laughing at you now.* Tears fell as she welcomed the frigid winter air into her lungs as she tried to control her humiliation.

Avion was so lost in her thoughts and anger she did not notice Ashley standing by her front door. And practically jumped clean out of her skin.

"Steady Avi." Ashley said leaning forward to touch her arm reassuringly. "Jeez, what's upset you?"

"Gabriel turned up at Mrs P's just now. It kinda gave me a shock." She let them into the flat and made a B line to the kitchenette, busying herself with making tea, to hide her trembling fingers.

"What brings you to my door Ash?" Avion tried to keep her voice calm.

"I came to ask you something." Ashley said as she watched Avion fight for control over her nerves.

"What?"

"First you have to sit down. Pour some tea and take a few deep breaths." Ashley advised. When this was done, Ashley nodded.

"I dared not visit you at the clinic, you know they have cameras everywhere, and I didn't want to be sacked for visiting. Since you've been out, that bastard has kept me really busy." Ashley rolled her eyes.

"Doing what?" Avi asked curiosity blooming where humiliation died.

"What if you could get your own back on Gabriel? Ashley asked, seriously.

"I'm more curious about what you were busy doing."

"I'm getting to that." Ashley said waving her hand airily.

"I don't know if I care enough anymore." Avion smiled meekly behind the tea mug.

"Judging from the state you were in just now, I'd say he still affects you." Avion looked away, it was true, Gabriel did still affect her and she hadn't realised by how much till she'd seen him.

"Are you still angry with him?"

"Well der, yes of course I am."

"Do you love him?" Ashley waited as Avion's mouth opened and closed again.

"What's any of this got to do with you being kept busy?" She opted for the change of uncomfortable subject.

"Because Nathan De Luca and his adorable wife are putting on a New Year party, and yours truly has been doing most of the bloody booking for it." Ashley beamed, like that explained the answer to the universe.

"So?" Avion reminded her, that she for one wasn't on the same page yet. Ashley rolled her eyes.

"If you love him and want to teach him a lesson, why not seduce him. He wouldn't expect that and definitely not from you." There was a pause before Avion broke out laughing.

"You're serious? Firstly it's a party. By definition one interacts with people at parties. Secondly. He hates me, remember? And if you need a third, I'm covered in scars."

"I know." Ashley said sorrow in her eyes. "Firstly, Gabriel hates parties. He'll sneak off first chance he gets. He normally goes to the pool room, it has dark glass and you can see out over the lawn where the party will be. It's also quiet in there. Secondly. He doesn't hate you. You've heard that saying about not knowing what you got till it's gone? That's him. Don't ask me how I know, just trust that I do, and thirdly wear a teddy, made of satin. Nothing screams sexy like satin and lace, and he won't see your scars." *But he already has*, Avion remembered sadly. Ashley rested her chin on the back of her hands and waited. It was tempting. Avion could almost imagine herself seducing the great love God that was Gabriel, but he was better than her at this type of thing, had so much more experience, and she pointed this out.

"Not if you're the one in control. Don't let him do anything to you, you don't want. I've a feeling no woman he's ever dated has seduced him."

"I'm not invited, so how do I get in?" Avion said screwing up her eyes shrewdly.

"I am, and I will sneak you in."

"I will have to think on it." Avion said, then remembered what Ashley had said about her scars.

"How do you know I have scars?"

It was Ashley's turn to look away.

"I found his phone on the floor, and I saw the text Damion sent him, and the um video. Gabriel had zoomed in on your stomach and, um, well." She shrugged embarrassed. Avion stared at her.
"Why would he find me attractive after seeing my scars?" She whispered, tears welling in her eyes.
"He still loves you." Ashley countered.
"He feels sorry for me."
"No. I heard him scream and roar and I heard the plate glass window crack when he punched it."
Avion's eyes were wide.
"Avi. If you can't forgive him, at least give him a good memory of you, one you can be certain he will never forget. What better revenge is there to be had, than making him understand what he has lost?" It was a thought. It was also a very powerful thought. Hadn't he played games with her? Hadn't he broken her heart? A small twitch of a smile touched Avi's lips
"Ok. I'm in."
Ashley grinned and nodded.

***

At the beginning of December Avion had everything in hand. The estate agent would put her flat on the market on the first working day after New Year. Her bags were all loaded into the boot of a small car she had brought for herself, she had emptied her bank account and stashed her funds all over her luggage and clothing, so that if anything got stolen, she wouldn't lose everything. She arrived at work and found herself sad to be leaving Mrs Parker. After all the months she had longed for escape, now it was almost here, she was suddenly both afraid and sad.
"Mrs Parker may I have a word?"
"Indeed." Mrs P said brightly.

"I am giving you notice that I shall be leaving in the New Year. I have written a letter for your records." Avion chewed her lower lip. Mrs Parker remained silent for a long time. When she spoke her voice was raspy and rough.
"I suppose I should be grateful you stayed as long as you did. I'm sorry about Gabriel." She bowed her head at another broken promise.
"It's not your fault, or his, he didn't know I was waiting for you to get off the phone. Though things could never go back to what they were, that bubble is well and truly shattered. He used me for his own selfish ends, and I had enough of that from Damion. I hope you can find someone else soon." She almost added to control, but thought it too cruel. Mrs Parker was already shedding tears, though she nodded, she understood.
"Thank you Avion, for your caring and company. I have never been *so* very fond of anyone as I am of you."
Avion didn't want to leave Mrs Parker like this, but she hadn't planned on staying any longer, she feared who might be visiting. Avion stood up and slowly put her jacket on, and as she walked slowly down the hallway, Mrs P called out.
"He always loved you, he just went about it in the wrong way."
He sure did. Avion thought as she closed the front door. *I never got to kiss him and thank the Gods I never slept with him. Small victories*, but that didn't stop the regret and sorrow. Love was like a razor, it left her soul bleeding.

Chapter 18

It was a mild winter without snow, but not lacking in freezing temperatures from time to time, and rain. Ashley had ensconced Avion into the pool room, which was a large upper room with a huge wall of darkened glass that over looked the main garden where the party was taking place. Ashley had warned her to stay away from the glass, as it was not one way, so anyone who happened to glance upwards, might see her silhouette. It was a mild evening and the party was in full swing. The water reflected the low lighting onto the ceiling, which rippled in a turquoise colour. There were a few large potted plants placed about the floor space, and a wide stone lounger or two which over looked the pool and gardens. There was also a stone bench that faced the large glass window. Avion had a comfortable chair to sit on, hidden behind a few strategically placed plants, as Ashley had indicated she would have a long wait. Gabriel had to be pleasantly present for at least part of the time, so Avion resisted chewing her nails to the bone, and instead tried to focus upon a book she had brought for just this purpose. Unfortunately, nerves prevented her from reading and plans dominated her mind. Her dress was unremarkable, black with a V neck and straps she could slide off her shoulders should things get that far, and Gabriel hadn't laughed her out of the last vestiges of self-esteem she had. She jumped at every sudden outburst of laughter, and nearby banging of doors, be them buildings or car. She hoped no one else knew of this room and hoped they wouldn't choose this night for a passionate rendezvous.

It was the quiet whoosh of the door downstairs that brought Avion's heart into her mouth. The steady footsteps that climbed the tiled stairs, and the slow pace that announced the arrival of Gabriel. Avion watched him with appreciative eyes, always taller than she remembered, always broader. He wore a perfectly fitting tuxedo, crisp white shirt and bow tie. She heard him kick off his shoes and sit on the stone bench overlooking the garden. She watched as he took out his phone, scrolled and began playing The Rose, as he looked through pictures. He was lost, leaning forward, elbows on his knees; lost to whatever memories he had on that phone. She felt a wave of pity for the man, who was alone and to her mind, lonely. She took a deep breath, and in her bare feet she stepped from her hiding spot, and walked over to him, always expecting him to turn around, but he didn't and she caught a glimpse of his very private memories, pictures of her. Pictures he hadn't taken, that showed her in moments of daily activity, close ups of her face, and expressions. She stepped to his side and watched as his head snapped around to see who had joined him. He stood slowly, placing the phone on the bench, still playing that haunting song. Avion stepped back away from the window, and he followed. He didn't dare speak, for fear if he were dreaming, he would wake and lose her all over again. She stepped closer to him once they were in the middle of the space, her eyes searched his, drank in his features, his smooth clean shaven face, his soft lips. She reached up and touched his hair, soft dark waves shorter around his ears. He watched her intently as she traced her fingers down his temple, feeling the softness of his skin. She watched his nostrils flare at her touch. His jaw tightened as those finger tips traced the scar down his cheek. They travelled back along his jaw to his ear, where she followed the shape of his lobe slowly. Gabriel closed his eyes, he was on fire. He ought to stop her but he couldn't. He was already lost from the moment she had appeared. Instead he breathed deeply of her scent, roses, and savoured the erotic, electrical sparks her fingers ignited against his skin. *Avion*, his mind called. *Avion*. When her fingers found his lips he parted them instinctively for her, and she traced their shape as he shivered intoxicated, his knees weak, his blood pounding in his ears. He lifted a hand but it felt too weighted, so he dropped it. When she pulled his bow tie undone he gasped involuntarily, opening his eyes, looking down at her soft features. He held his breath as her fingers slowly undid the top button of his shirt, then the next one, and the one after that. She pulled the shirt open exposing his neck, she watched the pulse beat hard in the artery and inhaled deeply of his scent, spices and soap. How she had missed that erotic perfume, she closed her eyes momentarily, and let her fingers linger at his throat. His amber gaze bore into her soul, she was the river and he was drowning.

Avion would've been content to stop there, but they were making a memory, one that would have to last their whole lives. If this were the only opportunity she would ever have, to know what love was, she would take it, and make it the most special memory she'd ever had, so she unbuttoned his shirt slowly and pushed the material to one side, exposing his toned chest, whose muscles bunched at the cooler air and her touch. Her eyes adored him, as they roamed over every inch of his impressive frame. He had scars just like she did, scars her fingers traced making him suck in his breath. His nipples hardened and his stomach tightened, as he suffered her touch, clenched his jaw, and suppressed the urge to take over and make her his. Her eyes looked up into orbs so dark he might have been a vampire, and then she stood on tip toe and softly, so softly brushed his lips with her breath, warm and seductive. Now he moaned, he couldn't not. His groin was on fire, surely she knew? Her lips moved over his chest, slowly, her tongue tasted, and her nose inhaled. To Avion he was exquisite, and she trembled as her own body responded to her administrations, she pulled the shirt down over his arms effectively pinning them at his sides, then she ran her fingers down his biceps and forearms, breaking him out in goose bumps. If she were dreaming then she never wanted to wake.

Gabriel watched her wordlessly, stunned by the sensations she evoked. Lost to the burning ache his whole body was crying out against; this amazing rawness stole his breath, made his throat dry, and he all he could do was watch her. From deep inside his chest a soft baritone moan escaped when her eye lashes left a trail of butterfly kisses over his pecs, and when she flipped the button on his trousers, he ripped the shirt from his arms, sending the gold cuff links dancing across the tiled floor. He stood unashamedly in his tight pants, which could hardly contain his arousal. He found the strength to raise his hands and push the straps of her dress over her shoulders, allowing the materiel to drop down her arms, exposing a black satin teddy tailored like a second skin to her torso. His pupils dilated even more. The black material clung to the swell of her breasts and her nipples strained against the silkiness, its colour complemented her cream skin. Gabriel feasted on the sight, committing every part of her to his memory. She stepped up to him, snaking her arms about his neck, pressing herself against him, absorbing his warmth. He slowly raised his arms and placed them about her, she was so warm, and her skin was so soft. He buried his head into her neck, and quietly died as her scent washed over him, as her hands caressed him, as those erotic fingertips traced sexual lines down his muscle tight back. She could feel his want, she could tell he was drowning by his laboured breathing, by his deep moans, by the way his hands now flat roamed over the satin of her teddy. Avion gasped softly and Gabriel undid her zip letting the dress fall away. She pulled away from him, enough so that his hands rested on her waist, then she pulled his head down to her lips, she hesitated, stretching the moment out until Gabriel growled his frustration, so she brushed her lips over his, pulling his bottom lip tantalisingly. Fire ripped down her nerves and Avion inhaled deeply. His lips were like petals, and they caressed her own so gently. How often had she imagined those lips, and now she tasted them. Slowly she pulled away, her eyelids unwilling to open, hesitant at what she might see in him, but she needn't have feared, his eyes were ebony, not a glimmer of amber to be seen. She smiled now, and he found himself returning it. She was always beautiful when she smiled, but this was a smile he had never seen, seductive, demure and his heart pounded up to his throat, his arousal throbbed and he wasn't at all certain for how much longer he could keep in control.

Avion kissed him again, but this kiss became deeper, hungrier, her tongue slipped easily between his lips and Gabriel was glad to finally feel her let go. Wrapping his arms about her again he picked her up, and she curled long legs about him pulling herself into him. He growled his pleasure, and walked her over to the wide recliner. His hands roamed her back and buttocks, silky satin and rough lace, God how alive he felt, if only she knew that she was his hunger and only she could feed his endless aching need. He stood astride the recliner lowering her down, not leaving her lips, but holding their kiss passionately. His fingers gently racked her long hair. He leaned her backwards, lowering himself atop her, her legs remained tightly around his waist, as soft grunts escaped his throat. His hands were gentle, his fingers buds of tenderness. Avion gasped as his lips trailed down her long neck, to the tender base of her throat. He knew the reason for the satin teddy, hadn't he already seen the scars? He had to wonder if this was her insecurity or her way of preventing the past from killing the moment, it didn't matter to him but his respect mattered to her, so he bit back on ripping the offensive garment from her, instead he wallowed in her sighs, in the way her fingers pulled his hair. He moved down her body, leaving kisses across her stomach, and between her legs. Avion bucked against him, fire burned her veins, passion ruled her heart, she wanted him, she needed him, and he didn't disappoint. Reading her mind he moved the teddy aside and propped himself up on his powerful arms, looking deliriously down into her flushed beautiful face. Her eyes begged him and he obeyed. He stripped, sliding himself into her, stopping inside to fight with every ounce of his being to make this matter, to make it bloody last, but she had pretty much burned that chance with all her erotic attentions. His nostrils flared as he fought for control, his chest heaved from the exertion, and slowly his body conceded, allowing him to move in long slow thrusts. Avion whimpered and the sound almost undid him.

***

He held her in his arms. He kissed her head, inhaling the scent of her hair. He felt sated, he had loved, but as he lay there, he realised that for the first time in his life he'd *known* love. He'd had to hide the tears that filled his eyes as he climaxed, the rush of joy that overwhelmed him. He'd whispered her name over and over, as his heart broke at the thought he would lose her. She had left her job already and he hadn't imagined he would ever see her again, yet here she was, and how alive she had been. He didn't want to imagine her reasons for this night, he had known love, he had received it and given it, and he understood what that meant. Understood what his parents and older brother had, something he now wanted for himself. Avion moved against him, and pushed herself up so that she looked into his dark amber eyes. He saw a sadness there, and his heart constricted. "Avi?" He whispered, but she shook her head softly, freeing herself, he saw the tears in her eyes, she didn't want to leave but she was leaving. He watched in numbness as she stepped into her dress and then paused. He swung his long legs over the side of the recliner, but she was already walking away. Panic filled him and he ran after her, but she was already at the bottom of the stairs and he was still naked.

"Avion." He called. He ran down the stairs and opened the door.

"Avion!" He yelled into the night. His voice fractured, and he swore, racing back up the stairs to dress himself. His shirt was torn where he'd ripped it off, he'd lost his cuff links, and as he fell to his knees, he saw the package under the stone seat. He pulled it out, frowning at the sight of his name on the label. He opened the parcel to discover a shirt and another label.

Debt repaid in full.

Gabriel howled. He stood in his trousers, his chest bare, hands pressed against the dark glass of the wall window, he searched the party goers counting down to midnight. She was gone. Avion was gone and this was her goodbye.

Chapter 19

Avion stood in the shadows of the pool house, her heart in her mouth, tears on her cheeks. She heard the door slam open and Gabriel's strangled yell of her name. She hadn't in her wildest imaginings expected to pull this night off, and worst still she hadn't imagined how wonderful it would be. Her heart was broken, but she feared to go back, how easy do so, to go back and let another man run her life for her. A part of her wanted that because the love was worth it, because the feel of his breath on her skin, said she could live with it, because the touch of his fingers told her she wanted it, and because his lips made it all tolerable. Why did Gabriel have to be so complicated? She eventually found the strength to move her feet, and they didn't take her back to the man she now knew she loved, instead Avion got into her car and headed off away from the fireworks that welcomed in the New Year.

***

Two Years Later

The spring sunshine warmed Gabriel's office nicely, and he was grateful for the air conditioning that stopped the room from becoming an oven. He sat at his desk sipping coffee, reading emails from hopeful entrepreneurs, folks looking for an investor for new business ideas. However he stopped after reading one such mail that began "Dear Gabriel" He checked the email address, "Al-paca-lunchbox" Not that he expected to find a name but he had wondered. He carried on reading.

"Dear Gabriel.

This isn't an easy letter to write, but you are our last hope, and frankly I have no idea how to proceed. I now live on a small Island in the Outer Hebrides along with a meagre population of twenty other Islanders. Our Laird is Robert Callum. He has fallen on hard times due to financial debt created by his younger son, (drugs and betting) and he is now forced to sell our Island to cover those debts. The interested party is Mrs Anna Noble of Noble VIP holidays, who has submitted plans to the council to turn our Island into an executive holiday venue. It would mean that all of us that call this Island home, will be told to leave, and we have nowhere else to go. The Island is primarily farm land, and the only farmer is Alasdair Campbell, who has sheep. I have the Alpaca walking business, and Mrs Campbell runs the pub as a B&B, so the income we get is not enough to help our Laird with his debts.

Quite apart from us, the Island has otters, seals, caves, Orcas and a mountain that grows a very rare orchid. I have tried to make this known to the council, but it seems my emails and letters are being ignored. An employee told me that Mrs Noble has her hand rather deeply imbedded into councillors pockets, and that she will get the Island at a significantly discounted price, on account of Laird Callum's situation.

Obviously we cannot afford to buy our Island, and we equally cannot afford exorbitant fees for solicitors, which leaves us all facing eviction and loss of livelihood. I am writing to you in desperation, given your extensive contacts, might you know of someone who can advise us, and won't charge more than we can afford?

Yours Avion.

Gabriel leaned back in his chair, swivelled it around to stare out of his window. She had a nerve. He could feel his irritation growing. Had this situation not occurred what were the chances he would ever have heard from her? Yet here she was facing hardship and who does she come running back to? He almost sneered at the irony. He read the letter again, so she had a business now, he felt a sense of relief, that she was, at least, settled into a life that provided a living, well for now. She hadn't stated a time line for the sale, so he didn't know how long he had in which to find someone who could advise them. He did, however, know Anna Noble, a divorcee with a ruthless touch, who had dated Cut for a short time some years back. Cut might've been the one to ask, but his association to Anna would be a conflict of interest, and besides, the relationship had not ended well. In truth, Gabriel had no intention of asking anyone to advise, he would do so himself. He wondered what Avion would think when she discovered she would have to face him again, after what she'd done two years ago. *You stole my heart.* He thought with a smile.

***

It was three days before Avion got her reply, and then she was terrified of opening the mail.

Dear Avion

It appears that Mrs Noble's interest in your Island is quite legitimate, and she is quite aware of the importance to protect the orchid, which is why she has proposed a site of environmental interest, whereby the orchid and other plant species will be given free range to grow in a specific area.

There are other Islands surrounding yours that would gladly absorb your neighbours and yourself, so you couldn't claim to be homeless.

In short, unless you can provide me with a suitable argument relating to the orchid and relocation of tenants, I am unable to fulfil your request.

Yours G. De Luca.

Avion read the email twice over and her heart sank. He wouldn't help but then why would he? And the way he'd signed off. She supposed it was because he was being professional, and he couldn't very well sign off Gabriel, but that didn't stop it from being a barb in her heart. He'd said he couldn't help, but hadn't offered anyone else, so did that mean no one could or did it mean he wouldn't allow it? Avion felt beaten, but her passion and emotion for her home screamed for justice. Why should they have to give up what little they had in life, for some rich cow who just wanted an easy sale of a cheap Island she could ruin?

Dear Mr De Luca

Thank you for your kind reply. The orchid grows extensively over the mountain, the same mountain Mrs Noble wants to create free climbing on, which means climbing boots crushing the flower. It cannot be contained to a small area, and she has not answered the question regarding policing that ground to ensure the orchid is respected. Likewise she has not provided a plan of protection for the otters and seals that use the beaches for breeding, nor has she offered any compensation to the neighbouring Islands in relation to noise from Jet Ski engines, motor boats, and other environmental pollutions.

The occupants of the Island have lived here for generations, but are expected to surrender their land for a pittance of the true value. Developers have no idea as to the community that exists here, or the time honoured traditions that come from living off the land.

Please invoice me for the time you have given this.

Avion.

Gabriel smiled, it had been a gamble, had she just given up he would've walked away, but he would also have known where she was. Thankfully she was defiant.

"Abi. Book me a flight to Scotland, and a helicopter to the Callum Island. Keep it discrete Avion lives there." He said flatly. Then smiling he drank his coffee. Abigail gasped when her boss told her why he was going to Scotland. She had never known what became of Avion; that was the agreement so she couldn't be found. Abigail wondered how her friend had suddenly been discovered, but she couldn't contact her to ask.

"There isn't a helipad on the Island Gabriel, you have to use the ferry."

"Find out where I can land a helicopter, and organise it." He growled. Abi sighed. It took her the rest of the morning on the phone to organise that adventure.

"You're expected day after tomorrow." She eventually told him.

"Under what name?" He asked.

"For now it is just as a guest. I'll inform them tomorrow, or when you leave."

"When I leave." Gabriel informed her.

***

Avion ducked as the loud noise of the helicopter deafened her and Robbie, sending the alpaca's into a panicked scatter across the field. She had been livid when Doug had called her mobile to tell her some bloke called Gabriel De Luca was arriving that afternoon by helicopter. Livid the miserable shit hadn't thought to let her know, even if she knew full well why, he was obviously not intending she should have a choice in this. It just confirmed her worst opinions about the De Luca men, all controlling.

"He likes to make an entrance don't he?" Robbie said as he ducked again, and the grass flattened from the down force of the rotor blades. They watched as the helicopter flew away towards the field Doug had organised to be clear for the landing.

"Yea he does." Avion said with more sadness than she had intended. Memories of her first ever meeting with Gabriel surfaced and she felt the pain in the same raw way.

"You'd better get going then, I can finish up here." Robbie smiled at her. He was a nice man, a year or two older than Avion, strong and good looking. He had wild red hair, stubble on his cheeks, a strong nose, which a sheep had broken once long ago, and full firm lips. His eyes were mischievous hazel, and he had the best, friendliest smile Avion had ever encountered. He also sported some serious arm muscle and during sheep shearing time, had shown off his impressive honed torso.

"Thanks." Avion answered and headed for the gate. She refused to be in any kind of hurry to see Gabriel, more it was with trepidation in every step that she walked down to the pub. He hadn't wanted to help, that much she was certain she had read clearly, yet here he was, so why?

She passed the half way memorial that reminded the villagers of the ten men who went to war twice, never to return. It reminded visitors that even Islanders answered the call to defend freedom. She watched an eagle soar on warm thermals gliding higher and higher in the blue sky. Could Gabriel even begin to appreciate this wildness? She didn't think so, he was a creature of the city, a man of business and contract, of control. As she approached the pub, the sea breeze whizzed around a building and caught her hair, tugging wildly at it to go and play. Avion giggled as she grabbed at her hair and tried to control it, at the same time entering the warm pub.

"Did yer not ride down?" Mairi asked as she watched Avion.

"Na, there's an idiot in a helicopter scaring the animals, so Robbie needs the bike to check the idiot didn't drive any sheep over the cliff." Avion said this in a loud voice so everyone could here. Everyone being Gabriel and two other folks, likely tourists. Mairi gave her a look as she gave Avi a glass of cider.

Even sitting down, Gabriel was taller than she remembered, and the thought scared her. She had forgotten how intimidating his gaze could be, and she felt herself shrink in his presence.

"Good afternoon Miss Chaplin." He crooned at her, straight faced and dashing in a bloody suit on an Outer Hebridean Island, what was he *thinking*? She nodded, unable to find a voice.

"I like the whiskey they serve here." He added by way of being conversational. "Have you tried it?"

Avion shook her head, she didn't like whiskey. She watched as he took a sip of the thick dark liquid from his shot glass.

"Why are *you* here?" She hissed when she finally found her voice. He looked affronted.

"You asked for help didn't you?"

"You refused it didn't you?" she shot back. He paused.

"I don't recall refusing." He frowned slightly. "I recall saying Mrs Noble has a legitimate interest and I recall pointing out that there are other Islands to live on. I also recall suggesting you come up with a more suitable argument for my involvement, but at no point did I refuse to help you." He smiled tightly. *Son of a bitch.* She squirmed inwardly.

"So are you here to help?" She asked slightly more defensibly than she intended.

"That rather depends on you." He replied, watching her with those amber hot eyes.

"How?" She tried to avoid his gaze.

"Firstly you have to get off your high moral ground, and listen to my advice. I am not going to spend my time here explaining myself every five minutes. I am bound to tread on sensibilities, you and these tenants are passionate about your home, which blinkers your point of view. I am a businessman

and I view this in that light." He leaned forward so that only she could hear what he said next.
"Do I make myself clear Avion?" The chill of his words slithered down her spine, and she wondered why it was she felt such profound disappointment.
"So is that a yes?" she asked in her coldest tone. He nodded.
"Then you're sacked." She said straight faced.
"Excuse me?" He growled. Avion stood up.
"We can't afford you and I can't afford you. I asked you to recommend someone we could afford."
"Then you lose it all because you can't afford anyone." He said matter-of-factly.
"Well you could've saved yourself the trip by emailing that to me." She replied. She'd be damned if she would owe him another debt.
"Obviously it never occurred to you that we do favours from time to time. Or perhaps it did, that was the reason you wrote in the first place right?" He said charmingly. Mairi was watching from the bar suspicious as to why Avi was on her high horse at the arrival of this stranger. Avion was boiling with annoyance. He knew damn well why she'd written, and now he wanted her to make a public declaration of the fact.
"I'm not a bloody charity." She growled at him.
"Yet you need me." He said, crossing one ankle over the other as he sprawled out along the bench.
Avion drew in a deep breath.
"No I needed someone who is capable of compassion, who would fight for us. I needed someone who didn't have a grudge against me, who could be impartial. What do you know about country living? Island life?" She was leaning over the table towards him, the scent of roses wafted into his nose, and he had to resist the instinct to close his eyes.
"You think me incapable of compassion? *Avion* what a short memory you have. Why would you think I'd have a grudge against you?" He asked in a silky sexy voice that brought out

goose bumps on Avion's skin, and made her blush. Was he referring to that New Year parting?

He had thrown her, she *did* remember, and she was uncomfortable about it. Gabriel watched in satisfaction as Avion fought her emotions. He also had to wonder why he was fighting his own. She was just as beautiful, perhaps more so, now she was windblown. Visions of her black teddy seeped into his memory and he had to supress them less they ruin his image completely.

"Why don't you sit down and tell me why an alpaca tour is so vital to this Island?" He changed his tone to his usual flatness. Avion did as asked.

"I don't know. I chose here, because of the views, because of the orchid, because it gives tourists an opportunity to photograph otters and seals and the dolphins, you know? It is flat but it is challenging, especially if you take the mountain trail. We get good feedback, so I think I chose it right." She sipped her cider. Gabriel had taken some notes.

"Don't the other Islands provide these things?"

"Mostly but they don't have Benn Dreki." Avion smiled, "And they don't have Dreki's orchid."

"I want you to show me this orchid." Gabriel decided. The plant was the key to this whole argument.

"Then you'll need to wear more suitable clothing than that outfit." She nodded at his suit, he ignored her.

"Tomorrow morning then? We'll take an alpaca walk." He suggested and Avion stared at him.

"What?" He asked in that same flat tone.

"I didn't take you for someone who might like alpacas." Gabriel frowned at her.

"I don't, but I am here on business and to do that business I have to understand what the tours entail. " He said.

Silly me for thinking he might be interested. Avion would have to remind herself constantly that he was here on business, and *only* business.

Chapter 20

Avion spent the night destroying her self-esteem slowly. What if this was just one big get back at her expense? What if he hated her business, would he still support it? What if he couldn't understand their way of life? By morning she was wishing she had never written to him. She trudged out of the small house she owned and over to the stables, where Robbie was already mucking out.
"Hey Robbie. I need two alpacas this morning. Mr De Luca wants to take the mountain tour to see where the orchid grows."
"Why so depressed?" Robbie asked, stopping his work to appraise his boss. Avion shrugged.
"Nerves I suppose. There is so much riding on this."
"Want me to take him?" It was tempting.
"No. My business, my responsibility." Avion said in a resigned tone.
"Take Gabriel then." Robbie suggested and Avion suddenly burst out laughing.
"I can't Robbie. I named the bloody animal after him."
Robbie grinned a beautiful broad smile, then began to laugh.
"I hope he innay that fucking awkward." He said chuckling.
"He is." Avion laughed.
"Well I hope you handle him better than his name sake." Robbie laughed.
"Hey I can handle Gabriel." Avion said in a mock defensive tone.
"Glad to hear it." Said the familiar flat tone. Avion turned at his voice, and Robbie looked away grinning.
"Erm, no. We were talking about Gabriel the alpaca." Avion said blushing. Gabriel cocked an eyebrow. Her eyes stared at

him, taking in his polo neck jumper that hugged his muscular form, slightly rolled up sleeves, showing off his forearms and scars, his jeans fit snuggly and he wore walking boots. She had never seen Gabriel in anything other than a suit, and her heart skipped at the sight of him.
"If you're ready?" He asked.
"Not quite, we need alpacas first." She turned to Robbie.
"Would you?"
He smiled, put two fingers in his mouth and let out a long high pitched whistle. Gabriel watched as alpacas came galloping over the field. A brown and white alpaca nuzzled Avion's hair and nibbled at it with velvet lips.
"Gabriel stop it." She said firmly, then turned to put the harness on.
"Well we have good looks in common." Gabriel observed with a smile, something else Avion had rarely seen on him, but his smile was endearing and captivating, giving his face a softer expression. She quickly had a white alpaca also harnessed, and they set off.
"I'd normally take tourists to see the otters, but it is breeding season, so we leave them alone. The path is that way, but we are going to go straight on." Avion explained, as she took the straight path along wild grass and heather.
"What got you into tourism?" Gabriel asked as he trudged along beside her.
"I was in Manchester and I met a couple who were buying alpacas at the animal auction. We got talking and then I worked for them for a bit, learning about the trade, then set out on my own." When he made no effort to further the conversation, she chanced a look at him, he was expressionless as he walked.
"Was there a reason that you asked?"
Gabriel shook his head, the wind caught the longer strands of hair and ruffled it playfully, making him look wilder, rugged and if possible more handsome. They walked on in an awkward silence, Gabriel looked about him and his name

sake copied, making Avion laugh. At the cliff tops she stopped.

"We're in luck." She pointed out to sea, at dolphins jumping and playing. Gabriel took out his camera and began taking pics. Avion sat on the grass watching.

"Mrs Noble will scare them off with acoustic deterrent devices. They say it is a kind way of making them move on, but it can cause deafness and some scientists claim mental dysfunction. Either way, this was their home before the Island was ours." Gabriel said nothing and Avion realised she had brought emotion into the conversation, she almost wanted to apologise.

"Can I ask why you're taking pictures?"

"For Krissy, to make her jealous." He grinned. Avion scowled.

"I thought this was business Gabriel, not a freebie bloody holiday."

"Perhaps if I charge you, I'll make it a working holiday." His face remained neutral, and his tone flat. She turned and retrieved a thermos flask with coffee in. She poured for them both.

"Why do I get the impression you're angry with me?" She asked after a while.

"I am not angry Avion. I am disappointed you did not want to share this with us, we are family, and we looked upon you as family." He did not look at her but out to sea.

"I'm sorry. I was afraid one of you would want to control me and tell me what to do." At that he did look at her, long and uncomfortably hard.

"By the nature of how we operate our businesses, control is something of a necessity. This is your business, not ours, we have no interest in controlling you. If I am honest, it hurts to think you would think of us in that way." He drank his coffee, and Avion had a feeling she had inadvertently stuck a knife in him.

"I'm sorry, I really am, but you controlled me before." She took a deep breath and watched as Gabriel tensed, the line of his jaw becoming tighter, his jumper stretched over his chest as he inhaled deeply himself. *Shit another knife*, but it was true. He took Gabriel's lead and began walking, acting as though nothing had just taken place. Perhaps she would do as well not to mention the past, after all it wasn't as though they had a future; so Avion kept walking, pointing out a rain cloud as it travelled across the water, depositing its contents into the sea. She talked about the sun rises and sunsets and the beauty of the Northern Lights, and through it all Gabriel said nothing else, making her wonder if she was doing the right thing or not.

Finally they arrived at the foot of the mountain and Avion stopped.
"This is where we eat lunch." She announced.
"Why do we not eat on the mountain?"
"Littering. And because of the orchid." She unpacked her alpaca and set the picnic rug over the grass.
"I keep it simple, Ploughman's style." She smiled as she watched Gabriel sit down and tuck in.
"Do you do the tours?"
"I muck in on busy days or cover if one of the other's goes sick. I normally leave it to Robbie and his sister Isla." She wondered why it mattered. Gabriel thought about this information. Robbie was good looking and around Avion's age, it irked him to think she might like him more than an employee.
"He your boyfriend?" Gabriel asked without emotion. Avion choked on her bread.
"Not that it's any of your business, but no. I choose to stay single." She noted the tic in Gabriel's jaw ease.
"Why?" He asked.
"I um, I just do that's all." It wasn't what she was expecting, and she could hardly tell him he was the reason she never wanted to fall in love again. He squinted at her.

"Why did you leave Avion?" He turned to face her now, his face serious his amber eyes intent.

"Arh, so you do have an alternative agenda!" Avion smiled softly but it died on her lips at the savage expression on Gabriel's face.

"Fine. I needed to get away from you all, from being used." She looked down, unable to meet his glare.

"What made you think you were being used?" He growled in a low tone. She shrugged.

"You mean you honestly don't know?"

He waited, and Avion knew she'd have to spell it out for him. "You let me think you cared about me but you didn't really, and it hurt, so I left."

"Did I fail your expectations?"

Avion's head snapped up. "I didn't know what to expect." She flustered, her face turning hot. It made him smile inwardly.

"I left because there could never be anything between us, but I still wanted to, mmm." She'd almost said too much, at the look on his face she knew she had. *Damn it.*

"Wanted to what Avion?" His voice was suddenly soft, bringing out goose bumps on her skin.

"What did you want so badly that only one night would do?" She could almost hear the hurt in his voice. Tears pricked at her eyes.

"Love you." She whispered. *Hurt you*, except it had hurt her more. She'd no idea what that night would be like, and when it was over, she had broken herself as much as she had hoped she had broken him. The silence fell instantly, just the breeze that danced between them, playing at pulling their hair. Gabriel had hardly heard her, yet she had confessed, he hadn't ever imagined she would.

"Was I worth it?" He asked distantly, his eyes still roamed over her face. She nodded because her voice had left home.

"You could've stayed." He said in the same soft tone. Again the silence floated down upon them. Avion was well aware he would've given his life for her that night, but that was the problem, she was too afraid to trust he would always love her, hadn't Damion been the same? So loving at first. She drew in a deep breath.

"No. I couldn't. You wouldn't understand." She swiped a stray tear from her eye.

"You never gave me the chance." His tone was a tad harsher now and she couldn't tell if it was anger or pain.

"I'm Sorry." She whispered again. "I. I really didn't think I'd go through with it, and um, when I did, I was sc, scared, and what if it didn't last? So um, I wanted the memory." Now she could no longer hold back the shame she felt, she had hurt him, not trusted him, not trusted herself.

Gabriel watched her shrivel visibly. He had wanted to hurt her, but seeing her and hearing her confession, he realised just how fragile she still was. She had made a memory, but he sorely doubted she had any idea of how priceless that memory was to him.

"Is the memory enough Avion? You could have had that every day for the rest of your life." The regret in his tone wasn't lost on her, she had thought it enough for the last two years, but now she realised she had been kidding herself, what she wanted more than life, was what he had just offered, but she also noted it was past tense, so he had no feelings for her now. She couldn't blame him.

"I'm no good to any man. I can't have kids, I have scars. Why would you want that when you could have someone who is beautiful to look at?" She spoke softly. Gabriel looked at her.

"Who are you to tell me what is or is not attractive?" He snarled. "I thought you were different from the shallow women I know, but you're not, you still think perfection is everything. Seems you're all the same, it's all about image." He got up and brushed himself down. He packed up the picnic and waited for her to dry her eyes, then they continued on their way in silence. Avion had not the heart to talk nor had she any intention of trying to persuade him. He had no intention of helping them, this was about his anger towards her, and she would pay the price by losing her home.

Midway along the trail Avion stopped and pointed to the ground. Gabriel had been lost in his anger, and wondered at first why he was supposed to be looking at the ground, then he saw the tiny orchid. A small flower that clung to the rocks; that was battered by the wind, and surrounded by harsh grasses. For some inexplicable reason, he immediately saw Avion as that rare flower, clinging onto life whilst being beaten by Damion. He let his eyes roam over the landscape, at all the tiny fragile plants that defiantly attempted to stand proud against all odds. Love wasn't a rose, it was a rare and tender orchid that survived in a volatile environment. That gave a glimmer of colour to an otherwise bleak landscape. Avion was that rare and tender thing.

***

Gabriel twiddled a pencil around his fingers. Thinking of Avion in her black satin teddy. The feel of it under his skin as he moved over her, the way her lips parted when he kissed her and the softness of them. He wanted her more than ever. In her company she made him whole, gave him a reason to inhale and exhale, without her he was adrift, quite lost. It was annoying how easily he had succumbed to her, yet it felt right, they were two halves of the same piece and they fit. He wondered if she felt that way too. She had not chosen to enter into another relationship, and he felt good about that, she loved him, otherwise why do that? The pencil snapped. It always snapped at the point he got frustrated. He glanced up at the clock, Anna Noble was, of course, running late. She liked to do that, to create an atmosphere and then seduce everyone by her charming femininity. Gabriel liked punctuality.

"Perhaps some more coffee?" The plump woman opposite him asked, but there was only so much coffee a person could drink before bladders needed emptying, and that meant more delays, he refused politely, glancing over at an older man, who looked to be in his early sixties, with slightly greying hair at his temples. This would be Laird Callum. A man who long ago lost the ability to sleep, and the tired bags sat in dark blotches under his eyes. His lips were thin and pressed together. Gabriel deduced he was another who disliked late arrivals. The plump woman opposite him was something to do with planning, and the thin man who looked anorexic with his gaunt cheeks and waxy complexion, was someone in the environmental department. There was a woman in her thirties who was something to do with housing, and had a problem with staring at Gabriel, who managed to make a professional example of ignoring her. Finally there was a young man who claimed to be a solicitor, whom Gabriel imagined was not long out of nappies, given he looked to be around twenty something and full of eagerness and energy.

Suddenly the doors slammed open announcing the dramatic arrival of Anna Noble. Gabriel wanted to roll his eyes, but kept them focused on the table.
"So glad you could join us." He mumbled to himself.
"Sorry for being late." Anna said in a fake breathless way, to make people think she had been rushing, when Gabriel had heard her stilettoes clipping up the hallway in a smart walk.
"Oh! Mr De Luca. How very nice to see you." She cooed when she set eyes on him. He nodded tersely, at her warm bright smile, he couldn't imagine why she was surprised to see him; she knew he would be here.
"How is Cuthbert?" She asked pointedly. Gabriel knew the reason for this, was to inform people of the conflict of interest in the room.
"He said to say hello." Gabriel replied, playing into the game. Her smile wavered slightly.
"Did he indeed?" She muttered softly, then sat down. Everyone had to go through the process of introductions again, which was more time wasting.

"Remind me again why we're here?" Anna asked as she looked about her at the people present.

"Mr De Luca wants permission for a scientific research team to assess the best way to protect the Beinn Dreki Orchid. The young solicitor said.

"We already did that Gabriel." Anna said smiling sweetly. "A designated area" She looked about the room. And all nodded in agreement. Gabriel lifted his own pictures up to the room. "That won't be enough. The orchid grows extensively around the mountain. I have learned that a team of scientists wanted to do a study only last year, but they were refused permission. I want to know why?"

"They hadn't got the right paperwork." The young solicitor said.

"From my own research, they were not permitted to apply for the right paperwork." Gabriel pointed out. The young solicitor frowned, and rustled through his papers.

"I beg your pardon Mr De Luca, but the records I have, show that they did not apply for the right paperwork."

"What is the right paperwork?" Gabriel asked. The young man flustered about before saying he didn't have that information at this time.

"You are lucky indeed to be working for such a deficient employer. Had you worked for me, you would be sacked now." Gabriel said in his usual drone tone. This got him some objections from the other board members.

"I can confirm that the right paperwork was applied for and blocked. I have the evidence right here, if your incompetent solicitor would like to reacquaint himself with it?" The young man flushed red.

"I never have given permission for anyone to study that orchid." Laird Callum said in a tired voice.

"Why not?" Gabriel asked. The man pinched his eyebrows.

"It would cost too much." He replied. Gabriel looked at the Laird with dark amber eyes that made the man shuffle uncomfortably.

"Interested parties aside, you cannot sell the Island without a scientific assessment of the orchid. It is already recorded as existing." Gabriel pointed out. The Laird shrugged.

"I believe you refuse permission because you already know that it will be classified as a rare plant, and therefore designated a sight of scientific interest."

"I have no such knowledge." Laid Cullum argued. "At this stage it is only guess work."

"Is this not a letter sent to you some ten years ago?" Gabriel said offering a copy of an old letter to the panel. Everyone denied knowledge of the letter that made the suggestion about the orchid.

"It is and you know from the contents, only suggested, which is why I didn't give permission for any research to take place." Laird Callum replied in a tired voice.

"I fail to see how this affects the sale?" Anna said, though the slight worry that crept into her voice was not lost on Gabriel.

"I am suggesting that we allow a study to be undertaken to prove the rarity of this flower or not." Gabriel informed her.

"Absolutely not." She snapped. "For goodness sake." She laughed nervously. "You know that will add unnecessary cost to the whole sale." She fluttered her false eyelashes at Gabriel. "Did Cuthbert put you up to this?"

"Mrs Noble, please leave my family out of this, we are all aware of your relationship to my brother, and there is no conflict of interest here. I am pointing out that you cannot buy the Island before an assessment has taken place. That has nothing to do with me or my family." He levelled a steady gaze at her, making her look away.

"Actually the Island can be sold." The young solicitor started but stopped when Gabriel held up his finger.

"I have already notified the authorities in Glasgow of the importance of the orchid. No sale can take place unless this study is undergone." The room erupted in objections.

"How dare you go behind my back." Mrs Noble said. Gabriel shrugged.

"Why is this of such importance to you? You're not an interested party here. I cannot think my tenants can afford your fees, so I want to know what is going on?" Laird Callum said, his ire not hidden.

"Your tenants are facing forced eviction in favour of extreme sports facilities. They would find it almost impossible to afford to return to the Island should it become designated a site of natural scientific interest. I also have evidence of bribes in that Mrs Rayner has acquired a substantial bonus this last two months, though in her capacity as an employee of the planning department, I can find no reason for it. Mr Fillerman has also received a substantial bonus, shall I go on? I am sure the Inland Revenue would be very interested in these bonuses, coming from an unknown source." Gabriel spoke in his flat tone, and watched as the colour drained from their faces.

"How dare you. That is my damn Island and I can sell it to anyone I damn well please." Laird Callum shouted.

"I agree." Gabriel said with an even tone. "What you cannot do is ignore the fact that an inconvenient flower has chosen your Island to be its home."

"Yes but Gabriel, we have said we will continue to protect the wretched thing." Anna protested.

"As I have already stated, the orchid grows all over the mountain. You should come and see it for yourself. It will not be enough to restrict it to an area of your choosing."

Anna Noble knew there would be arguing this with Gabriel until she visited the wretched mountain, so she begrudgingly agreed to do so. Gabriel smiled. *Small victories.* He thought smugly.

Chapter 21

Avion shivered in the morning chill. She was still trying to understand what Gabriel thought he would achieve by organising this visit to the orchid. She watched with Robbie, as the party trudged up the hill towards them.
"I still think it is not a good day to do this on." Robbie complained softly.
"I agree, but it isn't up to us." Avion looked out to sea watching the sky for any signs of rain, but apart from it being windy and grey, there were no signs of a storm.
"Aye, well perhaps we can get this done afore the weather changes." He added flatly. Nothing ever went well where weather was involved.
"Good Morning." Mrs Noble said as they arrived. She looked at the alpacas, one male one female, with apprehension, she was clearly not an animal sort of person. She introduced the people to each other, and then Robbie and Avion took the lead. Gabriel trailed behind the others keeping a watchful eye on Avion and Robbie. He found he hated the way the two of them walked so closely together, and memories of that one night flittered across his mind, making the feeling worse. He could not stand to imagine Avion with another man, and he almost wanted to confront Robbie about it, but that would be immature, yet that's how he was around Avion, madly jealous of anyone looking at her, or being too close. It didn't matter that she had said she wanted to stay single. He just couldn't help his feelings when he was around her. He trudged along hardly hearing any of the chatter going on, his eyes straying to the two leading the way, no matter how hard he tried not to stare; he did. The wind tugged at scarves and hoods, and pulled Avion's long hair upwards wherever it

could grab a loose strand from her ponytail. It tussled at Robbie's thick mass of red hair and rippled through the alpaca's woolly coats.

After half an hour of walking they had reached the base of the mountain. Avion and Robbie stopped, gathering the party about them.

"It is a bad day to be on the mountain, so we will each clip ourselves to a partner, the wind is gusty and can easily knock you off your feet, by being anchored to a partner, we reduce the chances of losing one of you." He grinned at them. Avion handed out belts which had a rope connection, she let the group decide who got clipped to whom, and found herself left with the woman from the housing department who kept looking at Gabriel. Gabriel found himself attached to Anna Noble, which was no surprise, and the anorexic man from the environment department was clipped to Robbie. Avion was glad of that, she didn't much care for the way the man eyed her. They began to proceed upwards, taking the pace slowly and bracing against the wind which seemed to get louder and stronger the higher they climbed. Gabriel found himself constantly having to haul Anna up as she often stumbled, making the whole group wait for them to catch up.

Eventually they made it to the area where the orchid grew. Everyone looked about them at the masses of orchids that carpeted the ground. The way the wind battered them savagely reminded Gabriel once more how like Avion they were, fragile yet strong, determined to keep their place in the world.

"You still think this extreme thing is such a good idea?" He shouted at Anna as she clung onto his arm, against the velocity of the wind that tugged and pushed at her. She nodded up at him, smiling.

"Exhilarating isn't it?" She shouted back. He looked over her head at Avion, bracing herself into the gale, her hair flying about her like an angry whip. He could understand her concerns now. The weather was unpredictable up here, and

that would lead to risks being ignored in favour of profits before safety. Robbie walked towards the cliff edge, and pointed out to sea. Avion joined him and they shared a conversation that no one else could hear. Avion nodded and as she turned to face the group, a violent gust of wind billowed up the cliff and knocked her off balance. In a heartbeat the woman she was attached to unclipped her belt, which left Avion without an anchor. She was swept over the edge. Gabriel and Robbie both screamed NO at the same time, instantly unclipping themselves from their anchors, both lunged towards where Avion had stood but moments before. Robbie was nearest, and was flat on his stomach as Gabriel arrived, landing flat on his. Avion had found a piece of jagged rock to cling to, her feet resting on a slim shelf. She looked up at both men, her face white as a sheet, her eyes filled with terror. Robbie got to his feet and ran to the female alpaca, grabbing a rope and flare he raced back to the cliff edge. Gabriel immediately held out a hand for the rope.
"What?" Robbie asked. Avion didn't have time for a discussion, so Gabriel sat on the edge and lowered himself over before Robbie could stop him. He signalled Robbie to make a loop and then he lowered it over his shoulders pulling it tight about his waist. Gabriel then found snags of rock for his fingers to grip, whilst his feet saught to do the same, often failing, yet he made a good pace getting to Avion as her fingers began to lose their grip. He wrapped his body around her, pinning her to the cliff.
"I got you." He shouted in her ear. She leaned her head back and he heard her sob into his neck.
"We're going to climb up." He told her loudly but she shook her head.
"My ankle is hurt." It was all he would get before the wind snatched her words away. Gabriel cursed his luck.
"Ok, turn around and face me slowly." Avion shook her head too terrified to try.

"Avi, trust me. Please this time. I promise I have you." His voice encouraged. She knew she had to trust him, and slowly she let one hand go and reached for his forearm, her feet immediately slipped as the shelf gave way a little. It was a blessed relief to hold that forearm with both hands, the ache in her fingers was unbearable and the cold wind made it worse. She twisted her upper torso around and when he nodded, she twisted her hips around to face him. He slammed into her, reaching for a better grip with his fingers, Avion flung her arms about his neck.

"It's ok honey, I got you." He said into her ear.

"I'm scared." She shouted back to him.

"I know, just wrap your legs around me and we will do this slowly ok?" She nodded into his neck, and he pressed against her as he reached for a point above them, then heaved them both upwards and the rope pulled him as he moved, helping to take the strain.

"Gabriel I'm sorry. I never wanted to leave you that night." Avion sobbed as he pressed against her to reach up again. She picked a fine time to get a guilt trip, but he knew why she was doing it, clearing her conscience in case he failed her again and they both died. He knew she was lying, had she wanted to stay she would've, she chose to walk away and he'd watched her go. His anger fuelled his determination to save them both, she likely would never know it but in that stupid statement she had given him a motive to succeed, and he pushed harder to get them up the cliff face. Strong arms reached over and grabbed his, pulling them both up over the edge. Gabriel didn't really care whether she spoke truth or not, his anger faded. He had saved her, and he was quick to wrap his arms around her, to hold her tightly to him, to remind himself if only for a moment just how precious and wonderful she was. Then the first splash of water hit him and another.

"We need to get to the cave." Robbie shouted over the wind. Gabriel nodded and followed where the younger man pointed.
"Take the rest of them, I'll follow with Avi." He shouted. Robbie nodded and then indicated the group should follow him.

Gabriel hugged Avion tightly unwilling to let her go, hiding the tears of relief he shed. Surely this would prove his ability to protect her, except had he been protecting her, she would've been shackled to him, not the stupid woman who wanted him to notice her. After a moment he realised she was hugging him too, clinging to him desperately despite the rain that now poured and stung viciously with icy sharpness. Reluctantly he pulled away, and wiped the strands of hair that had stuck to her face, her teeth were chattering, her lips blue. He stood, then stooped to scoop her into his arms, lifting her easily, he walked after Robbie.

They were all sheltered in a deep cave. The wind tore at the entrance and the rain did its best to cross the threshold, but to no avail. Gabriel allowed Robbie to look at Avion's swollen ankle and bandage it. The emergency torches came in handy for seeing in the dark.
"Mrs Parker never said anything about you being a free climber." Avion said softly through chattering teeth. She had not let go of Gabriel, too afraid the moment would be a dream.
"Used to do it a lot when I was your age." He said bashfully.
"Why did you give it up?" Robbie asked
Gabriel shrugged. "I suppose work took over and I never really got the time to do it again."
"I'd be too terrified to try it." Avion admitted.
"You did just fine." Gabriel told her and she snorted a laugh.
"I was wrapped around you." She pointed out, as Robbie finished his work.

"I disnay think it broken, but you'd best get it checked out." He suggested. Gabriel turned his stony gaze to the woman who had undone her belt allowing Avion to fall.

"Care to explain your reasons for attempted murder?" His voice held a chill to it that kept everyone quiet.

"If I hadn't done that we would both be dead now." The woman said defiantly.

"The whole point of tethering is to prevent that from happening. All you had to do was copy Avion." Robbie said in a stern voice.

"Well it wasn't attempted murder." The woman said angrily.

"You undid your belt on purpose. You intended for her to fall, how is it not attempted murder?" Gabriel said calmly. The woman paled.

"I was nay thinking of her, I was thinking of me." She said. "I feared for my life."

"Aye an at the risk of another's, you undid the belt." Robbie looked at her disgustedly.

"Well if you ask me, she just wanted Gabriel to hug her." Anna Noble put in, and when everyone turned to look at her, she shrugged adding, "Well she's been trying to get Gabriel to notice her all the time he's been here."

"That is not true." The woman shrieked, but everyone else was nodding in agreement.

When the sun came out an hour later, the rainbow it created straddled the Island and formed a perfect arch in front of the cave.

"What a beautiful sight." Anna Noble said as she walked to the front of the cave.

"A site we will lose when you evict us out of our homes, and one the Island loses when you build and block that view." Avion said softly.

"Time for us to be headed back down." Robbie piped up, though he cast a worried glance at Avion.

"I'll call my helicopter." Gabriel told him.

"Where will it land?" Robbie asked frowning.

"It won't." Gabriel smiled, and reached into his jeans for his phone.

Several minutes later, the party of investors had begun their decent leaving Avion and Gabriel alone waiting for the helicopter to arrive.

"I can't help thinking you're annoyed with me." Avion said into the silence that had enveloped the cave. Gabriel stood with his back to her, listening for the helicopter engine.

"That's the second time you've said that." His voice was deep and sounded tired.

"I'm sorry, it's just you seem distant." The silence fell again, then slowly he turned to face her.

"What do you want me to say Avion? I would hold you in my arms forever if I had my way, but you have other ideas about what you want from life, and I am not a part of your plans." He said frankly, his eyes roaming over her in that way that told her he was memorising every part of her. Avion was dumb struck, she hadn't seen that coming.

"Gabriel, I meant what I said. I never wanted to leave you."

"Then why did you?"

"I was scared." She dare not look at him, but when he made no answer, she looked up to find him scowling at her.

"Scared of what? Me?"

"In a way." She said meekly. Gabriel was surprised.

"What did *I* do to make you so scared of me, you would seduce me, screw me and fuck off?" His voice was harsh and angry.

"Maybe I didn't expect it to be like that, and no I have no idea what I expected, just not that." Her voice pleaded to him, but if Gabriel cared it didn't show.

"Yet you asked for my help." He stated, turning his back on her again. Avion felt the knife cut. She'd asked for his help *because* of who he was, yet who he was had been the reason she had run away. It was a painful reality to see.

"I'm sorry. I didn't mean to use you, I honestly had nowhere else to turn." The soft thrum of an engine floated in on the breeze and Gabriel set of the flare that would guide it to them. "Climb on my back." Gabriel instructed her, but Avion stayed put.

"I can't. I'm scared of heights." She said flatly. Gabriel stared at her, his eyes lowered to the blood that oozed from her raw fingertips, fingertips that had clung to the rock face in a desperate hope of being rescued. She hadn't just been scared of the incident, but of the height. He thought of the orchid clinging to the rock and fearing the wind that threatened to rip it free at any moment. He leaned over Avion and pulled her to her feet, placing her arms about his neck, he instructed her to wrap her legs around his waist as she had done before. The helicopter lowered a safety harness, which he looped over them both, and Avion clung on tightly with her eyes scrunched shut, as they were winched to safety.

Chapter 22

Avion sat on a hospital bed in nothing more than a hospital gown. The doctor who examined her was satisfied she had a sprained ankle, and the bruise on her hip which was huge, was a result of Gabriel's pressing against her during the rescue and her initial impact with the rock face. Her clothes were dirty, so she had texted Robbie to bring her some clean ones from the house, Her fingertips were dressed in plasters and bandages to help heal the jagged cuts they had sustained. The doctor had noted her stretch marks and scars, he had asked her about them but she had refused to say anything. She knew what would happen next, confidentiality be damned, Gabriel would be told and this time the truth would have to be told, if she refused he would never stop digging, so truth it would have to be. She was clutching her bag tightly when Robbie arrived. She dressed and the nursing staff called the doctor.
"Why are you leaving?" He asked kindly.
"I am quite well." Avion replied. "Thank you for your help."
"I would rather you stay here over night, you have mild hyperthermia." He insisted kindly.
"I am good honestly." Avion insisted
"Then you need to sign a form if you are discharging yourself." He said. She sighed and soon signed the form, grabbing Robbie by the arm and limping him smartly out of the ward.
"What's the hurry?" He asked pulling his arm back.
"I hate hospitals." She hissed at him.
"Ok." He put his arm around her waist and helped her along.
"Where are we going?" He asked as they hobbled down the entrance road.

"Can you call a taxi? I have to stop somewhere overnight."
"Sure, and *we* will be stopping overnight." He amended.
They ended up in a small hotel, in a single room. Avion knew Gabriel would be looking for two of them in a double room.
"I'll take the chair." Robbie offered as Avion was having trouble deciding. She flopped onto the bed exhausted.
"You're an odd one Avi Chaplin that's for sure." Robbie shook his head as he watched her lying on the bed.
"I hate hospitals and I hate doctors even more." She reiterated. "We can go home tomorrow. I just needed to get away from that place. Thanks for rescuing me." She lifted her head and smiled at him. Robbie spent an uncomfortable night listening to Avion whimper, watching the tears seep down the sides of her face. She had so many secrets and no one she trusted them with.

***

Anna Noble lounged on a chaise longue wearing a satin dress that hugged her curves, her tanned skin complimented her chiselled cheek bones, square jaw and chin. She held a champagne flue in one hand, as she eyed the handsome figure of Gabriel De Luca, who stood before her disrobed of his dinner jacket, a white shirt with bow tie open and hanging around his neck, black trousers and shoes finished him off perfectly. They had just enjoyed a very public dinner together at a very expensive restaurant in Glasgow. Avion was still being held in hospital, while she recovered from mild hyperthermia.
"So what is this all about?" Anna asked seductively, mentally undressing the fine figure of a man before her.
"Are you still intent upon acquiring the Island?" Gabriel asked sitting down in an opposite chair, his gaze intent on hers.

"Well of course silly." She replied smiling a blood red lipstick smile at him. He gave no response, just let his eyes roam over her body. Anna thrilled at his attention.

"You could always join the team." She offered. He seemed to consider this.

"You won't get the sale price. Once the science is done, that Island is going to be safe guarded. Callum knows this, it's the reason he's never allowed the study to go ahead."

"Gabriel darling, there are more ways than one to skin a cat." She smiled again, then sipped her champagne.

"Indeed there are." He smirked back at her. "Tell me why it matters so much to you to own this Island?" He leaned back lazily in the chair, stretching his long legs in front of him. Anna shrugged indifferently.

"It's going cheap, and I can get the price down even further. Look at all the potential there? The mountain is incidental, we can just close it off if the silly flower thing needs to be preserved. Think of the water sports, the gliding, the parachuting stuff, the biking trials and the zip line. So much going for it." Her eyes sparkled with excitement.

"The Island isn't large enough to support all that, you would need a heliport, a GP, rescue teams, not to mention staff, how do you propose to fit them all onto an Island that is two miles wide and three miles long?"

"Technicalities darling." Anna waved her drinking arm in a dismissive action. "I pay people to design my Islands."

"What happens when you are blocked by government until the orchid study is done?"

"I'll not wait. I can deal with that when and if it happens. It's a bargain Gabriel, can't you see that?" He could. He knew that the moment the orchid was listed, the Island became protected in law, and the price of it would drop through the floor. Any future owner would be obliged to safeguard the Island for future generations, making Anna Noble's plans hit the waste paper basket before they were ever read. The problem he had, was getting the Island protected before she brought it. If Anna Noble got the Island dirt cheap, she could then evict the tenants.

"What happens when the Island becomes listed and your plans don't materialise?" Gabriel asked.

"Who says it will become listed?" Anna smirked knowingly at him.

"I see." He smiled. So she was going to use backhanders and that would be expensive.

"Gabriel darling, there are no restrictions about neighbouring Islands being used for certain activities like water sports, and there are no restrictions on the owners' part to prevent anyone visiting the Island to view said orchids." Again she smirked, and Gabriel joined her. If she couldn't use the Island to build on, she would use neighbouring Islands and that meant she could allow visits to Callum Island, there wouldn't be anyone policing the area, so who cared if some tourists wanted to go see the rare orchid and climb the mountain? It was clever. His phone buzzed.

"Excuse me." He said retrieving it from his pocket. The message made him scowl momentarily.

"Problem darling?" Anna asked curiously.

"No, but I have to leave. I'm sorry." He stood and grabbed his jacket. He felt annoyance in one sense, he had so much sexual frustration bottled up because of Avion, he had intended to use Anna Noble in the most efficient way he knew, to relieve some of it. On the other hand, he also knew he didn't want Anna Noble beneath him, as ironic as such a position might be, he could only imagine Avion, and according to the text message, she had just signed herself out.

"What the fuck do you mean she has stretch marks?" He hissed as he marched along the road in front of the hotel he had just vacated. He waited while the other voice explained. He had no words. She had refused to explain them to a doctor and then she had signed herself out. He had no idea where to start searching for her, but the last thing he had been told was that Robbie was with her. Gabriel wanted to punch something, or someone, right now he didn't care which.

***

Gabriel knocked on the cottage door. He had waited for Avion to return home, as she was bound to do, her business was here, her home was here, so back to the Island she would come, all Gabriel had to do was wait. It had taken a whole twenty minutes of high blood pressure and panic two nights ago, before that sensible fact had surfaced. He again marvelled at how undone he became around Avion. He'd been surprised at how quickly she had returned, so having let her have another night to herself, he was now going to find out how she was faring, given she had mild hypothermia and a twisted ankle. He knocked again, heard the thump as she fell over, so he bowed his head to hide his smirk. She had obviously forgotten about her ankle. He listened as she bumped her way down wooden stairs and swore with virtually every hop on her way to the door. When she opened it Gabriel was grinning stupidly. He looked so young, so amazingly handsome. His smile had wrinkles at the corners of his mouth, and he had brilliant white very straight teeth. In return, as Avion gazed at him dumbly, he found himself looking into her wide brown eyes, eyes he drowned in if only she knew it. She wore an oversized male shirt, whose sleeves came down to her knuckles, and whose tail ends touched her knees. She was sex on beautiful shapely legs, and he found himself aching for her all over again.
"Good morning Avion, may I come in it's a tad chilly out here"
She stepped aside mutely and he walked in, taking in the small living area, low ceiling he could feel his hair brushing against. The ingle nook fireplace with thick wooden mantle, the logs neatly stacked on the hearth. He turned towards her, she was pale, her hands still bandaged.

"I bet you'd love a coffee about now." He said, smirking at her bandages. He headed towards the kitchen, so missed her sticking her tongue out at his back. He found an aga, which he filled with logs and coal then lit. He also filled an electric jug and switched that on. Avion had followed him and was now sitting at the small wooden table, carefully removing one layer of bandages leaving her fingers covered but free to move. Gabriel turned to face her.

"So, don't you want to know why I'm here?" He asked flatly. She shrugged. "I know why you're here. I signed myself out and you want to know why." He cocked his head to one side, waiting. The electric kettle clicked off, and he turned his back to make coffee.

"I hate hospitals." She stated flatly

"Any particular reason for that?" He asked without emotion. She did not answer, so he turned to find her looking at the table top, her bandaged fingers pressing hard into the wooden surface. He placed the coffee mug in front of her, resting himself against the butler sink. Still she did not move, nor attempt to look at him. Some things were easier to live with if they weren't spoken out loud. Gabriel watched as she fought herself over whether to say those things or not. She had scars, that in itself wasn't a reason to hate hospitals but death was. Gabriel's blood suddenly chilled to ice as he realised her inner struggle wasn't against self-image as he had thought, it was against grief. Her baby had died in a hospital. No wonder she had never mentioned having a child, no wonder she hated people seeing those stretch marks. Gabriel felt another unfamiliar emotion, sorrow. Profound sorrow. He had never felt it before, having never lost anyone close to him, but watching Avion struggle with her emotions of grief, somehow made him feel deep sorrow, he couldn't speak for several minutes.

"You lost your baby in a hospital." His voice was soft and barely above a whisper. Avion looked up at him, her pale face even paler; her eyes swimming in tears. Gabriel had no idea what it must feel like to lose a child, but all the pain of that memory was written all over her face, her bottom lip trembled as she fought for control.

"I'm sorry for your loss." He said in the same tone, his face a true reflection of that fact.

"Ain't grief." She whispered hoarsely. "It ain't grief. I know you think it is, but it ain't." He waited, this was the bit Avion was fighting over, the bit she had perhaps never admitted out loud; the hardest part of an inner truth. Her eyes roamed the room in a last attempt at finding escape, then with a deep breath and an agonising sob she found the words.

"It's guilt." The tears spilled, and she sucked on her lower lip fighting for control. He watched her silently.

"See Damion was right. I'm fucking useless." She nodded her head vigorously. "I couldn't keep him safe." Her voice trailed off into a whisper.

"I couldn't keep him safe. Couldn't even do that right."

Gabriel felt a cold rage seep up his spine. Damion had been the father, which meant this loss hadn't been so very long ago. Avion was hugging herself and rocking to and fro, then looking beside her, she saw her bag hanging on the chair next to her, she grabbed it and hugged it close.

"That's why I'm no good, see. I can't have kids. I ain't responsible enough." She looked up at Gabriel whose face was grey, his eyes like amber stones, the muscles in his arms bunched and taught where they folded over his chest.

"Responsibility takes two Avion." His voice was a deep growl of contained anger. She shook her head.

"N no. I couldn't afford the pill no more. Damion had every penny I earned, but he said it was my fault, my responsibility to take protection." She paused to gather herself. "Besides it was my responsibility to keep him safe. I was his mom."

"Safe from what?" Gabriel had a sick feeling he knew and he dreaded the words, hoped he was wrong. Avion shook her head, breathing deeply to get control. Then she looked up at him.

"He never wanted it. Never wanted to be a dad. He said I had to get rid of it." Her whole face pleaded for Gabriel to understand her point of view. She was guilty of keeping her child when she'd been told she had to get rid of it. For his part, Gabriel kept his face neutral.

"It was too late by the time he found out. He was furious." She had stopped crying, as she stared beyond the man in front of her.

"He said I was selfish, not thinking how he would be able to support it. Said I never thought of him. Except I did, every bloody day I did. I kept telling myself and the baby that he would come round, he'd see him and love him like I did, but we never got that far." She was staring into that distance again, seeing things Gabriel was glad to be blind to. A silence had fallen as she clutched her bag, her fingers squeezing it all over, then she smiled and blinked, evicting the last tears from her eyes.

"So, now you know why I hate hospitals." She forced a smile that failed to reassure anyone of anything. Gabriel watched her, his expression unreadable, he knew that wasn't the whole of it and nothing like the end of it, but it's all he would get for now.

"Then I'm fucking glad I smashed his face to a pulp." He said in a cold deep voice. Avion snapped her attention back to him.

"Yea. I killed the bastard." He watched her face for any expression, but she gave none.

"So we're both murderers." He decided to state the obvious to her so she could add that to her guilt. She wasn't a good judge of character choosing two men who turned out to be murderers, but Avion was on a guilt trip and no amount of common sense would appease her pain or suffering, she needed it, and God forgive him, he understood that entirely. The guilt he felt every day for failing to protect her, the pain and suffering he'd let Damion and Danny dish out on him had been punishment, and his pleasure, after all.

"You still need to rest Avi. Hospitals for the most part, do a pretty reasonable job of helping people. You cannot ignore that fact." He pushed himself off the butler sink and walked around to her side of the table, he offered his hand, and Avi stared at it for long moments. It was a large hand, one she remembered had warmth and strength. She saw the ragged scabs on his fingertips where he had climbed the rock face, the odd scratches on his forearms. She remembered what those fingers felt like when they traced her skin, when they moved across her back, when they linked into her own fingers. She didn't imagine she would ever feel that again. That was her deepest grief right now. She had long ago moved on from the loss of her son, it had taken this many years, but losing Gabriel's love was a heart break she couldn't face.

Chapter 23

Gabriel sat at the kitchen table, doing his best to push the images from his mind. He tried to focus on his work but the images of Avion kept floating in front of his vision. He had watched her change from a skinny half-starved creature to what she was now, a beautiful woman with confidence enough to step out on her own, and make it work, yet within she carried a guilt so deeply rooted it had evolved into a monster of her own making. He tried to focus on the email he wanted to send, but visions of her smile so bright and vibrant kept pushing the words from his mind. The softness of her skin, her scent; her beautiful brown eyes he drowned in. If he could wave a magic wand and make everything right, he would. If she would love him regardless of what he was, he would give her the world, yet his only memory of Avion was so vivid and intense he ached endlessly for her. That memory of satin against his groin finished off any effort to do any work at all, he was beyond frustrated and needed a shower for the excuse to relieve himself of the endless aching need she evoked.

Tiny whimpering noises drew him from his contemplation, and he got up to check on her. She had fallen asleep, but a thin sheen of sweat covered her face, tears leaked from the corners of her eyes. He knelt beside her and lifted her head into his arms and then held her against him. He couldn't imagine her nightmares, but he could tell her he was there, she didn't have to face them alone, yet so far it seemed she had chosen to do just that, perhaps it was her way of punishing herself, or maybe she just didn't think anyone would understand, either way he would be there until she was ready to open up. He felt her move her head away, she looked up at him confused. Deep dreams would do that, so when you woke you wondered where you were.

"Bad dream." He said in his matter-of-fact tone. Her eyes lingered on his, he wondered what she was looking for.

"Mind if I borrow your shower?" He asked eventually. She nodded gently. He lay her back down on the sofa, she couldn't run away with her ankle so swollen, so he left her to take his shower.

Her room was large enough to have a double bed in it, a standalone mirror in the corner, and a small wardrobe. The floor was varnished boards, and she had a small window set within thick stones. The bathroom was equally simple, a roll top bath sat in the middle of the room, with a shower attached to the taps. He stared at it disheartened at the thought it wasn't a proper shower, and he would have no relief under that, but as he turned to leave the room, he noticed the newer addition fixed to the wall. The room was a wet room. He smiled.

Gabriel arrived back in the kitchen quite a bit later than he ought to have been, sometimes a long shower in colder water could be an experience of discomfort and pain that was another kind of abnormal pleasure for him. He felt drained in more ways than one, but also revitalised, invigorated and perhaps ready to try again at that email. Firstly he checked on Avion, she was very quiet. He found her sleeping deeply. He stared at her now, so peaceful, so calm, her long lashes naturally curly against her pale skin, her lips full and inviting. Memories of those lips threatened to send him straight back upstairs for another cooling off session. He was about to leave her in peaceful slumber when he noticed her bag had fallen onto the floor, so he picked it up and placed it gently onto her stomach. He could never understand that of the things she had, she had never replaced the faded tatty material shoulder bag. He wondered what it meant to her, given the way she had clutched it so closely to her earlier, as though it kept a secret no one else could know.

He smiled down at her and went to take a step away, when he saw something scrunched up on the floor. He bent down and picked it up. *A rag*, he thought, but on closer inspection he discovered it was a cloth book. Curious he walked into the kitchen where the light was better. He sat at the table, pushing his lap top to one side and stared at the cover. It was embroidered in a strange thread, and when it occurred to him what the thread was, he sucked in his breath sharply. Tentatively he touched the thread, soft as satin, fine as the hair he realised it was. Each layer created a depth and shading to the words they wrote. He marvelled at the neatness, at the fineness of each stitch. Gently he opened the book and looked at the daisy, the detail was breathtaking. It looked like a sketch not an embroidery. He turned the pages finding other intricately stitched works of art, all made in hair. He found himself mesmerised by her detailed portrait of him, she had captured so much detail it was as if he were looking at himself in a mirror. When had she done this? How long did they take to create? She had even stitched a train ride, where he was standing behind her, his head bowed to her neck; his fingers touched her face, it broke his heart. This was a memory that was as precious to her as much as it was to him, every page was beautifully made and he found himself lost for words, overwhelmed with emotions, sadness being the strongest. He closed the book and bowed his head, running his hands through his damp hair, this was her secret, her own special memories that he'd bet his fortune, that no other human being had ever set eyes on. He'd seen her soul and it moved him more profoundly than anything else about her. He picked the cloth up and another piece of cloth dropped to the table top. It was carefully folded, he opened it up and stared at it, not believing his eyes.

Being told an event had taken place was one thing, knowing Avion had lost a son was that one thing, words he could take or leave, but now he found himself staring into the old pram, looking at a sleeping baby. The detail was breathtaking, his beautiful thick downy black hair that adorned his head, to the shadows the light cast over his perfect sleeping face, to the lashes of his closed eyes and his thick eyebrows, even his tiny pudgy nose, the child was real. The only indication he was dead at all, were the blue lips. Gabriel felt tears in his eyes, pain stabbed his heart, and he felt her grief as if it were his own. He felt it keenly in every careful stitch she had placed, with each perfect layer. He had never seen anything more beautiful or moving in all his life. He hadn't considered how old the baby had been when she'd lost him. He recalled her saying that Damion had told her to get rid of it, but it was too late for that by the time he discovered her. Now Gabriel wanted to know, yet he feared the truth. He couldn't kill Damion a second time, but he had to know, how this beautiful child died.

***

Avion's eyes fluttered open, to the crackling of the fire in the ingle nook. The house was eerily quiet, so she sat up, making her bag fall to the floor, she picked it up suddenly remembering she had been looking at her book, when Gabriel was running her water off in an endlessly long shower. She became frozen at the realisation said book was missing. She felt a rage overtake her, *how dare he*, but when she peeped over the back of the sofa, she saw him sitting at the kitchen table, his back to her, his hands raking his hair. He wore a tight fitting t-shirt, he always did now, and she could see the muscles bunch and move beneath its flimsy materiel. She had no doubt he'd found her secret, she knew he would look through it, and she wondered how it made him feel. Her heart sank at the same time, this was a violation of her privacy, one even Damion hadn't managed to destroy, but Gabriel? In the end she was surprised to think she wasn't as heartbroken as she had always feared she would be. It was out in the open now, he knew and at some level that was good to know, it meant he knew all of her, knew more than anyone ever had about her, and that was ok too. They might never have a future together, but at least he had all of her now, there was nothing left for him to know, which meant he would leave her alone, let her go. It wasn't reassuring.

Avion got off the sofa and hobbled her way into the kitchen, sitting in the chair opposite him, only then did he look up and see her. She watched as frustration worked through him, as anger and sorrow flashed in his beautiful eyes, as helplessness won over it all.

"It's me you'll end up hating." She said softly. "I'm the only one left, and I didn't protect him." The silence stretched as he looked at her, conveying nothing in either his expression or his eyes.

"I don't remember what got him so mad that day, never did take much to set im off, but he was proper mad at me for something." She paused to look at her bandaged hands.

"I'd grown complacent. While I was carrying, he'd hit my head, face, arms legs, but he never hit my stomach, so I thought I was safe." She gave a sad smile and looked away.

"I never said sorry. That was my mistake, thinking we were safe, but then he lost it." Her words faded away, she blinked back tears of regret. So many times she had wished she could go back, change it all, but in reality, Damion was always going to kill the child, because he never wanted him.

"The pain was awful. Made his punches like slaps in comparison. Never knew pain till then. He never heard me when I begged him to stop." She looked at Gabriel then, his stare was hard but she could see tears, she thought.

"You know what it's like when the rage takes over, don't you? He begs and that just feeds your anger, cos he has no right to beg." Gabriel knew it but was surprised at how easily Avion knew it. He'd never met anyone who understood when that boundary was crossed and stopping was beyond your control. Something in his eyes told her he understood.

"There was so much blood. I never *seen* so much blood." Again she paused at the memory. His fingers moved slightly on the table top, almost as though they wanted to reach out to her, but he stopped them.

"I come round in the hospital, and they told me, my, baby." She took a deep breath. "My baby was dead." She whispered. Gabriel's lips had thinned in his determination to keep his anger in check. Silence fell between them.

"Why wasn't he arrested?" He asked in a low gravelly voice. Avion smiled sadly again.

"Cos he told the police I fell down the stairs."

"They believed that?"

"The stairs are concrete, course they believed him, he was distraught with grief."

Gabriel considered asking why she hadn't spoken up but knew the answer to that, fear was a powerful incentive to stay quiet, and he'd bet anything Damion pumped her full of threats to ensure she stayed that way.

"You said before that you were both murderers, for what it's worth, you ain't the murderer he was. You saved me, you killed a monster. No matter what you say, you'll never be his kind of monster." She looked at Gabriel in earnest, hoping her expression would give strength to her words. He listened, knowing he was far more of a murderer than Damion was. Damion had killed once, he had killed far more times than that, but he felt no remorse for his past, he was what he was made to be, and he regretted nothing. Avion got up from the chair and turned to the aga putting the full kettle on it to boil.

"What did you name him?" Gabriel asked from a place far away. Avion paused with her back to him. She smiled up at the window in front of her.

"Been a long time since I thought of his name." she admitted, turning round to face Gabriel, keeping her hands behind her back as she leaned against the butler sink.

"I've never spoken it out loud before." She admitted tilting her head to one side, thinking for a moment if she wanted to say the name out loud.

"I gave birth to death, so I named him after death." She paused and smiled. "His name is Charon. Life is always ahead of you see, but if you turn around, death is right there, waiting for you. He follows you everywhere." She watched Gabriel's impassive face and smiled. "I am never alone, even if I feel lonely, Charon is always with me." She nodded to the book on the table.

"I bet you think me weird or mad." She laughed lightly.

Gabriel couldn't fathom his emotions right then. He understood her completely, she made absolute sense to him. She knew what the madness was when that rage took over, she knew what pain was, such as he welcomed. She knew his darker side like no one ever had, save perhaps his grandmother, but most importantly he saw Avion, and he loved her more in that moment than at any other time. She was more than a survivor, she was stronger than he'd ever believed she could be.

"So now you know who I am and what I am, it's time for you to go." She lowered her head. It damn near killed her to say the words but they had to be said.

"If you stay, you'll just come to hate me."

Gabriel stood up, he was tempted to follow her instructions, to walk away, and had it been only her emotions on the line, he would've.

"You *know* me so well?" He asked in that deep growl. Avion looked over to him, as the kettle began to whistle, she changed her focus to making tea.

"I know in time you'll resent me for not being able to have kids. I know in time you'll blame me, even if you never say so, it'll be there. An invisible wall that won't go away." He made no response, so she turned to look at him, he showed no emotion, but then he seldom ever did.

"I hear your words and I think you talk about yourself Avi. You have no idea what I am, or who I am." He had a point. She had never pushed to know about him, she had always assumed her own past was sufficient to ruin any relationships she might have.

"So who are you Gabriel De Luca?"

He watched her now. It was his turn to weigh up what he divulged, he had never shared his darker side with anyone, but if anyone could see him truly, it had to be her. He had to trust her, and that was a first; a revelation he didn't like at all. He paced about the small part of the kitchen he was in.

"I kill men who do wrong." He stated flatly, then paused to gauge her reaction. She played his game of keeping her face neutral. *Clever girl.* He thought.

"You have been told that we are all monsters, and we are Avion. We have all killed, but I am the one who thrives on suffering, on torture, on fighting. I pride myself of never dishing out what I haven't already received. My scars are mine because I allowed them, not because I got careless. Now who's the greater monster?" He asked, his eyes glued to hers, his face rigid; his jaw stark with tension.

"Bad people aren't innocent babies. I knew you knew pain when I saw your scars, and I knew you couldn't be that careless and have the reputation you have." Her own eyes remained steadfastly fixed on his, her voice remained low and calm.

"Your grandmother often told me that whatever monsters you boys were, none of you would strike a woman no matter how evil she was." She paused momentarily.

"And for what it's worth, I believe her." She turned to pour the tea.

"And knowing all that, you still think I would hate you? Resent you because you can't have kids? What makes you think I'd want them? What makes you think I'd be a good role model for a father?" His anger was starting to seep into his words, and he turned away from her, fighting to get his

control back. It always happened around Avion, he found it near impossible to control his own emotions, when all he wanted to do was hold her, protect her; love her. Avion placed his mug of tea on the table and sat down with her own. "Perhaps you're right, perhaps it is me that won't forgive myself, won't trust me to be responsible. Perhaps I don't yet deserve to be trusted." She sipped her tea, daydreaming at the table. Her heart was pounding with the stress, and yet she felt calm. So far he hadn't said anything she hadn't guessed already.
"For how long will you go on feeling sorry for yourself?" He asked in a menacing tone. She didn't answer, so he turned and walked over to the front door. He stopped, bracing his arms wide, resting his hands on either side of the door frame, against the stone wall. He bowed his head.
"I love you Avion." His voice was a husky whisper. "I'd not want to leave without you knowing that."
"Then you can't be a monster." Her soft, gentle voice was right behind him. "Monsters don't love."
She watched every muscle in his back tense right up, his arms bulged, and she swore his buttocks joined in, making her bite her lower lip slowly.
"Then you can't be a monster either." He said in a soft deep voice. He relaxed and let his arms fall from the wall as he turned to face her.
"How so?" She asked, her face alight with curiosity. He drank in how dark her eyes were, almost black, the way she sucked so seductively on her bottom lip, and that bloody shirt, with the sleeves too long, the front buttons undone to reveal a cleavage he remembered all to well. He found he had a lump in his throat almost the size of the one in his jeans.
"Because you told me you loved me two years ago." He said. His own eyes were orbs of molten amber, staring at her with such naked desire, she thought she had to be burning hotter than the sun.

"As I recall, I never spoke." She reminded him, in a voice that was gentle and seductive. He stepped closer to her, towering over her.

"You said it clearly when you said nothing at all."

Her arms slipped around his neck, her bandaged fingers stroked his face. He watched her eyes close, long lashes lowering, he watched her lips part; soft lips, lips he wanted, lips he lowered his head to feel upon his own. His eyes closed as the emotions washed over him, and he could no longer hold back, his arms wrapped around her, less than kindly, held her, less than gently, pulled her so close to him, he almost squeezed the life out of her, but her hands were dragging through his hair, driving him on. He lifted her leg to wrap around him, and she wrapped the other herself, he walked her back into the cottage, his heart pounding in his chest. His tongue searched her mouth, his lips pressed hard against hers, his hands roamed hungrily over her back. She had tugged his shirt up to his neck, so he gladly took it off. He found the stairs and needed two arms to steady himself against the walls, to get them both safely up them. He virtually flung her onto the bed, glaring at the offensive male shirt, he ripped it open easily and leaned over her. He paused letting his gaze take in her scars and stretch marks, his eyes walked up her whole body slowly, until they locked with hers. She looked afraid. He smiled then, reminding himself to slow down, to make this matter like she had, though he'd be damned if he was going to wait another two years before he could make love to her. He stood up, she only had pants on so she wasn't going to escape. He slowly undid his jeans, and pushed them down, stepping out of them, he watched with satisfaction as her eyes widened at his groin. He bent over the bed and kissed her ankle, the one without a thick bandage on it. He traced his lips up her shin bone, making her shiver. He paused at her knee, looking up her body to find her smiling, her hands clutched over her chest. He lowered his head and kissed up her thigh, she gasped. He paused at the top, trailing his fingers softly over her skin, along the hem of her pants, he moved upwards, kissing her soft abdomen, finding himself imagining what it would be like to see it swollen with a child, his child. The thought made him pause, he was shocked at what he had imagined, and had for a split second yearned for. She was right, he did want kids of his own. More than that, he wanted her to be their mother. He smiled against her skin, and continued to trail his kisses upwards, his hand cupped her breast, and he felt her ribs expand as she gasped lightly. He let his tongue taste and his teeth nip at her before drawing back and looking down at her. Avion, with her long brown hair splayed across the pillow, her eyes closed, her long lashes creating a dark curved line.

"Marry me." He told her, his voice molten lava. Her eyes snapped open. She stared at him hardly daring to think she had heard him right, but she had, given he had that look on his face that meant he wanted an answer. Her mouth opened and closed.

"Is that a yes?" He teased, straddling her hips, leaning his muscular torso over her. His lips came down against her neck, warm and tender. She arched her back into him.

"You say it best, when you say nothing at all." He reminded her, in a deep sexy whisper, as he trailed his tongue across the cuff of her ear. Her fingers tore at his pants, and he obliged her, allowing her a sight she hadn't had in two long years. A soft moan escaped her. He let his erection stroke her leg making himself shudder with delight.

"Say yes Avion." He coaxed in a voice that dripped desire, he stroked her leg again eliciting an anguished groan in her throat.

"Say yes, and you can have this for the rest of your life." He kissed her neck with tender lips, and nudged her legs open so he could fit between them.

"What do you want Avion, a life with me or without?" He moved to her stomach blowing softly against her skin, letting his own flesh skim over hers until he was hovering just above her, the strain on his arms must have been immense, but he held still. Avion opened her eyes and looked at his powerful arms, felt for his taught buttocks. There was no pretending, she loved him.

"With." She whispered, and his mouth claimed hers, his hands swiftly removed her undies and he made good on the deal. Her back arched, her throat strangled a cry of ecstasy, her fingers dug into his backside, pressing him into her more and more. Memories of the last time he had claimed her flooded her mind, and she let out a strangled cry as he brought back all the passion she had buried away. She arched her back, she clawed at his, and he followed her every whim, so that they both found release together.

He lay supported by his arms, his pelvis pressed hard against hers. His eyes closed. His breathing heavy, ribs pressing against muscle as he inhaled deeply. Slowly Gabriel opened his eyes, and found her staring back at him.

"You never said that before." She stated, sounding like a little girl more than a grown woman. He frowned.

"What?"

"You never said you loved me." She pointed out. He broke out a smile at that, and she stroked the side of his face.

"I never asked you to marry me before either." He added, then bent his head down and kissed her deeply. He rolled over to the side of her, pulling her on top of him.

"You're not going to walk out on me again are you?" He asked, though somehow he knew this time was just the first of a long life if he had his way.

"Not leaving, not ever." She said, bending down to kiss him, and knowing in her heart, the past had just been forgiven.

Chapter 24

Gabriel looked at his watch, it was two minutes on from the last time he had looked at it. As always Anna Noble was being unfashionably late, and today made it all the more irritating because Avion was arriving from Scotland and he wanted really badly to be at the heliport when she arrived. He was about to send her another text when Ashley announced the arrival of Mrs Noble, who sauntered into Gabriel's office as though she had every right to it. He watched her with a steady gaze, her cream suit with tight skirt that ended at her knees, almost as stylish as his sister would wear, but far tighter in fit. Her carefully arranged blouse, open just enough to be teasing, and her perfume preceding her by several miles. He resisted the instinct to wrinkle his nose, as his sinuses shut down at the intensity of it.

"Good morning Gabriel." She sounded airy and happy, which set off alarm bells, given she had nothing to be so cheery about. He nodded slightly, completely on alert now.

"May I?" She nodded at the chair in front of his desk. He gave another slight nod.

"You're a sly one Gabriel, you really are." Her eyes narrowed briefly, but she wore a smile. He waited.

"Putting a research team on the Island already and another to follow in as soon as they're done. Sly, sly." She reprimanded smiling seductively. He made no response.

"You must have paid that Laird a whack of money to get a team there at all." She paused, eyeing him up, though she knew better than to expect a man such as Gabriel to disclose what he did or didn't spend. When he made no response, she carried on.

"I am considering arguing about the teams you have, given they are associates of Raphael's." She tipped her head to one side.

"One team is, the other team are university scientists, nothing to do with anyone." His tone was as ever impassive.

"Well I'm sure Raphael's team can be disregarded immediately." She said with an airy wave of her hand. Gabriel leaned back in his chair, resting his elbows on the thick leather arm rests, he steepled his long fingers together and tapped his lips with his index fingers.

"It won't change the outcome. Covent garden have one of the orchids in their library of rare plants, one team or one hundred, won't change the fact that they have already stated that the orchid is rare and unique to that Island. The research is as much to find out why as it is to confirm the fact." His eyes remained impassively glued to Anna's.

"Why did you do it? I mean the Island is nothing to you. Surely you didn't do it because you got engaged to one of its residents? Which makes it a conflict of interest." She was relaxed, but she crossed one long very straight leg over the other. Gabriel noted the lack of shape and thought about Avion's very shapely legs. He resisted a smirk. Her only indication of annoyance was the way the crossed foot flipped up and down.

"News travels fast." He noted. Then removing his fingers from his lips, he rested his arms on the chair arms.

"It isn't a conflict of interest. I am a tenant now, the Island is as much a home to me as it is to the residents already there." Anna thought about that.

"Why are you here Anna?" he asked in a mild tone.

"I dislike being cheated." She said factually. Gabriel let his eyebrows make the slightest frown.

"The Island is useless to you Anna, it is a worthless lump of rock stuck out in the farthest regions of the Outer Hebrides. You could do nothing with it." He reminded her. Anna sighed.

"Arh Gabriel darling, has love blinded you? Given you amnesia? Did I not outline the bigger picture to you?" Her eyes were wide now, as she feigned hopelessness in the face of a failing student. "Get one Island dirt cheap, and developmental planning permission for the others. Now of course you scuppered the get one Island dirt cheap part, and though it'll cost me more, the developmental part can still go ahead." She smiled kindly at him. Gabriel really hadn't expected her to want to keep going with her ludicrously stupid plan. It occurred to him suddenly that this wasn't about the Islands at all any more, it was personal. She would spend years applying for any number of permissions to annoy, frustrate and drain the De Luca finances, because he was obligated to defend the Islanders. She was smiling as he realised all this. He kept his expression impassive, and let the silence stretch between them.

"Well I look forward to seeing you again soon." Anna said, abruptly standing, grinning confidently, she held out her hand to him but he refused to take it. He seldom shook hands with people, and only then if he made a mutual agreement. He watched as she turned and walked smartly out of his office.

***

The helicopter blades slowed, and the occupant opened the door. Gabriel smiled at the sight of her. He had made it in time, and he felt overwhelming relief to see her again. As soon as Avion stepped out of the helicopter, she found herself enveloped in his arms, and to her it felt wonderful, to have been missed so much. Once again he felt overwhelming emotions coarse through him. Why did she have this effect on him? It had taken him almost a year to stop thinking about her when she'd left, and now he was back to being constantly distracted.

"I missed you." He said softly into her ear, words only she could hear. It made him think of his parents, the way his father would stand so close to his mother, fingers on her hip, or waist or shoulder. The way he would place his head close to hers, and then she would blush or smile because he said something that only her ears should hear. Gabriel smiled inwardly, now he understood it. Michael had the same thing with his wife, so Gabriel deduced it was a trait of De Luca men to be possessive of their women, and to always keep them close.

"It hasn't been that long, but hell I missed you too." Avion admitted as she snaked her arms around his neck. It was an odd sensation to miss somebody so much, just like losing a limb or her shadow. His lips claimed hers in a long lingering kiss, and his arms reacquainted themselves with her back. He didn't think Avion would ever really know just how passionately he loved her, he wasn't the kind of man who spoke openly about his emotions, but he wanted to tell her, yet words seemed not enough.

"You'd best put this on then. Seems word of our engagement has spread already." He said matter-of-factly. Avion looked down at the red rubies and white diamonds on the golden ring. Her eyes widened as she watched him slip it onto her ring finger.

"Gabriel." She whispered, tears in her eyes.

"What?" He asked concerned. "Don't you like it?"

Avion nodded too emotional to speak. He smiled at her.

"Red rubies means you have my heart. White diamonds means you have my soul." He informed her. She looked up at him, utterly devoid of words, and just cried happy tears, that he wiped away as fast as they fell.

"Sorry. I just... I don't know. I didn't expect this."

"I believe that normally a man would have the ring with him at the point of asking a woman to marry him. I hadn't imagined I'd be asking you that, when I did." He grinned at her boyishly, making her hiccup at his sudden glow of youth.

"Who knows we are engaged?" Avion asked suddenly remembering what he'd said.

"Oh Mrs Noble knows. I imagine someone on the Island told her, and if she knows, I guarantee the whole world knows, or they will soon enough." He looked slightly annoyed.

"Oh." Avion felt a little dejected, maybe the ring wasn't as well meant as she had first imagined.

"If you're thinking what I think you're thinking, then don't. I want to tell the whole world you are mine, but that didn't go so well last time." He hesitated and Avion placed a finger on his lips.

"I'm ok with that now. I want the whole world to know I am yours and that you are mine." She smiled. He let out a breath of relief.

"We should get going." He stepped away taking her hand in his, he led her to the car, sitting in the back with her, his arm about her shoulders. He made a call.

"Stewart. You were right. We need to go ahead with the WHS, seems Mrs Noble isn't done with us yet." He paused, letting his fingers stroke Avion's neck absently. "Yea, all of them." He added, then hung up.

"Am I allowed to ask?" Avion raised her head to face him.

"Mrs Noble thinks she can use the other Islands to acquire business contracts so that she can still use the area for extreme sports. By making the Islands a World Heritage Site, she can do nothing remotely close to them." He smiled. Avion smiled.

"Avi, there is another problem I need to talk to you about." His voice was filled with seriousness that sent shivers down her spine. Gabriel struggled to know how to begin, but found himself stopped by those tender finger tips.

"I missed you Gabriel. I don't just mean that I missed your company, I missed *all* of you. I don't think I could stay on the Island without you, so I think it would be best if I stayed with you in London, if that's ok?" She looked at him with worried eyes. Gabriel stared at her long and hard.

"You mean that?" He asked frowning slightly.

"I still own Al-Paca-Lunchbox, but I made Robbie my manager, so I can be with you. If things work out ok, I can let him buy the business off me in a few years." She bit her lower lip hesitantly. Gabriel let the words sink in, then he let the meaning of them soak into his being. She was giving up her business and her home to be with him, the same man she had run away from just two years ago.

"Is that what you were wanting to talk about?" She asked, suddenly afraid she has misread his intentions. A slow smile crept over his lips.

"It was, and none of that was part of my thinking." He replied.

"What was your thinking?" she asked softly, playing with his collar.

"That was the problem and I didn't know the solution." He said, as his eyes darkened. She trailed her finger idly over his jaw line, and he inhaled deeply.

"If you don't stop that, I am going to get the driver to pull over and he will have to watch me and I am quite sure you don't want that?" He pointed out, placing her hand on his groin so she understood exactly what he was talking about. Avion gasped and grinned wickedly.

"Where are we going?"

"Home. Think I can put this off any longer?" He spoke softly to her, not wanting his driver to know the extent of his discomfort.

"Oh, really? I was so hoping we could visit Mrs P, I want her to see my new ring." Avi held up her hand twisting it this way and that, so the light made the diamond and rubies sparkle.

Gabriel gave a low chuckle, he didn't imagine for a moment that she had forgiven his grandmother.

"Later honey. I have more pressing things to deal with." He pulled her closer to him.

***

Gabriel's flat was typically bachelor. An Attic apartment, it opened into a large living area with low square windows all around, nearer the floor than the ceiling. To the left was a galley kitchenette and a breakfast bar along the front, dividing it from the living area, which contained a large sofa, a coffee table with a glass top and antler legs, and a modern gas fire that glowed warm flame behind a glass exterior. He had a large TV to one side of the room, and at the back were a set of stairs which led to a mezzanine balcony which ran along the living area and led to a door, which opened onto a small garden area. To the left of the balcony was the bedroom, containing a large super king-size bed, a dressing room and bathroom were adjoined. Not that Avion got to take it all in at first, given Gabriel had begun his seduction of her from the moment they had entered the private lift. He had started to undress her the moment they entered the place, and she got mere snippets of glimpses of the cosiness of his home. He made his way to the kitchenette, undressing her as he moved, kissing her with heated passion. He paused long enough to remove his jacket and shirt, revealing his scarred torso taut with muscle. His hungry lips trailed down her neck, as his hands clasped her ribs, he burned for her, eager to feel her once more, he made his emotions say what words could not, with every caress, with every kiss, with every moan and gasp, he told her what she meant to him.

Avion clung to his neck, her hands tore through his hair, as she kissed him as hungrily as he did her, her fingers quickly raced over his skin, his scars, all the muscle that rippled beneath her touch. She had never wanted anyone as much as she did Gabriel, and she had never loved anyone like she loved him. He was power, he was strength and he was all hers forever. She didn't care what he was or who he was, he was someone who loved her, and she was pretty sure that he never got quite this hot and bothered around any other female he might have bedded. He lifted her onto him, powerful arms holding her as she instinctively rocked, as they gasped and groaned their way to completeness. He felt emotions with Avion, he felt alive and he would never let her go. He knew joy with every moan she let escape her, with every delicious shiver his fingers created in her, and he never wanted the love making to end, to feel her, to know her, to be a part of her.

"Forgive me. I know not what I do." His voice was deep and husky, making her shiver with delight.

"Forgive me Avi. I can't stop loving you."

Printed in Great Britain
by Amazon

What is Love?

For Avion it was pain, a constant endless rain of punches and kicks, of bruises, cuts and broken bones. Of being blamed. Of believing she was worthless. She had resigned herself to the hopelessness of her life, that one day she would not wake up from a beating, so who'd have thought salvation came in the form of a ninety year old blind woman?

Gabriel was a monster, a killer, a shrewd business millionaire. A man without feelings, who languished in dishing out pain. What made him so very dangerous was his love of being in pain, of surviving it. They said he had no heart to give, and he liked that until he met Avion.

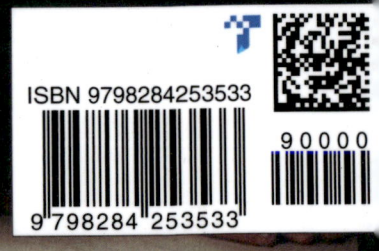

ISBN 9798284253533